Civil War Two

America's Second Attempt At Suicide

James Stewart

Published by FastPencil Publishing

America's Second Attempt At Suicide

Second Edition

Print edition ISBN: 9781499906790

http://www.fastpencil.com

Printed in the United States of America

Reviews for Civil War Two; America's Second Attempt At Suicide

Although a fictional account, this book contains plenty of today's reality mixed in to make this a fun read, yet chillingly frightening.
Richard D. – Vancouver, Washington

This is a must read for those who care about the future of their country! It presents a world that, sadly, may just come to be because we weren't paying enough attention to our leadership.
Peter S. – San Diego, California

Stewart delivers a well written work which tackles the current difficult social and political situation in the US from a unique future perspective. This creative perspective allows for an unbiased patriotic perspective encouraging the reader to tackle these important topics in their own terms.
Dr Ron K. – Portland, Oregon

A gripping thriller that is all too realistic. Great challenges for where we are going and how to avoid it.
Tony C. – San Diego, California

A well-written and suspenseful peek into a bleak possible near future. The documentary style of writing enhances the realism and gives a voice to the players shaping the events as they unfold. Part military tactical action piece, part political statement, and at all times a harsh mirror upon the current societal divisions and the way we can demonize the so-called enemy so easily; even when they are our neighbors, friends, family. The message is clear and timely. Time to start loving America.
Dylan S. – Seattle, Washington

This book is an American nightmare that is too close to a viable possibility. Written with believable imagination and expertise, it's discomforting and engaging at the same time.
Anonymous

This book is dedicated to my wife and family
who regularly give me examples of
what life is truly about.

❧

About the author

James Stewart is a first time fiction author. He is a regular science fiction, fantasy and military fiction reader and is enchanted by writers that weave technology throughout their work to create new worlds.

James has become ever increasingly worried about the political state of affairs in the United States. He became inspired to write this book after Donald Trump was elected as the 45th President and political commentary on both sides of the aisle became seriously toxic.

He hopes that the terrible events described in this novel will never come to fruition and that balanced conversation and respectful dialogue between parties can be renewed. This is a tall order, but if saner minds don't prevail, Civil War Two; America's Second Attempt At Suicide may very well be the road we go down as a country.

God help us if that is our collective fate...

Forward

Two weeks after the collapse of the United States Federal Government, I was summoned from my home in Reno, Nevada for special duties. And summoned is the right word. An email titled “Let’s talk” lands in my Inbox containing a very simple message.

“You have come to us highly recommended by important people from your past. If you want to help your country emerge from its current condition, we would like to talk to you. A driver will arrive at your current location at 8:00 AM tomorrow. If you are not on the curb, we move on without you; time is of the essence. Pack for two weeks of international travel in cold climate.”

The driver arrived promptly at eight and rolled down the window. “Patrick, I assume?” “Yes.” “Please get in and we can cover a few items. Afterward, if you still want to go to the airport, we go. If not? No harm, no foul.” “OK.”

“The top envelope has your itinerary, logistics, boarding passes and some information about your destination. The bottom envelope contains contact information, a pre-paid cell phone, and enough US cash to cover incidentals plus some.” “OK.”

“You’re going to Finland. It’s a hard place to get to.” “It’s also winter.” “Yes. It will be cold. You have packed for a cold climate, no? Like your instructions said?” “Yes. I’ll be fine.”

“Your travel arrangements are on private jets and private helicopters, so you must be a very important person.” “Not really.” “Well, I think you might be mistaken. My employers do not waste time with idiots.” “I’ll try not to disappoint them.”

I followed my summons per the itinerary in the top envelope with long and boring flights on tiny jets and even smaller helicopters. Never was there more than one other passenger on board. But none of them were going to the same place I was going. What is this, a private jet bus route? Crap, what have I gotten myself into?

The service was immaculate and the food and drink even better. I had the feeling that this was the peak of my experience down this path; the recruiting perks so to speak. And thinking this, well, I go forward anyway.

Twenty two hours after saying "goodbye" and "thank you" to the driver, I was indeed in a cold (correction, make that frigid) climate and headed to a think tank funded by some of the richest people in the world. They gathered this meeting in a polar circle resort of all places. In winter no less. Eclectic.

Eclectic and frigid.

My new think tank had the self-proclaimed missions of 1) preventing global violence, and 2) halting the spread of violence that does break out. I think that preventing and halting violence are great goals. I'm not at all convinced anyone can do it, but I like the intent, so I go forward again and attend the meetings.

Mine was not the only message that was sent out. There were many recognizables and professionals in similar circumstance in attendance at the briefings. After two weeks of these silly and serious at the same time, freeze-my-flesh meetings, I was able to pull together a story that led me to believe that I am simply one part of a complex, underground team being assembled to <u>observe</u> and <u>report</u> and ultimately <u>influence</u> the outcome of the ever increasing violence in America.

My particular role was simply to report. I was given the assignment to contact whomever I saw fit and to record <u>their</u> observations, <u>their</u> experiences, and <u>their</u> attempts at influence. The job was to create a factual record of events that had occurred during the war with the ultimate goal of being better able to predict what might occur in the future.

I was given an infinite budget (as far I was concerned) including piles of cash of all denominations and currencies. I was given no particular time goals except for "periodic" report deliveries.

"You'll know when to send information."

My parting gifts were passports and visas and various identities to allow me to travel across the world and across all of America without friction. I was even implanted with something that stung like hell but supposedly allows me to prove my sponsorship to any government in the world.

Really? So my right wrist is now a Customs magic wand? Really?

But, given a chance to lend a hand to my country vs. standing there and watching it come unglued, I go forward yet again and lean into the opportunity. I dropped everything in my day to day life, bought recording equipment and cameras and laptops and phones and SD cards and thumb drives and luggage and tickets and reservations and began the task.

And for years I've done the task. And the research. And the travel. And the interviews. And the reports. And once every year or so I attend a general meeting back in cold Finland at that polar circle resort. I eventually came to treat these trips as a little vacation. I could actually sit still for a week or so and that was not normal.

I don't actually know what was done with the material I generated. It just disappeared. It was never in the news. I mean, the news covered the events I was researching, so there was a lot of overlap. But most of my studies were of past events to try to set facts in place and this research is yesterday's news. I would think that at least some of the more drastic discoveries, even if historical, would ring some bells and go public. But nothing; nada; zero. Everything just fell into a big, black hole.

So after years of frustration and not feeling very influential at all, I decided to publish my research on my own and bring my discoveries into public view. The unbelievable occurrences I've been made privy to cannot go untold. Visibility into the cruelness and the hideousness of rampant human bad behavior must be left for our children.

Someone once said: "Those who don't learn from the past are doomed to repeat it." That cannot be allowed to happen. These times are too crude and ugly to remain hidden.

We should never tread these pathways again.

Preamble

If you sit back and think about it, it isn't hard to understand how things would proceed as America's next war began to unfold. I call it "Civil War Two; America's Second Attempt At Suicide". For years the tensions across the United States grew and grew. For years the divide between the haves and the have-nots amplified. For years the anger between political parties brewed from a dull simmer to cauldrons of hate.

There were many forces at work shaping the world and its connection to what was going on in America at that time. Economic forces had their cycles and political issues across the globe contributed in seen and unseen ways. Third world situations had their impact and highlighted the disparity between the powerful and the powerless. Not to be forgotten, climate change controversy and increased occurrences of natural disasters helped perch the world on edge.

Alliances of convenience which have always been a part of the world seemed to morph from day to day, hour to hour, and minute to minute. "Enemies of my enemies are my friends" was obsolete thinking and infrequent hidden daggers became well, shall we say, not so hidden and all too common.

And daggers weren't the only thing out in the open. Guns in America began to take a greater and greater toll on the population. Gang warfare in urban areas had always been the greatest gun killer, but random mass shootings of innocent civilians chased for second place.

Many Americans called for drastic gun control measures to stem the violence. Others called for stronger response to the criminals that committed these heinous acts. All called out for better solutions for drug addicts and the insane, but even with agreement, there was never legislation passed that made a difference.

Technology evolution was rampant and the advance of social media dominated generation upon generation. Visibility into the vagaries of the American political condition rose to all-time highs and confidence in leadership fell to all-time lows. Committee after committee, panel after panel, and subpoena after subpoena, much was said and much less done. Politicians soap boxed and pointed fingers and raised money for re-election, but there was never anti-violence legislation passed that made any difference.

So the US became a powder keg. And the richest, most powerful country in the history of the world - the country that was once the tip of the spear - became the country that was now the tip of a fuse. But a fuse and powder keg are not a good analogy in this case. The fuse is lit and a powder keg explodes with damaging glory, suddenly and all at once. The damage is done and recovery follows.

America's powder keg would ignite slowly and intermittently. It would flash and spit and smoke and stink, only to sink back into a pseudo status quo for periods. Then it would re-ignite again with new fury and fashion to reach a new crescendo that would only be replaced in magnitude by the next event or the one after that.

And so it began - the unraveling of yet another empire of sorts that had grown too arrogant to stay on top of what is important; to pay attention to the factors required for long term stability and careful evolution. The haves that lust to be in charge and call the shots ignored the cries of distress from the have-nots that rightfully demanded consideration and respect. The bosses that wielded tools of power ignored the proletariats, whom having come into their own, were demanding seats at the table.

The population of the United States was changing in age and complexion and size and stature - again. Yes, population change in America has happened before with huge influxes of people from other parts of the world. It started with Europeans invading North America, laying waste to the natives who lived there and seizing control of just about everything.

It continued with the import of thousands and thousands of dark skinned Africans to provide labor for households and plantations. It struck again when thousands more came from Asia to escape unlivable conditions there and trade them for unlivable conditions here. And it continued again as famines and wars in Europe drove yet thousands more to give up everything to find food and shelter and employment.

Yet, even as the "haves" vs. the "have-nots" theme eventually emerged, the early days destabilizers were not that way. In the beginning, it was the haves vs the haves that set the stage for America's mass unrest. The have-nots were too powerless to influence the country's agenda; too busy making ends meet to have time for leadership aspirations.

But the haves in America had plenty of everything and wanted more. Those with positions of power did everything possible to remain in power so that they could continue to get more. Those not in positions of power did everything possible to enter those positions of power so that they could get their more.

Politics in America had always been less about policy and programs and more about power and decision making. If you had the power, then you influence decisions to make more come your way and make even more come the way of your family, friends and supporters.

Winning an election no longer meant that the electorate was dictating policy changes to resolve this issue or that issue. It simply meant that those that win elections get to choose how power is allocated and who gets to get more and more and more. While those that lose an election see their power ebb; they no longer get their share of the spoils.

The platforms of the Democrat and Republican parties were once carefully assembled systems to drive growth and prosperity. The platform differences were about different means to the same end; growth and prosperity for the people.

But not now; the platforms of the Republican and Democrat parties are now carefully assembled show pieces to attract more and more campaign funding. And more campaign funding is the only way to attract more votes. Modern political platforms have much less to do with growth and prosperity for the people than they do with growth and prosperity for the people in charge.

The left leaning Democrat platforms and the right leaning Republican platforms are paraded in front of the voters in much the same way as new fashions are shown by models on a runway. In this way, money is raised and votes are cast and the prettiest platform wins the election.

But when is the platform implemented? When are the policies and programs brought to the floors of government and turned into law to achieve growth and prosperity for the people?

The answer? Never. Elections simply change the people who have the power to influence decisions to get more to come the way of themselves, and their family, friends and supporters. And once the graft engine is assembled and operating, it's time once more to identify the next pretty platform.

I use the colors blue and red synonymously with Democrats and Republicans as that has become standard language. The reality of Civil War Two was that it was brought on by the red-haves in positions of power in angry partnership with the blue-haves in positions of power. For the most part, the have-nots of both colors watched on in vast despair as life in America came unglued.

Blue and red, Democrat and Republican; it wasn't always that way. In the middle of the 20th century as black and white television was replaced by color, who was blue and who was red flip-flopped back and forth. Sometimes the Democrats were red and the Republicans were blue. Sometimes it was the other way around. Since this was during the middle of the Cold War, no one wanted to be associated with red which was the color of the free world's enemy - the Soviet Union.

As the cold war ended and significance of the colors faded, the mass media had its way and the Democrats now remain permanently blue and the Republicans are permanently red. This is just one example of the way politicians spend their time in wasteful fashion. Instead of working together bilaterally and implementing platforms to solve societal problems of the day, way too much time is spent in defining colors, drawing lines, and highlighting differences that will be built into the next pretty platform.

Way too much time is spent focusing on the other's faults and calling each other names and unleashing legal teams in public fashion to create boogie men where none exist. As the first quarter of the twenty-first century came to an end, the Blues in the government and the Reds in the government polarized dramatically to the left and to the right. They became locked in endless battle over trivialities and inconsequential things while the unrest in the population grew and grew and grew.

It's worthwhile to study election results in this red and blue language to better understand why America fell apart the way it did. In the map below are the electoral vote results by state from the 2016 presidential race. Notice the blue strongholds in the states on the west coast, in the northeast, some in the north central US, and the middle southwest. The remainder of the nation's states declared themselves red.

Population-wise, red and blue headcount was split almost down the middle. Half of the people plus or minus were red and half of the people were blue. Hillary Clinton actually received more individual votes than Donald Trump that year, and those blue votes came from the heavily populated urban areas. Donald

Trump won the election via electoral count, a process that is designed to keep balance between large and small and ensure equity between dense and sparse.

The power brokers on both sides saw these election results as an opportunity to declare voter fraud and change how elections were decided. Neither party spent much time studying the underlying energies that were separating the people. Instead, they hardened their hearts and their platforms and spun tales to move people right or left. Middle ground was a death trap for a referendum or a politician. Take a side or be mowed down in public. Reach across the aisle and have your hand cut off.

As federal polarization neared its peak, the ability to get anything done, to actually create and implement meaningful legislation ground to a halt. There were little or no bilateral approaches to any serious topic. If Blue was in charge, the government drove wildly to the left; if Red was in charge, the government veered frighteningly to the right. This grab-the-wheel steerage eventually made the people being governed nauseous. Anything to get off of the ride was better than clinging to the whipsaw of the federal government.

Parties strengthened their polarity and America's forward progress became stunted. Hardening of the parties became an epidemic and America's political vital signs dropped to new lows. Very little remedial work was done to build bridges between parties and the only bills that passed were budgets and further increases to the national debt. Absolutely nothing was done by the people in charge to improve things for the people they supposedly worked for.

Well, except to ensure that their graft engines were working well for them and theirs. That and, oh yes, also to identify and amplify their new pretty platforms for the next election. But we just talked about this didn't we; let's move on.

People grew more and more frustrated. This frustration led to focusing more attention on what was going on locally and in their state. In many cases, people uprooted to be in areas that were more to their liking, to live closer to their families and their values.

What was once the melting pot of the world continued to separate into oil and water, and everyone knows that oil and water do not mix.

Another tell-tale view of the US population comes from studying the same election results displayed above, but at the county level instead of the state level. At this level of detail, the granularity of the state boundaries is broken down and the very large geographies of blue states become dramatically smaller parcels of real estate. In compensation, these smaller parcels are even more intensely blue, driven by the huge concentrations of like-minded Democrats.

Vast areas of red span from sea to shining sea and the less dense, conservative country-side fills the void between islands of liberal blueness.

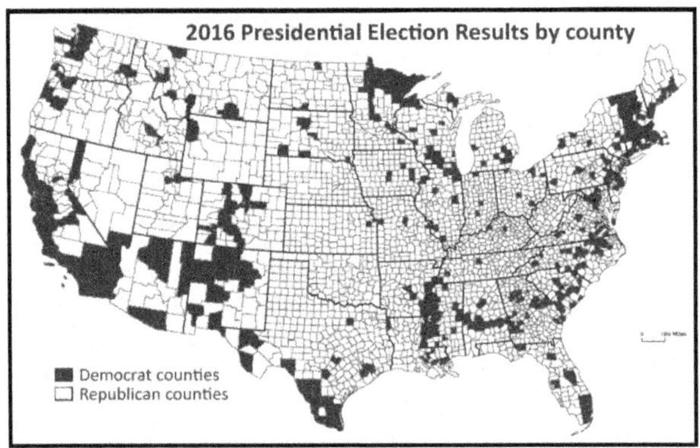

Looking at the map more closely points to a few things that are worth noting. Take for example the deep blue mega-cities of Seattle, Portland, the Bay Area, the Los Angeles basin, Las Vegas, Albuquerque, Santa Fe, Denver, Minneapolis/St Paul, Chicago, Detroit, Boston, New York, Washington DC, and Atlanta. These cities drove election results and turned their states blue. Most of these cities became blue urban strongholds during the war.

Examine also the blue areas along the US southern border; San Diego and Imperial counties of California, Tucson and south in Arizona, Texas along the Rio Grande, and Miami/Dade County. These blue communities are blue to their core on a per capita basis, but on the political side, they had mixed impact at the state level. Composed mostly of immigrants of meager resources, these border zones were not successful in driving state politics. Some of these border areas were among the first battlefields. It wasn't a pretty picture; not at all.

Another area of note can be designated as the deep blue south which appears as an arc that extends roughly from Memphis, Tennessee and points south to Jackson, Mississippi , then east towards Birmingham, Alabama and Atlanta, Georgia. From there it curls gradually northeast to connect to the Washington DC area. When law and order went out the window as States rights failed, this area of conflict wasn't a pretty picture either.

So why does all of this matter? Why are we even bringing up these locations and issues all over again? Good question.

As Civil War Two unfolded, it is best explained in three separate phases. The first phase is the time when public violence became greater and greater, but also a time in which the Federal government was active and pretending to operate. Concerns and issues about civil unrest were shared broadly across all of America through the national news media. Politicians argued back and forth about causes and solutions, yet no action was taken due to polarization and in-fighting. Violence occurring during this phase seemed random and unorganized, mostly individuals lashing out after reaching their own trigger frustration level. Pun intended.

Neighbors teamed with neighbors to protect themselves from marauding forces. Blue marauders sought consolidation of geography by ousting or eliminating red traitors within the urban areas. Red marauders consolidated in their own way by eradicated opposing political thought in the blue towns and cities sprinkled across the vast red sea of rural America.

Civil War Two's second phase opened with the demise of the Federal government; when the states were left on their own to maintain peace and order. During this time renegade militias formed in dozens of locations with the aim of either defending, to keep control of the state, or attacking, to take the state government away from the other party.

The National Guard was brought to bear in the support of parties in power. This was effective in stabilizing things in states where the politics of the capitol matched the politics of the surrounding areas. When the <blue/red> National Guard commander worked with the <same color> local political leader; well then, things were copasetic.

But when the <red/blue> National Guard worked with the <other color> local political leader; well, that was more complicated.

California's state capitol has been in Sacramento since 1879. The city itself is deep blue in political leaning, but if you look at the map more broadly, it is adjacent to red countryside to the north and east. Austin, Texas is another example in that Travis County is driven by blue political thinking, but surrounded on all sides by deep red neighbors. Let me amplify that: "all sides" means three hundred and sixty geographical degrees of political disagreement.

In Austin, the phase two militias staged a capitol takeover by force and by blockade. Eventually all of Austin became red; there were no more blue residents living there. All of the Austin blues had been converted, relocated, or eliminated, and all of Texas north of the border is now red. The government changed hands and now all Texas state government affairs are run by the Republicans.

In Sacramento, the Governor realized they were in a precarious position that felt a lot like Denver. Denver was on the front lines of a serious blue/red borderline and they were always in the news. So orders were given to evacuate Sacramento and move the government lock, stock and barrel to San Francisco. The government did not change hands and the California Blue Zone is still run by Democrats for Democrats.

One unforeseen effect of the second phase of war was to de-emphasize state lines which led to the obliteration of state mentalities. As people of like political leanings grouped together and ramped up to a war footing, state lines no longer had meaning. If I'm blue and my neighbors are blue, I work with them and they work with me; it's the same on the red side.

Violence across the America became more widespread and more damaging as tools of anger migrated from individuals with a handful of guns to militias armed with the heavy weapons owned and operated by trained personnel from the now-disbanding National Guard units.

As the second phase of the war drew to an end, the blue region of America's map coagulated into nine different areas. Five of the areas grew from metropolitan centers: 1) the Pacific Northwest which stretched from the Canadian border south through middle Oregon, 2) the California coast which stretched from northern California to Orange County and hugged the Pacific Ocean, 3) the middle southwest stretching from northern Colorado south to New Mexico, 4) north middle America from Chicago north to the Canadian border in Michigan,

Wisconsin and Minnesota, and 5) the east coast, hugging the Atlantic Ocean stretching from Washington DC up through Boston and areas further north.

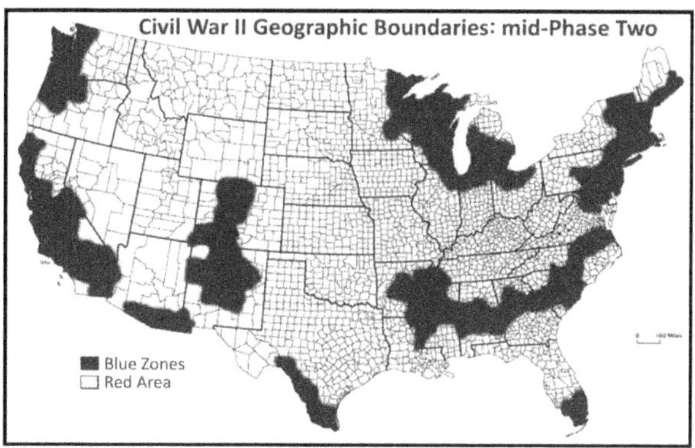

Three of the areas were dominated by immigrant populations; southern Florida, southern Texas, and a band along the Mexican border that stretched from Tucson almost to Yuma. The last blue dominant region was a curved ovoid across Mississippi, Alabama, and Georgia with stretches of control into Arkansas, North Carolina, and southern Virginia.

During the first and second phases of the war, the official military branches, i.e. Army, Navy, Air Force, Marines, and Coast Guard, remained neutral and were not engaged in the ever widening conflicts. During the first phase they were still commanded by the federal government through the President, the Joints Chiefs of Staff, Secretary of Defense, the National Security Council, and the Homeland Security Council. The chain of command of the military stopped with the executive branch and the President, and executive order after executive order was issued to mobilize the military for peace enforcement.

Judges from both colors would participate in the legal fracas that would trail each executive order into oblivion. Not one ordered troop deployment survived the gauntlet; no soldiers ever left their bases.

The legislative branch was split and dysfunctional on this topic as well. They tossed roadblock after roadblock in front of themselves to stop any legislation offered that utilized the military to halt the growing violence in the streets.

Any move to use the military required a common belief on who was to blame for increasing atrocities. If a legislative suggestion was made to use the military to hunt down people responsible for an urban attack in a clearly blue territory, countermanding legislation was produced to stop the blues from red-cleansing the suburbs surrounding blue regions. The end effect of this lack of agreement on blame was that the military was benched and remained behind their fences in their very secure bases during all of Phase One.

As Phase Two unfolded and street violence reached new levels, executive orders issued by the governors were also ineffective. As soon as an executive order was written, a judge in the affected territory would issue a stay preventing any immediate action. These dilemmas would again be swarmed by armies of legal teams and since the courts were also split in red and blue, it took months to deliberate and deliver a decision.

By this time there were new levels of nastiness in new areas of unrest and the problems trying to be solved shifted in intensity and location much more quickly than the legal system could resolve. Even declaring states of emergency were ineffective at freeing up and focusing the military to squelch street violence. Again no soldiers ever left their bases.

It's important to note that even though the official military branches remained out-of-battle for Phases One and Two, there are significant differences between these phases from a military leadership perspective. During Phase One, the traditional command and control remained in place, homed in the Joint Chiefs of Staff and the President. However with the collapse of the federal government signaling the beginning of Phase Two, there was no President, and no Chiefs of Staff. Leadership of the military forces fell to the local commanding officer of each military base and installation.

One of the last actions taken by the President and his team was to issue a call-up of the reserve forces across all areas of the country. These reserve forces were en route to their assignments when the government collapsed and had the end effect of reinforcing the already strong military in the already strong bases and further strengthening the autonomy of the local commanders.

The third phase of the America's second Civil War is still underway. It is impossible to know whether we are at the beginning of Phase Three or the middle of Phase Three. We're certainly not near the end of Phase Three. The violence is still increasing. The death toll is still accelerating. And there's no call emerging for establishing some sort of armistice. There has also been significant discovery of international players involving themselves in subversive ways and I for one am afraid that America's Civil War Two may rapidly be turning into Earth's World War Three.

I will keep researching and interviewing and recording the events of Civil War Two as it unfolds. And I'll keep sending my reports to my sponsors and hope it leads to something good. But I will also compile and publish my findings periodically to the American public.

People have a right to know what is going on.

What is really going on...

CHAPTER 1

Route 91 Harvest Music Festival - wikipedia.org article

On the night of October 1, 2017, a gunman opened fire on a crowd of concertgoers at the Route 91 Harvest music festival on the Las Vegas Strip in Nevada. Perpetrator Stephen Paddock, 64, of Mesquite, Nevada, fired more than 1,100 rounds from his suite on the 32nd floor of the nearby Mandalay Bay hotel, killing 58 people and leaving 851 injured, over 400 of them by gunfire and hundreds more in the ensuing panic. The shooting occurred between 10:05 and 10:15 p.m. PDT; about an hour later Paddock was found dead in his room from a self-inflicted gunshot wound. His motive remains unknown.

The incident is the deadliest mass shooting committed by an individual in the United States. It reignited debate about gun laws in the U.S. and focused attention on bump stocks, which Paddock used to help him fire shots in rapid succession and with results compared to automatic weapon fire.

The Las Vegas Metropolitan Police Department released a preliminary report on the event on January 18, 2018. Police speculate that Paddock acted alone and have not determined his motive. No links have been identified to any hate groups, terrorist groups or ideologies, and he did not record a reason for his actions.

On February 2, 2018, Douglas Haig, an Arizonan ammunition dealer, was charged in a Nevada federal court with "conspiracy to manufacture and sell armor-piercing ammunition without a license" after his fingerprints were discovered on unfired armor-piercing ammunition inside Paddock's suite.

Final investigative report:

On August 3, 2018, Las Vegas Sheriff Joe Lombardo held a press conference on the release of the "LVMPD Criminal Investigative Report of the 1 October Mass Casualty Shooting". He said the ten month investigation had revealed no evidence of conspiracy or a second gunman, and that the gunman's motive had not been definitely determined. Lombardo said "What we have been able to answer are the questions of who, what, when, where and how... what we have not been able to definitively answer is why Stephen Paddock committed this act."

CHAPTER 2

Route 91 Harvest Music Festival - Excerpts from an FBI report

On the night of October 1, 2017, a gunman opened fire on a crowd of concertgoers at the Route 91 Harvest music festival on the Las Vegas Strip in Nevada. Perpetrator Stephen Paddock, 64, of Mesquite, Nevada, fired more than 1,100 rounds from his suite on the 32nd floor of the nearby Mandalay Bay hotel, killing 58 people and leaving 851 injured, over 400 of them by gunfire and hundreds more in the ensuing panic. The shooting occurred between 10:05 and 10:15 p.m. PDT.

The investigation into this crime conducted by local law enforcement officials was concluded on August 3, 2018 with a published report that indicated that "*no evidence of conspiracy or a second gunman, and that the gunman's motive had not been definitely determined...*"

Another investigation into this crime conducted by the FBI has come to a distinctly different conclusion than that published by local law enforcement.

In cooperation with the local officials, the investigation into this atrocious act was split into two separate efforts. One was driven by local law enforcement and eventually reported findings to the public. The second investigation conducted in parallel with the first was driven by the Federal Bureau of Investigation and eventually resulted in this report, which has been shared only with the Director of the FBI, the Attorney General, the President of the United States, and the Mayor and the Chief of Police of Las Vegas. No one outside of this small circle of people knows of these investigative results.

The evidence from the crime scene was also split into two paths. Most of the evidence was processed by local resources in regular fashion, i.e. the police, other EMT elements, state investigators, and hired security firms. They also conducted interviews with witnesses and injured victims, developed time sequence studies, and led the perpetrator background research.

Due to the magnitude of the human carnage and the nature of the weaponry employed, the FBI was given jurisdiction over the ballistics studies, the handling of the perpetrators remains, and security video analyses.

Most of the results of the FBI investigations were shared with the local authorities to help them build their best understanding of what transpired that terrible evening. The public report summarized in the prior chapter is a well-developed amalgam of the local public investigation and the public portions of the FBI's mostly private investigation.

However, there were several separate pieces of evidence that were not shared with the local authorities. Believed to be unnecessary for public consumption and probably too controversial to track down in public view, these materials have been shared only with the "group of five".

<u>New Data: Mandalay Bay Hotel Visitors</u>

The Mandalay Bay hotel internal security video analyses showed multiple visitors to the perpetrator's room during times in question. Four local prostitutes entered and exited the room prior to the shooting event, one each day in the two days before the shooting and two separate visits on the day of the shooting. The first visit on the shooting day was a single prostitute in the morning and the second visit was by a pair of prostitutes in the afternoon. One of the pair was a new person, but one was also the morning visitor. "Come back later and bring a friend."

We have thoroughly interviewed and accomplished background checks on all of the prostitutes and are confident that none of them knew anything about the perpetrator's shooting plans.

There were also two visits by an as-yet unidentified male individual; one visit on the day prior to the shooting and one visit on the day of the shooting. On the day prior, in the mid-afternoon, the individual was empty handed and came and went within fifteen minutes. There is no record that we can find regarding the intent or content of that visit.

On the day of the event, the visitor returned, this time carrying a gym bag. He entered the perpetrator's room approximately one hour prior to the shooting event. Fifteen minutes prior to the start of the shooting, the perpetrator himself exited his hotel room and blackened the hallway security camera lens with a piece of duct tape.

We have no evidence of the visitor leaving the hotel room after the second visit as the camera was still covered with tape. The gym bag he carried into the hotel room was found there and contained boxes of ammunition matching many of the firearms present, including armor piercing bullets and clips for the AR style weapons.

New Data: Fingerprints

There was fingerprint evidence all over the two rooms used during the shooting event. Those prints included the perpetrator, the four prostitutes, the hotel staff, and a local gun dealer whose prints were found on some of the unopened boxes of bullets in the gym bag. The local gun dealer has since been prosecuted for selling illegal armor piercing ammunition.

There was no fingerprint evidence found that has been associated with the unknown visitor. We find this unusual as according to video analysis, the visitor was not wearing gloves during either of his visits.

During the weapons analysis conducted in Washington DC, there was fingerprint evidence from the perpetrator on all but two of AR-15s. There was absolutely no fingerprint evidence on these last two AR-15s, even though they had been fired during the event. Lab estimates indicate that these two AR-15s may have unleashed as many as 150 rounds during the shooting.

The gym bag which was carried into the room with the visitor's bare hands also did not contain any fingerprint evidence. However, upon detailed video review, the bag handles may have been wrapped in cellophane or some other similar material, and later removed and discarded elsewhere.

New Data: DNA evidence

DNA was also gathered during the investigation. Similar to the fingerprint evidence, there is DNA present from the perpetrator, the prostitutes, hotel staff, and the gun dealer. There were also numerous samples from other persons, and most of these samples, if not all of them, were probably from prior hotel room guests. These samples were processed and data submitted to all available law enforcement and military DNA databases, but after eighteen months of study with no hits of any nature, this avenue of investigation was halted.

New Data: Video Analysis

The videos from security cameras from the Mandalay Bay hotel and from other buildings nearby displayed nothing of note. These include the Luxor, the Four Seasons, the Excaliber and the Tropicana. This was a surprising result. We expanded our search radius and came up with one video recording that contained possibly related imagery.

A Terrible Herbst Convenience Store camera on the west side of I-15 captures a distant image of the backside of the Mandalay Bay hotel. At approximately 10:18 PM, there is a faint image of an object descending from the roof of the tower to the roof of the casino. If the object was indeed a human, the images are not clear enough to lead to any identification.

A rope long enough and strong enough for rappelling from the roof of the hotel was found on the roof of the casino two days after the event. Extensive follow-up identified the source of the rope, but it is a common brand, material, color and length and the investigation connected it to no other leads. There was no finger print evidence from the rope. Gloves that were probably used during rappelling were not found.

New Data: Lock Tampering

The hotel roof access door employs a building code compliant security lock as well as a commercial alarm circuit. There was no evidence of the roof door ever being opened on the day prior, the day of, or the day after the shooting event.

An FBI expert showed the lock to be readily picked by a person with that sort of knowledge. Additionally, the alarm device had been tampered with as well, also by someone with that sort of knowledge.

During a simulation, the lock was picked by the FBI and the door opened for testing. No alarms sounded in the hotel security room. When the tampering device was removed, the alarm functioned properly and sounded in the hotel security room as expected.

New Data: Perpetrator Autopsy Results

The final bit of undisclosed evidence is the most disturbing. The autopsy of the perpetrator indicated that death was caused by a handgun shot into the right temple at close range as reported in the Las Vegas police reports. The bullet that caused death was found in a wall of the hotel room and was in very, very poor condition from a ballistics standpoint after entering and exiting the perpetrator's skull and becoming lodged in a metal stud in the hotel room wall.

Detailed ballistics studies indicate that this bullet was not fired from any of the weapons found in the room after the shooting event. Most likely the caliber was 9mm and the handgun was probably a Glock, based on the very minimal remaining scoring on the bullet itself. This identification is an educated guess, not a provable fact.

Based on all of these findings - and this is not conclusive, but a very plausible story - the FBI investigation team believes that the visitor who entered the room prior to the shooting event assisted the perpetrator before and during the mass shooting itself. We believe the visitor was standing watch over the hotel room hallway during final preparations and was the one responsible for shooting the hotel security officer that was injured prior to the start of the mass shooting.

This visitor then also participated in the shooting event itself with the AR-15s brought into the room previously by the perpetrator; the visitor basically took turns with the perpetrator during the ten minutes of shooting into the crowd.

After the event concluded, or perhaps <u>why</u> the event concluded, the visitor used an un-yet-identified 9mm handgun to shoot the perpetrator in the right temple at close range.

We also believe that the perpetrator took a service elevator to the top of the hotel, gained access to the roof, rappelled down and escaped undetected.

FBI teams have re-created this sequence of events and have determined that a well-trained person could have murdered the perpetrator, performed the escape, and been driving away in a previously parked car within a span of six to eight minutes. Our best agent time during simulations of this escape was six minutes forty-two seconds.

We made measurements of the time from the end of the shooting event to the mystery person's escape from the hotel property. Given a few simple assumptions that may or may not be accurate - this guy did it in five minutes sixteen seconds. If this measurement is accurate, the visitor was knowledgeable, well-prepared and very, very fast.

Regarding motive for committing this heinous act, we have not explicitly found anything to cite - no notes, no social media, no other email, no character interview reports - absolutely nothing.

One analysis completed does lead to an interesting perspective. The event across the street that was attacked that day was a country western music concert. Research into these types of events indicates that country and western concert attendees are mostly white, rural and Republican in their political affiliation. This concert was actually attended by 68% conservative, 24% liberal, and 8% independent in their leanings.

We have studied the analyses by the NRA regarding the composition of the killed and injured; they were looking for anything to point to liberal hate groups and gun control supporters. We also have studied the similar analyses completed by the mass media and anti-gun groups who were looking for anything to support their point of view. The actual killed and wounded statistics were 50% conservative, 44% liberal and 6% unaffiliated. Based on these actual numbers, neither report was able to declare reasonable bias in either direction.

However, bullets have a way of creating their own statistics, and it is very possible that even though this conclusion is not supported by casualty count, the mass shooting could have been a politically motivated event.

Actual results in any single sample of a statistical norm may show significant deviation. If this was the case and the reason victim statistics were not the same as crowd statistics is just plain old bad luck, it is possible that the largest mass shooting in US history could very well have been a hate crime against the conservative half of the population. Please be reminded that this hypothesis is not provable and is only an educated possibility generated by the researchers at FBI headquarters. We believe it, but we can't prove it.

The Las Vegas mass shooting case has been closed down by the local law enforcement agencies; however, the FBI still has an open file. The unknown visitor still remains a person of interest, even though all credible leads have been exhausted to no avail.

CHAPTER 3

PVC Pipe Bomber - Interview with a bomb defuser

Interviewer: As I understand it, your name is Robert Johnson, and you're part of the team that helped defuse all the PVC bombs that were mailed in late 2018. Is that true?

Johnson: Yes that's true. Please, call me Bob. I'd prefer that.

Interviewer: OK thanks, Bob. Let me provide a bit of backdrop before we get started. I won't give you my name, as what I'm doing is very hush hush, but I can tell you I've been asked to interview as many people as I can to give insight into what started all of the violence that's going on these days. This is all very confidential and I won't include your name in my report, although I will keep it in my records in case I need to get a hold of you again. Is this going to be OK?

Johnson: No problem with me, anything I can do to help out. I was just doing my job anyway.

Interviewer: A little bit more information might be useful for you. Periodically I send my interview results to a top secret part of the government. Their purpose as I understand it is to try and recreate a factual sequence of events over the past years. Good decision making requires good data and it has become way too obvious that normal information sources about the violence are not reliable for producing unbiased facts. I'm sure you can relate to that.

Johnson: I know what you're saying. I can't even watch the news anymore. All that's going on is really terrible, no one knows what to do about it, and every time I turn around the story changes, someone else is to blame and the violence just gets worse and worse.

Interviewer: Yes, yes, I get it. That's why I've been assigned to talk to a lot of people who were actually there and get their stories written down as best I can. I don't know where all of this this leads, but my sponsors are pretty intent on finding out the facts.

Bob, do you have any more questions?

Johnson: Not really. <pause> Well, maybe one thing. Can I get into any trouble with this? I don't want to lose my job and I don't want my family in danger.

Interviewer: That's a good question. If I were in your position I'd be nervous about talking about anything to anybody these days. And I'll be straight. I cannot guarantee 100% that what we discuss here won't be heard somewhere and make someone upset. And this someone may have the power and the reach to, well, make some moves that might splash on us. But I for one, and I think you are this way too, we can't just sit by and watch the slaughter.

My sponsors think we've taken great measures to protect everyone by making this Top Secret and only allowing "need to know" information access. I'm going to give you a special phone number and a secure e-mail address that you can use to contact me again in case something starts making you nervous or if you want to provide me additional information.

Johnson: OK, that's good. Like I said, I want to help if I can.

Interviewer: So let's get started shall we? <Johnson nods> I've found the best way to handle the session is to let you talk about your experience without any guidance from me. We want your un-influenced experience and you don't have to force everything to make sense or go in order. So why don't you just tell me the story about these pipe bombs and what you went through at the time.

Johnson: OK, no problem. It all started when I got a call from my captain and he ordered me to be part of a team of bomb defusers. This was in NY City and there were only six of us that could do the dirty work, but there were teams all over the country looking into this situation and there were dozens and dozens of investigators involved.

Some of the stuff that we all heard on the news was totally correct. I mean they were like fifteen boxes sent to a bunch of Democrat officials and movie stars and each one of them was addressed by hand and had a return address made out to Debbie Wasserman Schultz; totally strange.

The bombs themselves were middle-of–the-road sophisticated; a battery with a trigger mechanism in a plastic box, a PVC pipe filled with explosives, a little computer board, wires to the battery and bombs, that sort of thing. They probably got the plans off the internet. I told the Feds this part of the story and most of it ended up on the news. It's what I told them that didn't end up on the news is what's interesting.

The first weird things were the batteries and I mean batteries, plural. Usually a bomb will have one power source, like a nine volt cell that will run the whole system for maybe a week. But this one had two batteries connected to separate parts of the bomb. The first one powered all the electronics, and those electronics were pretty sophisticated, mind you. The second battery was wired to ignite the pipe bomb; so bomb control and pipe activation were two separate parts of the design.

That might not seem too weird just by itself, but the battery to detonate the bomb was not even connected! The batteries were still in their plastic wrappers from wherever they got the damn things. So when the News told us all that the bombs couldn't even detonate, they were kind of being truthful because there was no battery attached. But I will tell you that if those batteries were connected and if those things did go off, it would have been nasty.

Those guys knew what they were doing. I mean everything was there to make a good bomb. Plug in the battery and BOOM! The computer board was also really smart because when we tapped into it, the lab laptop had a virus invasion and was out of commission for like twelve days. That virus was nasty, nasty, nasty. To this day, we do not know how they did that and we should've thought about it before plugging in.

Well, we did actually - think about it that is. The lab test equipment is in its own room on its own electricity and has its own little mini-network to totally isolate it from everything. When we plugged into the bomb computer, this virus jumped into the primary laptop at the speed of light, and then it infected all the smart devices in the test setup in like five seconds. I actually went to the tool chest, grabbed a hammer and smashed the laptop to stop everything. It was a nightmare. Like I said, twelve days to get re-certified.

But that that wasn't the worst part of the story.

They never told us about the notes, did they? Not a word of this in the press, no-siree; nada; nothing. Every single one of those bombs had an identical note in it that basically said "You know these bombs could've gone off, right? Consider this a warning. We can crank these out by the dozen any time we want. Next time we connect the batteries..." Scary, huh?

And then there was this one last weird thing. Remember that some of the news talked about shrapnel and nails in each of the boxes? Yeah that was true alright. But they didn't talk about the shrapnel itself very much. In each and every one of those boxes were handfuls of ten penny nails and on the head of each one was a little sticker. Half of the stickers were of Jesus and half were swastikas. Talk about crazy; the bomb makers are good at making bombs <u>and</u> they're nuts.

Now that's really scary.

CHAPTER 4

Voter Fraud - Interview with a Florida election supervisor

Interviewer: OK, I have a recorder running and you've agreed to go on record as long as we don't use your real name. So I'm going call you Annette. Is that alright?

Annette: I love my new name. I had a friend in grade school called Annette and I always envied her. So when you asked for an alias, it was easy for me to go there.

And yes, I want to help out with your report or whatever it is, but I don't want to get into trouble. I mean, I'm a pretty good person all-in-all, but I'm not stupid either.

Interviewer: OK, Annette. <she giggles> I understand. We're doing a great job of keeping our sources out of trouble, and you're behind several screens of protection. Please trust me on this.

Now getting started, the reason we're talking together is that you currently serve as one of Florida's supervisor of elections. Is that correct?

Annette: Yes, down in south Florida, near the swamps. That's where I currently am, but I've also done this job in two other counties and one other state. I've been doing election work my whole life.

Interviewer: Your credentials certainly are deep, so thank you for your public service all these years. The system doesn't work without people like you. Yeah, for sure, thanks.

Annette: Well, you're welcome. It's been an absolute pleasure. <more giggles>

Interviewer: So let's talk about this public service of yours. But not really just your service, I need a state-wide look at things. I'm following up on the last mid-term elections and the anomalies in a few locations, including Broward County. You and I were put in contact by some mutual friends and what I understand is that you perhaps can explain Broward election issues in some detail.

Annette: Yes, yes, yes. Been there; done that. I don't mind helping out with your project. Things have gotten really, really bad out there with the violence and if anything I can do will help, then so be it.

<thinking aloud> Where do I start? Mmm, OK; I'm ready.

What you really need to understand is that the Florida election machine is pretty well oiled for the most part. Most states including Florida have pretty good systems and the results are accurate and timely. Millions and millions of votes get cast and tallied; most of the time it is done and finished within a few hours of closing the last polling location.

Interviewer: Voting and counting is done pretty well most of the time almost everywhere. So what about Broward County? What happened there? There was a lot of controversy about fraud.

Annette: OK, I hear you. I'll talk about it this way. Running an election has two sides; the system itself, and the people that run the system. These are two totally different things. And in Broward County the system worked just as well as anywhere else. Sometimes, like this time, there have been problems with the people that run the Broward system.

Interviewer: Yes, yes; this is good. Why don't you just keep going here and tell me anything that you think would be good for my report.

Annette: Mmm, no problem. Like I said, we all operate the same machine pretty much and it works really well if you follow the process. It's pretty straight forward once things get started and if you follow procedures, votes come in and tallies go out. Even Broward County runs well when there are no hiccups.

But when things change, then you have to shift gears and jump to a new set of procedures. Folks in Broward County don't know how to shift gears very well; especially at the top. New procedures require a supervisor to actually do some things, you know, as opposed to watching other people do all the work.

Interviewer: I'm a bit lost. You're talking about changes and new procedures and different jobs. Why would that happen?

Annette: Well, most of the time changes don't happen and that's because elections typically come in as expected for the most part. But when the elections results are, how should we say?, "not as expected...", hmm, maybe even "not as desired..." , then sometimes some changes might occur.

It works this way. Basically, you get a call from the state office and they remind you that there is another block of votes ready for pickup. Then you have to run an errand, a personal errand by the supervisor I remind you. Go pick up a few boxes and then do a few more things to get the boxes into the counting process before the end of the day.

Interviewer: And in Broward County?

Annette: Yes, Broward County. Poor Barbara wasn't able to follow instructions in Broward County. And it's not the first time, either. A couple of years ago she had the same issue; she just plain old didn't follow instructions. The procedures are all very well designed to add a couple of boxes anonymously to the election stream in a way that no one really knows where they came from, not exactly anyway. Nor do they care.

You want as few as people as possible to really know about the changes and new procedures, so the super has to do a few precise things at precise times. Like picking up the boxes on your own and dropping them at a collection site on the dock a couple of minutes before a standard route is delivered.

But no, Barbara...

Interviewer: <interrupting> Excuse me, we're talking about Barbara Sikes here right? Just for the record.

Annette: Yes, of course, Barbara Sikes; the goddess of Broward vote counting. She sends people to pick up the boxes instead of going herself, has them placed into her car or her office and then she forgets where she put the damn things. Not all the time, just once every now and then. But her boo-boos are often enough that she's probably not going to be doing this much longer; not here, not anywhere.

Interviewer: OK, so Barbara just messed up?

Annette: Royally; super royally. The procedures worked everywhere in Florida, <u>except</u> Broward County.

Interviewer: What do you mean, "worked everywhere..."?

Annette: You don't think we'd be stupid enough to change things in a big way all at once in one location do you? If a change is needed, it comes in a box or two here and a box or two there. A couple of dozen change orders and pretty soon you can get some real numbers. So when I get a call to tell me about another vote pickup, it's not just me that receives an order. There are probably a few dozen busy little supervisors on a day like that.

Interviewer: So it's simple? A call from headquarters, a couple of errands run, some anonymous drop offs and boom, election results change. Really, is it that simple?

Annette: Pretty much; until someone doesn't follow procedures and gets caught. Then everything goes haywire for a while so we lay low and wait for the next election.

Interviewer: You make it sound like this is an everyday, or rather an every-election occurrence. Are you exaggerating? Every election?

Annette: I hate to blow your confidence in the American systems of voting and counting, but yes, there are change procedures in every state of the union - heck every county almost. You have to achieve a large number of really small changes for this to work without kicking up a stink. So you can't flip a big downside vote, but you can shift a few points here and a few points there and change some endings if you're careful <u>and</u> you follow the procedures.

<pause> Here's a funny aside before we move on.

OK, take all of the news coverage on Broward County and a few places similar, pile on some questionable FOX pundits to fog things up along the way, and a lot of America thinks that if this really ever happens, for sure it is the Democrats that do it.

Interviewer: So why is that funny? This is a pretty disconcerting topic if it were to go public.

Annette: You've got two things there and they're connected. First, these shenanigans go pubic all the time, but politicians and media both stomp the stories down and they just go away after a few weeks; only to blow up again a few years later. It's been going on forever, frankly. And the reason it gets stomped down boils down to the money.

Interviewer: The money? OK, tie this all together for me, please.

Annette: The change procedures are very expensive to implement, right? Lots of preparation to build and make ready thousands of ballots and records and people's names and addresses and inventory of boxes and ballots and thousands of pens and markers for balloting and the fabrication and combining forms and assembling into cartons and delivering to dozens or hundreds of locations all at the wave of a hand?

Plus, you never know where the pushes and pulls are required, so the pre-work has to be done for every race that may need some help across all levels of elections and for all parties and candidates.

Interviewer: <interrupting> Wait a second, every race, all parties and candidates? I'm lost again.

Annette: That's what's really funny. There is a whole industry centered on having boxes of ballots ready to use in an election. The parties and the local governments don't have the wherewithal or the smarts to prepare a farce of this magnitude. So there are a few very, very private companies - most of them non-profit, by the way - that make their sales numbers based on providing exactly the right number of boxes in exactly the right locations at exactly the right time.

These companies have huge stores of pre-printed, pre-voted, and pre-signed ballots, most of the time prepared for all major candidates in a race. Based on exit polling and other statistics, the party bosses request changes and these change requests result in orders being placed on the third party companies.

Sometimes the company gets orders from both parties and it gets really expensive, really fast. The highest bid wins.

Once election day has finalized and all orders placed in transit, the entire inventory of "other" ballots is disposed of and within maybe twelve hours of the polls closing there is no evidence of anything of a voting nature. Quite a gimmick if you ask me.

And the really, really funny thing for me is that people think it's a Democrat thing in general, yet the Republicans are way deep in this as well. Most of the time the Democrats benefit, not because "they're doing it..." It's because they're buying it! They have a lot more money than the Republicans and they are really excellent at making good deals in exactly the right places. So in Florida, maybe 85% of the boxes come in stacked for the Democrats. Elsewhere, like in Kansas and places like that, the numbers are more like 50/50, but here the Democrats definitely win the bidding wars for the most part.

Plus, this whole thing about "Who's doing it?" is just a sign of the innocence and ignorance of the US public. This vote-buying is happening in every state for sure, and sometimes in almost every county of the big states. Both parties buy votes in critical election areas and for sure it's not legal in anyone's imagination. But what's really not legal is the fact that there is an entire industry that exists around providing these stacked boxes; shadow companies that provide cases and cases of ballots and make mounds and mounds of dollars in the process.

My opinion? I think the companies are run by the Mafia families. I have no proof, but who else can do something this big and comprehensive and not have it splattered all over the internet? The President can't even fart without a press splatter. But with the Mafia, if you're involved and you open your big mouth, you literally get splattered and it's with a car or in your house or during a mugging or whatever works for the occasion.

Changing election outcomes has become a way of life in America. It's been going on for years and as long as there is money to be had, it'll be going on for a lot longer. Most of the time it's invisible and most of the time it really doesn't have a huge impact; not in the scheme of things.

But every now and then a party scores a big win and you get something like an unexpected piece of shit at the top, if you catch my drift.

CHAPTER 5

The New Socialists - wikipedia.org information

lexandria Ocasio-Cortez - US Representative – New York's 14th District

On June 26, 2018, Ocasio-Cortez drew national recognition when she won the Democratic Party's primary election for the 14th congressional district, defeating the ten-term incumbent Congressman, Democratic Caucus Chair Joe Crowley, in one of the biggest upset victories in the 2018 midterm election primaries. She beat Republican opponent Anthony Pappas in the November 6, 2018 general election, and at age 29, became the youngest woman ever to serve in the United States Congress.

A member of the Democratic Socialists of America, Ocasio-Cortez has advocated for a progressive platform that includes Medicare For All, a federal jobs guarantee, guaranteed family leave, abolishing U.S. Immigration and Customs Enforcement, free public college and trade school, infrastructure projects for renewable energy, and a 70% marginal tax rate for incomes above $10 million.

Favorite quote regarding Medicare For All: "People often say, how are you gonna pay for it? And I find the question so puzzling because, how do you pay for something that's more affordable? How do you pay for cheaper rent? How do you pay for - you just pay for it."

Green New Deal - part of a fourteen page resolution

"Guaranteeing a job with a family-sustaining wage, adequate family and medical leave, paid vacations, and retirement security to all people of the United States."

"Providing all people of the United States with – (i) high-quality health care; (ii) affordable, safe, and adequate housing; (iii) economic security; and (iv) access to clean water, clean air, healthy and affordable food, and nature."

"Providing resources, training, and high-quality education, including higher education, to all people of the United States."

"Meeting 100 percent of the power demand in the United States through clean, renewable, and zero-emission energy sources."

"Repairing and upgrading the infrastructure in the United States, including ... eliminating pollution and greenhouse gas emissions as much as technologically feasible."

"Building or upgrading to energy-efficient, distributed, and 'smart' power grids, and working to ensure affordable access to electricity."

"Upgrading all existing buildings in the United States and building new buildings to achieve maximal energy efficiency, water efficiency, safety, affordability, comfort, and durability, including through electrification."

"Overhauling transportation systems in the United States to eliminate pollution and greenhouse gas emissions from the transportation sector as much as is technologically feasible, including through investment in - (i) zero-emission vehicle infrastructure and manufacturing; (ii) clean, affordable, and accessible public transportation; and (iii) high-speed rail."

"Spurring massive growth in clean manufacturing in the United States and removing pollution and greenhouse gas emissions from manufacturing and industry as much as is technologically feasible."

"Working collaboratively with farmers and ranchers in the United States to eliminate pollution and greenhouse gas emissions from the agricultural sector as much as is technologically feasible."

Rashida Tlaib - US Representative – Michigan's 13th District

Rashida Tlaib, born July 24, 1976, is an American politician and lawyer serving as the U.S. Representative for Michigan's 13th congressional district since 2019. The district includes the western half of Detroit, along with several of its western suburbs and much of the Downriver area.

A member of the Democratic Party, Tlaib represented the 6th and 12th districts of the Michigan House of Representatives before her election to Congress.She was the first Muslim woman to serve in the Michigan legislature. In 2018, Tlaib won the Democratic nomination for the United States House of Representatives seat from Michigan's 13th congressional district. She ran unopposed in the general election and became the first Palestinian-American woman in Congress and one of the first two Muslim women elected to Congress, alongside Ilhan Omar (D-MN). She is a member of the Democratic Socialists of America and, along with Alexandria Ocasio-Cortez, one of two DSA members currently serving in the House of Representatives.

Favorite quote regarding Trump: "We're going to impeach the motherf***er"

Ilhan Omar – US Representative – Minnesota's 5th District

Ilhan Abdullahi Omar, born October 4, 1982 is an American politician serving as the U.S. Representative for Minnesota's 5th congressional district since 2019. The district includes all of Minneapolis and some of its suburbs.

Omar is a member of the Congressional Progressive Caucus and has advocated for a living wage, affordable housing and universal healthcare, student loan forgiveness, the protection of Deferred Action for Childhood Arrivals, and abolishing U.S. Immigration and Customs Enforcement (ICE). She has strongly opposed the immigration policies of the Trump administration, including the Trump travel ban. She has been the subject of several conspiracy theories, death threats, and other harassment by political opponents.

Ayanna Pressley – US Representative – Massachusetts 7th District

Ayanna Soyini Pressley, born February 3 1974, is an American politician serving as the U.S Representative for Massachusetts' 7th congressional district since 2019. Her district, which was once represented by John F. Kennedy and Tip O'Neill, includes the northern three-fourths of Boston, most of Cambridge, parts of Milton, as well as all of Chelsea, Everett, Randolph, and Somerville.

Pressley is the first African American woman elected to represent Massachusetts in Congress. With the November election victory of Jahana Hayes in Connecticut's 5th congressional district they are the first women of color to be elected to Congress from New England.

Pressley is a member of the informal group known as "The Squad", whose members form a unified front to push for progressive changes such as the Green New Deal and Medicare For All. The other members of "The Squad" ar Ilhan Omar (D-MN), Rashida Tlaib (D-MI), an Alexandria Ocasio-Cortez (D-NY).

In an interview with The Boston Globe in July 2019, Pressley said her office has received death threats after president Trump's tweets of July 14, 2019 and in general since her election.

In May 2019, Pressley gave the commencement address to the graduates of University of Massachusetts Boston, saying they are "President Trump's worst nightmare." In her speech she said, "Represented here today are dreamers and doers, immigrants, people of every race identity, every gender identity and sexuality, sisters rocking Senegalese twists and hijabs."

CHAPTER 6

The Young Believers - Interview with government interns

Interviewer: We've gone over the reason for my visit and you've agreed to participate in this important piece of capturing history for future generations. Before we proceed however, I need you each to put your hands on the Bibles you have in front of you and say after me: "I swear to tell the truth, the whole truth and nothing but the truth, so help me God."

Three voices: "I swear to tell the truth the whole truth and nothing but the truth, so help me God."

Interviewee #1: Don't we say "amen" as well?

Interviewee #2: Don't be stupid, that's just in church.

Interviewee #1: Don't call me stupid; it was a good question I think.

Interviewee #3: OK, chill ladies - otherwise we're going to be here all night.

Interviewer: Yes, yes. So let me jump back in. I'm turning on a recorder and first I need to provide some background information. Then I'll seed your discussion with a question. When that runs out of steam, I'll start something else until we think it's all been said. Does that work for you three?

Three voices: <general agreement>

Interviewer: OK; some background for the audience. Who we have here are Sabrina and Stephanie and Tom. They are all interns for various freshmen Representatives. They have been chosen for these interviews as they individually support three politicians that claim membership with the Democrat Socialists of America; Alexandria Ocasio-Cortez, Ilhan Omar, and Rashida Tlaib.

These interns here are in their own rights quite active in the political scene on their respective campuses, and we are treating this interview as a mini-focus group. We want them not only to share what they know of the politicians they support, but their own opinions as well, and also their collective thinking on the feelings of the rest of their friends and peers back at the universities. Got it? <n-ods>

OK, so why don't each of you share some basic personal info: name, age, university, program of study, and maybe something unique about you that none of us know. Sabrina, please go first; then Tom, then Stephanie.

Sabrina: OK, I'm Sabrina and I'm nineteen years old and I go to Columbia - the New York campus. I'm studying to be a lawyer someday. I've lived in New York City my whole life and I wouldn't want to live anywhere else, except for maybe London, Paris, Milan, someplace like that, but I don't have any plans yet.

Tom: My turn. Hi, I'm Tom. I'm twenty-two and I go to Berkeley. I'm just starting my graduate work in community organization, and well, something different is that I spent a year in the Peace Corps after high school and was in Venezuela when their elections went south. Things there got really, really flaky for a while; scary flaky.

Stephanie: My turn now. Hi, again. I'm Stephanie and I'm twenty-one. I'm a senior at Portland State University. I'm getting a degree in women's studies and will pursue a graduate degree in urban social systems at Stanford.

Interviewer: Why did you pick Stanford?

Stephanie: Well, because my family is from the Bay Area and it's a lot warmer and drier there.

Interviewer: I get it. I get it. Shall we proceed? <nods> OK, and thank you for your opening introductions by the way.

The first topic here has to do with some of the common elements in your politician's platforms and we'll pick three of everyone's favorites to start with. Let's talk about minimum wage, Medicare For All and pro-choice/pro-life. I'm just going to throw those ideas out there and then sit back and listen. Talk to each other in free-form and cover your politician as well as your own opinions and ideas. Start with $15 an hour, if that's OK.

Tom: Hey, I'll bite... First of all, $15 an hour isn't enough. I mean it's OK for now in most places, but not forever. And it doesn't even work in some places now. I live in the Bay Area and $15 is a joke. Just to share an apartment with three others and cover rent and food, let alone college, I'd have to work probably twenty-five hours a week at $15 an hour. And go to school for another twelve or thirteen hours, not counting any homework on top of that.

My friends in this situation never have any money - never. AOC thinks that before her term is out, we'll be asking for $20 an hour and even $25 in the big cities.

Stephanie: I like it. In Portland the minimum wage is $12 and going up to $12.50 or something stupid like that. Portland's cheaper to live in than the Bay Area, but not that much. A Starbucks coffee costs almost the same everywhere. Plus, when I go to Stanford, $15 won't cover anything.

Sabrina: <laughing> Tell me about it. My dad gives me an allowance of $15 an hour just for going to classes and that barely covers Uber rides. So things have to go up eventually. <swooning> Or we're all doomed!

Stephanie: In the Oregon country side, minimum wage is like $2.00 less or something like that. It seems to work for them.

Sabrina: Yeah, but you can get a burger in little town for $8. I saw that price on vacation last year. You go out for a decent burger and beer dinner in Manhattan and it's probably going to hit $75 for a couple, maybe a $100 if you go fancy. For burgers! So for me, it's not so much dollars per hour as much as it is dollars per month.

My burn rate here in DC with a roommate, no car, and a starvation diet is like $2000 a month with shared rent and utilities included, no gas bill, no cable, no parking. So do the math; one hundred and thirty-three hours a month for work to make two grand, so like thirty-three hours each week, just to break even. Not including taxes and fees and crap, so round up to forty hours a week. Full time for rent and a meager existence for the privilege of having a name brand diploma and a pile of debt when I'm done!

Tom: Yeah, so $15 is a joke and it's heading north. What do Omar and Tlaib think about minimum wage?

Sabrina: Ilhan thinks the entire concept of hourly wage to be archaic. Everyone has to live one hundred and sixty-eight hours per week, so that is the existential concern, not an earning rate per hour. It definitely moves her to stipend checks vs. a stance on minimum wage. Again, do the math.

Stephanie: What Tlaib thinks on this; I'm not really sure. She has me assigned to other issues and I don't get to go to many staff meetings. But if I offered what I think is her opinion on minimum wage it would be that it is a temporary concern and we all ought to be concerned about larger issues. Like who is in the White House and why is that bastard still there.

But I do want to talk about Medicare For All. She is very clear on this and very vocal as well. In her opinion, health care is a test of faith and obedience for a society; "Care for the least of us all..." and that sort of thing. And it is an indicator of self-pride, greed and sinfulness to focus on profit and achieve instead exploitation of society as a whole. Bottom line - healthcare should be provided for all as a basic right, right?

Tom: Well, I agree with that stance personally, and nearly everyone I know at school agrees with that too. AOC is especially sharp on this topic as it is an anchor issue on a whole variety of economic concerns. Without a universal stance for the health of individuals being resolved into policy, other economic factors like housing, food, utilities, transportation, entertainment, etc., become non sequitur. Crack universal healthcare and you crack universal everything.

Sabrina: Now wouldn't that be nice. At least that's what I think. There is just so much greed and pride that gets in the way; so much testosterone.

Ilhan shares all of these ideas about the future of health care, some with greater anxiety and some with less. On top of these ideas she also cites that health care costs are ridiculous and that fundamental restructuring of the health care supply chain profit pools is required to achieve sustained improvement. One of her favorite stories in private is that in order to save money in the long run, we're going to have to sue the ever loving crap out of everyone who makes a profit in the short run. I don't know how that will work, but that's the motto.

Interviewer: Wow, OK, so pretty strong support from all of the politicians. What about you and your friends? What do college students think of Medicare For All?

Tom: I already said I agree with Medicare For All. I don't know why we call it that, though. It's universal healthcare and it's a human right - no matter what the cost. Everyone in my network thinks the same way.

Stephanie: Bay Area, ditto, and Portland ditto for sure. Some of my friends from outside Portland are not so sure. There are lots of questions about cost to provide this, but no one, left or right, urban or rural, seems to have good data on the cost side. Report after report after article after article and you just can't get to corroborating numbers that add up. So mostly my friends believe in Medicare For All because it just seems right. It makes sense.

I'm still worried about the cost though. My aunt got really sick with breast cancer and her bills were like $100K in one year. She couldn't pay enough on time and I don't think she got the best meds as a result. Plus her credit score got hammered, so that sucks. So if everyone gets breast cancer and we all have $100K worth of stuff done, who pays for all of this? I know I don't make that much money.

Sabrina: It's all a profit farce. Everybody in corporate land behind all those costs basically sandbag their pricing and availability and anything that gets in the way of their profit. As soon as we get all of this public and managed by the government, then we'll realize that health care without fat cat profit is really not that expensive after all. And after a couple of Ilhan's lawsuits, the real problem of corporate greed and stupid tax reductions will come to fruition and the whole system becomes fully paid for. One of my professors even claims that once corporate profits are removed, USA health care will actually become a huge tourist draw because it will be the best and now the cheapest healthcare in the world.

Tom: I like that idea a lot. Think about it. What we're paying for healthcare is a farce because of corporate profits and protection of status quo. When the walls come down, we realize that health care doesn't really cost that much, so it should be free. Free of cost for the citizen and free of profit for the capitalist; sounds fair to me. Too many greedy people have been involved in healthcare for too long for the system not to be out of balance now.

Stephanie: I can see the bumper sticker now: "Bring balance to health care... Tom for President."

Interviewer: OK, wages and insurance seems to be pretty agreeable topics. What about pro-choice? What policy stance and strategies should we expect this year? Stephanie - how about you first?

Stephanie: No worries. To be frank with you, Representative Tlaib and what I understand about Islam seem a bit at odds on abortion. Islam itself seems very close to Christianity on this topic in many ways. Abortion is discouraged overall, but allowed, and only allowed in certain circumstances like very early term and extenuating circumstances like rape and incest and danger to the mom. Many different views on what early term is actually, like weeks or months or whatever. But the general stance is, you know, "please don't".

But Tlaib is much more supportive of a liberal pro-choice platform than her religion would indicate. I could talk about this a long time, but she is clearly of the view that there are simply too many people on the planet and if we can slow down birth rates voluntarily, so be it. I like her stance here, but I don't like really late term abortions, so I struggle with leaning too far left when policies lead to actualities.

Sabrina: Do we collectively understand that we will have eight point three billion people on earth twenty years from now? Where are they all going to live? South of Holister? Who cares how many of us decide to leave a fetus behind? For every one of us that say "no" to motherhood, there are three others that are going to say "yes". So no matter what the abortion rate is or when it occurs during term, we're still going to outgrow this planet.

Tom: AOC has a very clear stance on this - Pro-Choice. At the bottom of her thinking is that there are too many areas where women do not really have choice, so we need to stand in uniform support of this choice for all women. No ifs, ands, or buts. Pro-Choice means woman's choice and whatever the woman wants to do, that's her damn business.

Stephanie: Amen, brother. Do what is right for you. And it should be totally included in Medicare For All. My team of me, myself, and I decide what to do. It gets done and the bills get paid. Then me, myself, and I move forward. Tlaib is totally on board and she's also on a leadership vector here. Finally we have someone that can push loud enough for all of America to hear, and hear loud and clear. I really like it when she talks her mind. "Me, too." "Me, too."

Stephanie: Can we talk about Israel now? I'm really curious about what Alexandria and Ilhan think about that. I know it's not on your agenda, but I really want to know more.

Sabrina: Yeah, that's a good idea. Ilhan's stance is predictable; the infidels must go. She won't talk about this on TV or anything, but we let our hair down once and it was pretty clear that she's strongly Muslim on the Israel topic. Me? I have a lot less anger towards the Jews, but why do they insist on being in Palestine? I mean there are a gazillion nice places on earth and maybe they should just pick one and go there. Plus, have you seen that part of the world on TV? What a pit. Anywhere else would be better.

Tom: Well, I have a different view on this topic, I think. AOC is with you guys, pretty much. Single state solution - that is, a non-Jewish single state is the only long term answer, so let's keep the world moving in that direction.

My view? I'm Jewish. I should really say I was raised Jewish and had my bah mitzvah and such, but I don't actively practice being a Jew. When it comes to Israel, I don't understand why everyone hates them and why they are always on the defensive? This is over hundreds and hundreds of years. So I'm intellectually for a two-state solution, but only if there is some sort of disarmament along the way so that there can really be peace between the Israelis and the Palestinians. Can't we just all get along?

Stephanie: So what is the hold up? Years and years of conflict and strife and within ten minutes we all agree - the Jews should just move out! Why isn't that on the table at the UN or someplace?

Tom: It's more than just "move out..." I don't know why, it just is. My family spent hours and hours at the dinner table talking all around this topic and it was always the same discussion over and over and again. It felt like I was watching reruns of the same episode of CSPAN every night.

Others: < in unison> Nightmare! <long pause>

Interviewer: I have an idea. We've been going at it awhile. Let's take a flat white break and re-convene in a little while. There are a few other things to cover this afternoon.

CHAPTER 7

The Young Believers (Part Two) - Interview with interns - continued

Interviewer: Thanks for coming back so promptly and are we all ready for round two? <affirmations> OK, next topic is the Green New Deal. Tell me about what you think about that agenda.

Tom: I want to go first. Is that OK with you guys? This is my area of focus for AOC and I know a ton of the details. Can I go? <nods> OK, let me start with a story first. Pretend it is five hundred years from now and we've finally met people from another planet. Imagine how the conversation would go when it comes to fossil fuels:

"OK, let me get this straight. You guys used to take complex hydrocarbons in various states of decomposition out of the ground, burn them and then release the gasses into the air you breathe." "Yes." "And sometimes you would make products out of these hydrocarbons, like a gel that you would spread over parts of your body and use it like things for flu treatments and burn wounds." "Yes." "And then you actually would use some of these hydrocarbons to store your food in." "Yes." "And sometimes you would take food wrapped in hydrocarbon-based films and then put it into a machine that would bombard the hydrocarbon wrapped food with microwaves just before consuming it." "Yes." "And you drank a lot of water that came in hydrocarbon based bottles." "Yes." "And sometimes these bottles had been sitting out of doors or in the sun and got really hot, but then when it cooled, you drank it anyway." "Yes." "And then you threw these bottles and canisters and a billion other pieces of hydrocarbon based trash into landfills that sometimes drain into your watershed." "Yes." "And you dumped a bunch of this hydrocarbon trash into the ocean so that all of your seafood could eventually absorb some of it." "Yes." "No wonder you guys are dying..." "Yes."

Anyway, when you put it that way we seem stupid, but that's only one of the industrial demons we have to attack. The human race has dozens of ways to poison itself and there are people in the world who are getting sicker and sicker and sicker every day; hence the Green New Deal. No more fossil fuels; no more nuclear. Wind, solar, waves, thermal; move to 100% renewable energy within twenty years. Require compliance on a global scale. Look, we only have a few years before things really start falling apart.

The bottom line for me? AOC and the Green New Deal are right on target and just about the only way we can avoid environmental catastrophe!

Stephanie: Amen to that brother. The world's been dropping babies and trashing the planet for centuries and the piper has come to be paid. Sign me up.

Sabrina: Me too, me too. The science on climate change is totally uncontestable. It's only old people that think what we're witnessing on a global scale is a natural cycle. Would we really be losing the ice caps if there were only five hundred million people on the planet again? I don't think so.

Tom: AOC thinks that we're going to have to get pretty radical to make the sorts of changes that are required. Too many of those big wigs we talked about are in positions of real power. Some of them are just going to have to go. We can't wait for them to die off to make changes; we need action now.

Interviewer: That sounds interesting. What do you mean by getting radical?

Tom: A lot of people laughed at AOC when she brought up the Green New Deal. Republicans especially, but even some Democrats as well; mostly the older ones. Making the Green New Deal happen is going to take all the arms of government working together. Since almost all politics is split around fifty-fifty these days, we have to activate people that don't vote now and swamp the election results. Things like dropping the voting age to sixteen needs to be done. That and restoring voting rights for felons and bringing in more people from outside the US. All of this added up is pretty radical when compared to the status quo.

Sabrina: Plus some other out of the box thinking would be useful. I personally believe we have the wrong formula for voting. The young people that have to live in a future created by new laws should be part of the voting process for sure. It's the old people that shouldn't be voting; like everyone over fifty. They've screwed up things enough already. When you get to the end of your useful life, you shouldn't be deciding things for future generations; the future generations should be deciding those things.

Stephanie: I like that, but like we talked about that $15 an hour is just too low, maybe fifty years old is just too high. Maybe no voting after forty would be better.

Tom: I like it! Let's get really radical. The new voting age will be fourteen to forty. I don't think my mom and dad will like the change, but I'll just tell them to get back to their martinis and not worry about things anymore.

Sabrina: Red wine for my folks. Or margaritas.

Stephanie: I can just see it now. Universal health care; Green New Deal; leave women's rights alone; profit reduction and restructuring. These are things that need to be done and it's feeling pretty radical. Plus we'll add voting age change; fourteen to forty, but after forty, well, you get free martinis.

Sabrina: Or red wine.

Tom: Or margaritas.

CHAPTER 8

Sub-cabinet Meeting - Interview with a DNC eavesdropper

Interviewer: We've gone over the reason for my visit and you've agreed, under anonymity, to provide your version of an important meeting you were privy to. Is that correct?

Interviewee: Yes that's true.

Interviewer: And you're agreeing to the data provider's fee we discussed and in exchange, I get the truth, the whole truth and nothing but the truth. Understand?

Interviewee: Yes I understand.

Interviewer: So I am going to make a recording and let you tell the story. Please proceed.

Interviewee: OK. <whew> One of my roles with the Democratic National Committee is to gather video and audio information on whomever and whenever. My team and I have been doing this for a few years now. We have like ten thousand terabytes of information, or is that how much we record per month? I don't know anymore. Anyway, almost all of this is TV style interviews and it's all very well planned out. We have global reach, but 80% of our information is from the US. We cover all fifty states, but there are about fifteen states that make up 70% of our intake. And we cover all major cities pretty heavily but truthfully, rural towns and villages are included only when stories go there.

All this information is archived in three formats - Raw, Edited, and Headline. It is made available to DNC member organizations as appropriate and most of our partners pay for this content. We have a security level coding system that organizes the information to share into four categories: 1) general access - this is the free stuff, 2) regional access - this is for local news broadcasts, 3) in-depth topics, like special interest areas, and 4) need-to-know-only. That last category is determined and dispensed by the Chairman of the DNC and two other senior staff members that come and go.

About eighteen months before the 2020 elections, one of our sources was invited to a sub-cabinet meeting. Sub-cabinet means cabinet level people, but not the entire cabinet; just the members important to the topic. Plus special guests as determined by who knows who. It's like a sub-committee, but sub-committees are more long lasting; some are even permanent. These sub-cabinet meetings are always forming and disbanding and hibernating. They're really self-forming squads to deal with various depth topics. Sometimes they last a day; sometimes a month; never longer really.

This sub-cabinet team was meeting to talk about the recent government shutdown and next steps on the border security topic. Modest funding for building the wall was an outcome of the negotiations and this team was eager to spend it. Our source was responsible for managing fund flow on this part of the national budget, so she was invited. She contacted us after the meeting and let us know that she had some information to share.

What we didn't know at the time was that she had recorded the whole meeting with her phone in a purse pocket. She just turned on her voice recorder in the ladies room and turned it off when she got back to her car. Dangerous as hell, but she got away with it. If she would have been caught, she would be prison bound for sure. But her balls were our blessing and we got some seventeen minutes of totally awesome audio recordings. Some of it is hard to understand at times, but it has some really good parts that are clear as a bell.

There were seven people in this particular meeting: the President, the Vice President, Secretary of State, the Attorney General, our source and two unidentified men that stood in the back and never spoke out loud. One or two whispers to wrists, our source said, but they weren't really part of the meeting.

They could've been Secret Service, but the Secret Service never attends other sub-cab meetings, so I don't think so. They could've been FBI and one looked pretty senior, but we still don't know who they were. They could have been Russians for all I know. Our source didn't pay much attention to them.

I knew we were going to talk about this today, so I edited the original recording into a shorter piece with most of the stuff you can actually hear well. There were lots of side conversations and silent periods, so what we have here is about six minutes of meat; solid meat. Over half of it is need-to-know content, so a good three minutes of impeachment evidence if you ask me. Here, let me just turn on Itunes and we can play the material. You can simply copy my recording later if that will work for you; that should save us a lot of time.

< playback setup and testing>

OK, back to the beginning, then "play". That should work.

<playback starts>

POTUS: So then I get a double bogie on #12 when it took me two swings to get out of a sand trap. It was a total screw up and it blew my round and my weekend. I really hate traveling to Florida and back just to dent my handicap. I either have to play a lot more or play a lot less. I don't know. Mariana and I did have a great dinner and I got some movie time in with Bryan, but I tell you, I was being dragged down into a pit by that double bogie. That is, until I got your text that the spending bill had finally passed.

VPOTUS: Yes, Mr. President, I sent that immediately after the vote passed. Seven weeks of government shutdown, but we finally got a decent amount of wall money.

POTUS: Now Max, you know better than I. We can't call it wall money anymore. It's border security emergency funding now.

VPOTUS: Well, whatever we call it, it's billions of dollars and it's authorized for the executive branch to spend.

POTUS: Took long enough, but that's water over the dam now. Mr. Pampas, I'm guessing that you have completed that high priority list of Mexican officials that we need to compensate? They did a great job of complaining about the caravans and staging a few newsworthy protests. For that I am grateful.

SEC STATE: Yes sir, just like we discussed, I have the top three players in each of the six Mexican states along the border identified, plus a handful of our partners in Mexico City. They get funded in two days. We have a separate reserve set up for local Mexican law enforcement to use when the wall really starts getting going, but the reserve will be spent on an as-needed basis when tensions get high.

POTUS: Very good, very good. Building a wall is just like building a fancy hotel. You have to keep everyone who lives nearby happy, otherwise a project gets tied up in legal knots. A little recognition here, a little cash there, and pretty soon the project is flowing along smoothly. People just don't understand how to get work done.

I talked to the Chairman of the Joint Chiefs of Staff on the way back to Washington and he said that final prep for deploying the Corps of Engineers into Texas, New Mexico, and Arizona is on schedule. The ground breaking for the next ten sections of our border security barrier will start in about two weeks. California is still a mess with Nonsense in the governor's office, but they have the most border wall already, so that can come with time.

Speaking of Nonsense, have we heard anything else back from that joker on my demand to get our federal grant money back from them for that zero-speed bullet train they're pretending to build? Somebody take an action item to get the latest and update me next week.

But let's get back to the wall for now. Do we have the funding stream figured out? I mean the Executive branch and DOD budgets and now our border security emergency funding? There are a lot of moving pieces, and we have to make sure the compensation for our south of the border friends doesn't set off alarms anywhere.

SOURCE: Yes sir, Mr. President. GAAP compliant accounting across lots of line items and organizations, but checks will be written, sir.

POTUS: OK good, very good.Thank you.

Another topic: did any of you see the CNN coverage of Francine this morning? <laughing> Classic! She's going to win the election for me. <whispers of agreement> Do you think there's something wrong with her? Like health-wise? I couldn't understand a bunch of her words, let alone a full sentence. I mean, is it me? Am I the only one that thinks she's babbling? It's embarrassing. <pause>

OK, another different topic. Hey AG, talk to me about the new kids in town.

AG: Yes sir, thank you for asking. We've identified at least six new congressmen - men and women, both actually - that are way, way left of center. All are universally critical of the wall. Plenty of other hard of left policy statements as well, so these are a new breed of players. And they are in real numbers now, not just lone wolves.

You've seen the news coverage. Four of them are really visible as you know. The others are not hidden, just not as apparent on a national scale. Also, there could be a few more in the mix that we don't know about yet.

POTUS: Anything to worry about? I mean, they're being pretty pointed with their comments; socialism straight off the shelf. And mean, nasty mouths if you know what I mean.

AG: No worries, not yet. No. We're developing dossiers as we discussed; basically normal background checking. But we're also talking to neighbors and lifelong friends under the guise of screening them for security clearances. We should be able to brief you in detail, perhaps next week. Nothing out of line so far, but we've just started. Odds are that they won't make it through the next election, but it's better to be safe than sorry.

POTUS: I like what you're doing, but I'm still nervous. They are stirring up a shit storm in some channels, and I don't like their language a bit. Plus they've got Francine acting like a love struck school girl, so that makes we wonder. I want you to put a full court press together and really dig deep. We need to be prepared. And keep it on the hush-hush. If they keep going over the edge, then we'll need something on them to take the wind out of their sails; something to remind them of who's really in charge.

AG: Yes, sir, but how will we keep it quiet if we start moving people on and off of projects? That'll raise a few eyebrows.

POTUS: Yeah, OK. I see your point. Let me think for a second. <pause> OK, what about this? You move just a couple more of your people onto the dossiers and not so many as to make it look out of the ordinary. I'll get back to the Chairman and see if he can re-direct some of his JAG team to help. Assuming so, then they'll get a hold of you personally and you can coordinate with them however you want. With DOD budgets and such, this should be easy to hide. Plus it's a matter of national security so I feel fine about blurring budget lines.

AG: That sounds workable; a little risky maybe, but not impossible for sure.

POTUS: And we can figure this out too? Money-wise? We're back to the Executive branch - DOD budgeting thing again.

SOURCE: Yes, sir. Not a problem. We can't do it right now because, well, we haven't ever talked about it before. But soon, in like a day or two at the most. This is not a big issue to fix.

POTUS: OK, that's good. Gentlemen, gentlewomen, I think we're done on this for today; let's get on to the next meeting. What is it? Oh yes; some god-awful lunch with some god-awful idiot from some poverty stricken god-awful place from the bad side of the planet. This is something I should delegate. Mark, are you available to host this god-awful waste of America's time and tax dollars?

SEC STATE: Uh, no sir, not this time. Normally I'd fall on a sword for you, but I'm double booked already and if you want us to tighten up our border security barrier timeline, I have to meet with Jonathan and Susan right now - that can't wait even one day. In fact, I'm running late to meet with them as it is. Is anyone going to the Capitol? I've got a ride waiting out front if you want to join me.

POTUS: OK, Mark, but next time you go. And then when you're talking trash to the trash, I'll get back to not making another double-bogie. I have to play more golf; it's that simple. Maybe I can get back to Mar-a-Lago this weekend.

<meeting ending, chairs shuffling, conversations muffle>

POTUS: Have I ever told you - "You do a good job."?

<door opens to crowd noise>

SOURCE: Yes sir, you tell me that on a regular basis.

POTUS: Well you do. You really do. Thanks. I like having you on my team.

CHAPTER 9

Sub-cabinet Meeting (Part Two) - Interview with a DNC eavesdropper - continued

Interviewer: So the material from the sub-cabinet meeting was very enlightening. You said you have some interesting stuff beyond that one meeting, is that correct?

Interviewee: What I told you is that we have like a hundred or a million terabytes of video and audio recordings from all sorts of people in and around Washington DC. Not all of this is from the cabinet mind you; just some of it is.

Interviewer: What would be the best way to get to the juicy pieces - I mean the newsworthy pieces - that would be nice for my project?

Interviewee: It takes a lot of searching and reviewing to find things, so let's not do that right now because of time. Send me a list of keywords and topics. I can search through the database and find out if there are recordings that would be interesting for you. I did bring one other recording for today that I find pretty funny and you might find useful. Are you interested?

Interviewer: Of course I'm interested. But before we go there, let me just write down a list of those keywords you wanted. Then we can switch to what you've got. <pause> OK, here you go. Let's start with these ten terms and see where it takes us. Depending on results maybe we can do some more or maybe we'll have enough for now. How do these look?

Interviewee: Let's see the list; Russians, Ukraine, collusion, payments, Congress, the wall. OK, I catch your drift. This is a good list. It will definitely get some hits.

Do you just want executive branch info? Or are other important people on your radar screen?

Interviewer: My research goes way beyond the executive branch so a broader filter is best. By the way, when you finish using this keyword list, would you mind shredding the paper? I want to stay as low profile as possible.

Interviewee: No problem. Let me share this next recording with you, and then I have to go. Do you remember right before the election when the Access Hollywood tape was published? And then there were all these discussions about Gump with hookers in a hotel in Moscow or something?

Interviewer: Yes I remember; lots of back and forth about some really nasty behaviors. Unbelievable really; probably all rumors, so it went away. Why you ask?

Interviewee: Well, this next piece comes from a recording we got out of the President's personal limousine. Sometimes we'll drop a bug into a secret service pocket or a senator's briefcase or substitute a sequin on Mariana's gown and we get some interesting tidbits this way. I think this was one of those sequin bugs that got this recording and it's between Mariana and President Gump on the way to a ball or some art function or whatever. Anyway I skipped through all the preliminary discussions and just started with the funny part. Here goes. <pause> The first voice is Mariana's of course.

MG: Daniel, it was one thing to have to put up with all of that Access Hollywood stuff. And you know that I know that you play around every now and then and I don't mean a round of golf. I don't like it, but I am European and as long as you don't do anything stupid like create a baby or fall in love, I'll survive. We'll survive. But this story about you in Moscow with a hooker and peeing on her or her peeing on you is really making me question whether I know you very well at all. I am not very happy about any of this and you need to talk to me - right now!

POTUS: Mariana, Mariana, we've talked about this over and over again. You know the media is out to get me in any way they can and they use fake news all the time. It's a witch hunt!

MG: Yes I know that, but this is different. This peeing thing is not a natural sexual behavior and that makes me wonder whether you really are a pervert. You've never responded on Twitter to anybody who has posted on this topic and you usually tweet the garbage out of someone that attacks you like this. Mostly you are a pitbull, but this time you're acting like a little poodle with its little furry tail between its little furry legs and that is not like you. It makes me wonder very hard and you need to talk to me on this.

POTUS: OK, OK. I hear you. But the whole thing is kind of embarrassing, so I've been quiet on this one. I don't get embarrassed very often, but when I do sometimes I don't know how to react. This is one of those times.

Remember when I was going to Russia every other month or so? Most of the trips were pretty inert; the same thing over and over again. I arrive at the airport. They pick me up and take me to my hotel. They come get me later and we go to dinner and drink a little vodka. And then I go back to the hotel and go to bed. Two or three days of that and then business is done and I come home.

MG: Daniel, you don't drink. Why you telling me about vodka?

POTUS: You're right, Mariana, I don't drink. Until I do, like when I'm in Russia trying to build a new hotel and make hundreds of millions of dollars. As they say: when in Russia, do as the Russians do. But I always just have a little bit, you know, just to be sociable; to build trust with the locals. They all drink vodka and if you don't, they don't trust you. If they don't trust you, you don't get to build a building.

MG: So this is interesting. Next time I ask you to have a glass of wine with me, you must say yes.

POTUS: Well, we'll see. But let me finish the story. Like I said, it's embarrassing. So this is like my third trip over there, and the second night of my visit. I'm still jet lagged and we had a long day of negotiations. I was tired. After dinner, instead of having vodka at the dinner table or the restaurant bar, they took me to one of those loud nightclubs you see in the movies with the strobe lights and the electric music and the scantily clad women. It was a waste of time and annoying, but when in Russia... Did I tell you, you look beautiful tonight, Mariana? You really do.

MG: Nice try, Daniel; back on topic please. So you're sitting in this loud bar with all of these cute women around, and then what?

POTUS: And then they start giving me Vodka. Vodka with a capital V! Like five hundred dollars a bottle Vodka. And more Vodka. And more Vodka. And some beers to wash the Vodka down. I said "no" over and over again and I turned my glass over many times, but the toasts just kept coming. And we were talking good business, so I wanted to stay connected. But then there was all the Vodka.

So after may be an hour, we get up to leave. There were six of us then; the three of us talking business and these three girls. The girls were very cute. Not as cute as you, mind you, but I knew it was all a set up to get me in my room with one of them. For sure there would be a camera and some blackmail down the road. For sure.

MG: So this sounds a lot like what has been on the news. I'm still not happy and your story is not helping one bit.

POTUS: Mariana, let me speed it up for you then. So we're all driving in this big limo back to the hotel and there's more vodka and more beer and I'm feeling pretty lightheaded actually. We get back to the hotel and I get out of the car and one of the young women follows me inside. My hosts are really smiling, ear to ear, and that tells me for sure it's a setup. So I'm going up to the penthouse with this young lady hanging on to my coat tails and me trying to figure out how to ditch her.

Believe me, there was no invitation on my part and no interest to get involved. By now I was really lightheaded and just wanted to go to sleep, but the girl was relentless. I'll be honest; when I opened the hotel room, she followed me inside and was all over me. I mean kisses and hugs and nothing more. And I wanted nothing more than to go to sleep; my head was really starting to hurt and my stomach was upset.

MG: Where is this going, Daniel, you need to get to the point or I'm going to pack my bags and fly to New York.

POTUS: OK, OK. It all boils down to the vodka. I've never had so much to drink before. Not since being a teenager. But there's this girl in my room and she's hugging and kissing and I just lost it.

MG: Daniel, you lost it? What exactly did you lose Mr. Gump?

POTUS: It's not what you think, Mariana. I lost control of my stomach. I threw up right in the girl's face; bull's eye. Not a lot, just a little puke, but it was disgusting. So she got really mad, screamed a little bit and cussed me out in Russian, but it must have happened to her before because she just cleaned up in the bathroom and left. I gave her a thousand dollar tip to make things up. I wasn't happy with how that went, but it got her to leave so I liked the outcome. That's about it, Mariana.

MG: That's it? Really? The truth, the whole truth and nothing but the truth, Daniel.

POTUS: OK, well, there is one other thing and that's the embarrassing part. <pause>

MG: Daniel, we're almost at the Arts Center. You need to finish the story, or I am going to pack my bags and fly to New York.

POTUS: OK, OK. Remember the fake news part about peeing on the call girl? Well, I didn't pee on the call girl, I peed on myself. When I got up the next morning, I had wet the bed. I never even woke up through it. I don't remember anything after the girl left, but when I came out of the shower in the morning, the hotel maid was taking a photograph of yellow bed sheets; it's probably in some KGB file now. So when they fake newsed the whole "peeing on the hooker" story, I thought that was better than a peeing on me story, so I just let it ride. It's much more macho that way.

MG: Daniel, you're sick.

POTUS: I know, I know; it's embarrassing. But when I get back to my real life after being the President and we finish the Gump Tower in Moscow, you and I get a free penthouse suite for life. That's what I negotiated over the Vodka. That was the whole reason for the entire trip! But even though I don't drink, I've got to stop drinking, especially when I'm over there.

MG: After we have that glass of wine.

POTUS: Yeah, OK. But make it wine with a capital W…

CHAPTER 10

Celebrity Death - CNN News commentator

"CNN is truly sad to inform our listening audience that Secretary Hinton has died. Details are sketchy at this time, but the NY State Medical Examiner has confirmed that Mrs. Hinton's body was removed from her limousine after a traffic incident and taken to a local hospital where she was pronounced dead-on-arrival. No further information has been provided to CNN regarding her passing other than to indicate that all involved were heroic in their efforts to save her life. The family has asked that details on her passing not be shared at this time.

As we understand, there will be a very private, family only funeral service for Elizabeth a week from this coming Thursday. They also plan to enter a month long mourning period immediately afterward with no public appearances during that time. The family is asking that in lieu of flowers and other such gestures, donations should be sent to the Democratic National Committee to be used in the next election cycle.

God bless Elizabeth Rodda Hinton and may she rest in peace. She was an American hero across her entire life and she leaves us all with a hole in our broken hearts."

CHAPTER 11

Hinton's Death - Interview with a kidnapper

Interviewer: My notes tell me that you are Petrov Kiminski, an ex-KGB agent and you are serving a life sentence here in the Guantanamo Bay internment facility. I've also been told officially that there is no Petrov Kiminski here in Guantanamo. And for that matter, no ex-KGB Petrov Kiminski has ever been anywhere in the United States. Can you explain this to me?

Petrov: Yes, of course. I've been promised a nice steak dinner and a senorita tonight if I cooperate with you. I am not going anywhere anytime soon and no one knows I am here, so what have I got to lose? How can I help you?

Interviewer: You can start by telling me how you got here; from the beginning. Well, not the beginning, just the story of the last several years. You've been in Guantanamo for eighteen months, right?

Petrov: Actually it's been nineteen months, one week and four days. But who is counting? And I came to the United States four months and three days before being escorted to this lovely facility. So I have been in America for twenty-three months and exactly two weeks.

This is not my first trip to the good old USA. I was here three decades ago on official Soviet government business; that trip was not in the records either, by the way. It was a long time ago and a short trip; just two weeks of business and a week of sightseeing in your beautiful National Parks.

But I digress, I think. Back to current events. <pause>

It is so easy to get into the United States. You know that don't you. For this second trip, I came into New York's JFK Airport Customs with the name of Jarvik

Spack. I was on a business trip from Budapest to buy farming equipment. At least that is what my identification and cover story read.

After US Customs, I immediately connected to a flight that took me to a trade show in Milwaukee. There I had lunches and dinners with tractor salespeople and a day and a half later I returned to our company apartment in the Queens.

It was a nice apartment actually; top floor, very quiet, with a view of the river and Manhattan. That place is where I met up with my partners in crime. It took two months for us to get ready, one day to execute, and two more months plus one more day for me to get caught.

Interviewer: Wait a second. You said it took "us", plural, two months to prep and then it took two more months for "me", singular, to get caught. Explain, please.

Petrov: Oh. So you want the gory details, I see. You must understand first of all that this was a retirement mission. According to my bosses, who didn't tell me this at the time by the way, it was a retirement mission for me. Enter the U.S.; do the deed; then get found dead at the scene of the crime. I would be an easy scapegoat for the authorities to focus on; and being dead was a sure-fire way for the KGB to not have to pay my pension.

I guess I have outlived my usefulness to my bosses and I regret that it has come to this. Many long years - even decades of loyal service and it is worth nothing to them. But years of loyal service did teach me to listen to my gut. So when our deed was done, my partners in crime, how do you say, got weird? Is that a good way to say it?

My gut was definitely screaming; loudly and clearly. So when my partners in crime turned their backs on me to get the knife that was to go into my back? Well, I changed their assignment and then they died.

They died quickly, efficiently and just a wee bit messy. I made it look like an argument between kidnappers gone bad. The nasty criminals who no longer had a mission tried to take care of an unused interrogation scene and then well, instead, they took care of each other. You know, the American image of crooks - that they are stupid hotheads and can't even succeed at crime. Anyway, I digress again.

I did a very good job of making it look like my partners in crime killed each other, but even I cannot clean up a crime scene totally. There were broken things and blood all over the place. Let alone two bodies which had been in close quarters with me for days on end. You can't hide what has really happened from a good forensics team in that sort of situation. Too much of my DNA around and too many hand washed blood splatters. That might fool a street cop, but a good forensics team would find out in short order that there had been another person in that room.

So with my partners in crime out of commission, no witnesses, and a KGB-class cover story, I found myself alone and on the road. My best guess was that I had twenty-four hours before the FBI would know someone else had been in that room. I was already late for disappearing. The original plan had me flying back to eastern Europe via Brazil and surprisingly Cuba. I got to Cuba alright, just on a different day and through a different path.

Someone must have been assigned by my bosses to do a crime scene follow up that day. So my bosses knew what had really happened in maybe, what, one hour? Two hours? Even before the local police. The follow-up person found that my partners in crime were dead instead of me and placed a quick phone call to the KGB.

I returned to the company apartment immediately to prepare a hasty departure, and then everything changed. After that follow-up person's phone call, my bosses were quite fast in sending out new orders. Maybe they had them planned already, just in case. I am good at what I do and my partners in crime were not very good at what they do. Or should I say what they used to do.

It was 7:00 PM that evening when the lights went out in the apartment <u>and</u> in a lot of other places in my life. They cancelled the lease and utilities and closed off all bank access. They canceled credit cards and rent cars and plane tickets. Lights on! Lights off! At least I still had a lot of cash.

My bosses also prepared an Interpol alert and they sent that out. It was silly; someone forgot that I still had high level communications priority so I received a text of the announcement. It read in effect, "One Mr. Jarvik Spack is on the loose in America with intent to do harm..." They even included fresh copies of all of my new identity pieces, including the address of the apartment that I was standing in; wasn't that nice of them.

So I filled a backpack, left the apartment within twenty minutes and disappeared. I traveled lightly and off the beaten paths, and stayed out of everyone's way for two months. I traded locations, clothes, cars and motels every other day or so.

But the arm of the law in America is very long and very persistent and in four months and three days after coming to the United States, I was greeted at my motel room very early one morning by four huge goons and invited to attend some very pivotal meetings with FBI officials. Long story short, I received a free one-way ticket to Guantanamo Bay in exchange for a lot of cooperation. <long pause>

It's not a bad life here. I mean the alternative is that I get found by the KGB and permanently retired. They <u>will</u> find me if I leave; I am a, how do you say it? A loose end. They will find me and they will retire me.

So three meals a day in a tropical paradise with some simple restrictions on not going anywhere is OK with me. My family was gone long ago. I have plenty of books to read and movies to watch. I get to swim in the ocean once a week. I negotiated that part of my deal myself.

Interviewer: OK, we're off track. Let's get back to the day of the event. Tell me about the kidnapping itself.

Petrov: Yes, yes, of course. Our entire adventure was designed to look like an open attack on the Democrats by the Republicans. A direct knife thrust into the soul of the Democrat half of the nation. The entire world knows of USA, ahh, instability shall we say, and my bosses thought that it might be fun to help. I mean, we help with your elections after all, so why don't we help with the in-fighting that was going on at that time?

The crime day plans were straight forward; kidnap, hide, beat up, stage a scene, then leave the country. But we didn't even get through the "kidnap" part before the plan came unglued.

We knew that taking an-ex Secretary of State who was also an ex-first lady and who was also a presidential candidate would be tricky. Do you know that Mrs. Elizabeth Hinton is under seven by twenty-four Secret Service protection? She doesn't drive herself anywhere, and has a team of a dozen agents assigned to the family. So that had to be overcome, but there were a few chinks in the armor. Elizabeth evidently has, or had I should say, a social calendar that would embarrass a third world president, a shopping budget that would shame a mid-west town's annual budget, and a food habit that makes Wolfgang Puck jealous.

So she was always on the road and that brings uncertainty and opportunity. Plus, she is truly a witch and I mean that in every sense of the word and in every language that I know. Her enemies hate her, her allies hate her, her family all but hates her, and her Secret Service staff really hates her. They call it seven by forty-eight coverage, because each hour seems like two; most of the time even her husband won't travel with her.

The most abused members of her protective staff are the drivers - oh my God! They have this rotation schedule that indeed rotates very quickly. These unfortunate drivers must be very ill of health because they call in sick all of the time and there are often last minute no-shows. The effect is that the drivers are changing all the time and Mrs. Elizabeth Hinton does not even know her driver's names anymore.

My bosses have many assets in the United States of America; many, many assets. You never know when you will need some inside help. While we were back in Mother Russia planning our little interference play, we linked our asset list up to the potential target list and voila', Mrs. Elizabeth Rodda Hinton was connected to one of our assets. It just so happened that one of our men was on her driver rotation schedule; how convenient!

Our interference plans didn't require involving the Hintons, it just worked out that way. There were a few raised glasses in Moscow that night. She has no friends in my country you know; so we all liked the choice of the victim. It felt right to us, you know? Serendipity. Sound of Music. <smile>

People think that the KGB is full of mean and nasty people with no remorse for anything we do. That is simply not true. Most of the time our targets are decent people; good people that are just in the way and we say a prayer for the family of each person we kill. But in this case, our prayers were prayers of joy; it's not often that a target is so universally welcome onto our hit list. And we weren't going to kill her after all, just make a few bumps and bruises and leave her in an interrogation room with a lot of far-right propaganda.

We picked a busy holiday weekend when our asset-driver was scheduled to work. There was a major economic conference going on in New York that same weekend which would help keep everyone's security forces very busy.

Our man deliberately made a few wrong turns with the "intention" of losing Elizabeth's commie tails and the paparazzi, and ended up in lines of honking cars over and over. Mrs. Hinton would have none of that and became angrier and angrier by the minute. After thirty minutes into a terrible traffic jam on a freeway, Elizabeth was at a cussing wit's end and the limousine was finally able to separate from the chase cars without suspicion.

You must understand that there are always two chase cars for Elizabeth and they listen to the conversation in the lead car for security reasons to know always what is going on in the limousine. So when the freeway traffic was at a standstill, the chase cars knew all about the verbal abuse that was being unleashed. And they didn't pity the poor schmuck that was driving either. They had all been in that situation before.

So when the driver responded "I'm out of here at Exit 16, catch up when you can..." everyone understood and no one cared. The driver had decided to proceed on side streets and all of them know every possible path on the way; it's all been pre-planned. They were only six stopped cars behind the limousine. They would indeed catch up in a few minutes and everything would be business as usual. At least that's what they thought.

But they never did catch up to Elizabeth. The limousine driver turned down the volume of the chase car audio feed so the listeners could hear the yelling, but not the words. As he came off of the freeway at his pre-planned exit, he took a path that had been set for a two mile looping spiral back in the opposite direction of Elizabeth's destination. The driver turned off his own cell phone and dialed a programmed number on the prepaid phone he had picked up at Walmart the day prior and dropped it into his coat pocket. Elizabeth's phone was electronically jammed, the security handheld radios in the limousine were powered down and the little black box no one talks about was turned off.

Two minutes later the two chase cars were coming down the Exit 16 ramp following the limousine and an agent in the second car saw Elizabeth's armored car below him. He thought to himself "That's not right, they should be in front of us on Hunter's Point Avenue heading west to the tunnel. Elizabeth is heading south on 43rd Street and going really, really fast!"

Just as this thought emerged, the limo below him plunged into an underpass tunnel right below the still-sitting-in-traffic chase car. The agent's head flipped rapidly around to the left to follow the car, and he found himself staring at an almost empty on-ramp to the Brooklyn-Queens Expressway south towards Brooklyn with a four ton black rocket flying onto the freeway and heading away at upwards of a hundred miles an hour.

The agent's wrist popped automatically to his mouth and he sputtered almost uncontrollably, "We've got a runner. Repeat: We've got a runner. This is no drill. I just saw the Secretary's limo fly underneath us and get on the freeway to

Brooklyn. This is no drill; the limo was travelling at an extremely high rate of speed and is off of all of our planned travel routes."

This call went out to his partner agents in the front seat of his chase car, the three agents in the first chase car, and to an oversight handler at a local FBI field office. Unbeknownst to them, the call was also being heard by me and my two partners in crime. We were staged at an empty warehouse in Queens and being able to monitor the Secret Service communications put us thick in the middle of things.

The plan was for the limo driver to go rogue and get lost in traffic eventually heading north on I-278, back to Queens where we were waiting. Then we would have a talk with the Secretary and let things unfold from there.

It was unfortunate that the driver had been spotted getting on the freeway, even if it was heading south at the time. We had ordered him to disappear into the city, not get tagged within two minutes of getting out of sight. It's hard to get good help, but no one can predict traffic, so I returned to the conversation instead of griping.

Another agent's voice followed the first. This time it was from the driver of the leading chase car, "Look, we are jammed as hell on this exit ramp and we have maybe two traffic light cycles before we get free and can pursue. Oversight, are you there? Are you listening?" "Yes, I am, Lieutenant. I have already dialed into the VIP hotline and will have three borough's Emergency and SWAT team leaders in a call in just a moment." "Perfect and thank you. The Secretary will be gone in sixty seconds and we are in no position to pursue. Hand it over to the locals and we'll join the party when we catch up." "Yes, sir. Is there anything else?" "No, not unless you can change the traffic lights from there." "No can do, sir; sorry about that. Wait, the calls are coming on line...gotta go, sir." "By all means. Over and out."

It was very useful for me and my partners in crime to hear the Secret Service conversations. And we had another conversation coming in as well. The disposable phone that the driver had dialed just a few moments earlier opened up a call with us directly and we could hear very clearly what was going on in the limousine.

Secretary Hinton: Why are we going so fast? I want to be on time for my appointment, but this is ridiculous! Where are the chase cars? I don't see them anywhere.

Driver: Yes, ma'am. We lost a lot of time in traffic and I'm high tailing it now that we have a clear road. The chase cars are right behind us, but they got caught in the jam and will be meeting up soon. I suggest you put your seat belt on in case we hit some bumps.

Secretary Hinton: Yeah, well, if you hadn't been such an a**hole and gotten caught in traffic, then none of this would have happened and I wouldn't have to have a seat belt on, now would I?

Driver: Yes, ma'am. I'm trying to get you to your meeting on time and you should put your seat belt on.

Secretary Hinton: Quit calling me "ma'am" and just shut up. This whole situation is happening because you're a dork. I'm going to get you reassigned off of my team.

Driver: Yes, ma'am; whatever you'd like, ma'am.

The driver's rogue routing plan had him leaving the freeway at the first possible exit and then U-turning back onto I-278, this time going east towards Queens and our waiting interview session. I think that when he approached his U-turn underpass there was another traffic jam and soon he was driving into Greenpoint.

Driver: Shit – another jam. There's a go around on Van Dam to Bridgewater to Norman; I'll take that route. Please put your seat belt on ma'am.

Secretary Hinton: Screw you and your seat belt. Just get me to my luncheon.

The traffic was light on the side streets and when the driver headed east on Norman, he got back up to speed. We could hear horns and Elizabeth's cussing and she must've been getting tossed around. He knew he had a few minutes to get back onto the freeway going east, but he didn't know that he had been spotted by the chase car agent and an all-points bulletin had been issued to every cop within ten miles.

The conversation in the chase cars had continued as we listened to both sets of communications channels. When the street cops in Greenpoint spotted a limousine flying down Norman, a chase was inevitable. I won't tell you every street and every turn unless you want me too, but suffice it to say that the limo and the chasing cops made for a lot of excitement that day.

Secretary Hinton: Why are we being chased by police cars? Why are we still going so fast?

Driver: That's a police escort, ma'am. They're helping clear traffic for us. Please put your seat belt on.

Secretary Hinton: Quit calling me "ma'am", a**hole.

When the driver went off-road and flew into McCarren Park, there were six police cars in pursuit and they chased many, many lunchtime walkers off of the paths and into the bushes. Somewhere among the doughnuts in the grass and hopping curbs Elizabeth must've have taken a good jolt, because her cussing stopped and the moaning began.

Driver: I think you should put your seat belt on, ma'am.

Eventually the limo and the chasing police cars got back onto Meeker Avenue below the freeway and that's where the Secret Service chase cars caught up to the parade. At the height of the chase there were over ten cars in pursuit and the driver was alternating between the road and the sidewalk down Meeker. We heard lots of bouncing and scraping and horns and sirens from both the cell phone and the chase car audio feeds and it seemed to last forever.

The driver did everything he could to get away, but the pursuit was relentless and there was one more off-road session around the statue of George Washington in the Continental Army Plaza. The driver eventually made it onto the on-ramp of the Williamsburg Bridge. Sirens and bumps and horns continued, but the moaning in the back of the limousine became silent at some point.

The train of a lead limousine with ten fully lit and loud siren cars in pursuit must have been something to see. Plus, there were other cop cars coming from Manhattan at that time and all of the traffic on the bridge pulled over to the right, making a clean lane for high speed travel across the East River.

They eventually published a full accident report a few days later. The limousine was traveling above ninety miles an hour when a Volkswagen beetle pulled out in front of it. The beetle had been behind a stationary cement truck in the right lane and evidently the driver was oblivious to what was going on. A few seconds after pausing in a fully jammed right lane, the beetle jumped out into the fully empty left lane, only to be smashed by the full speed four ton limo.

Actually, it wasn't smashed. The left front fender and entire hood of the beetle were sheared away from the rest of the car and continued with Hinton and the driver as the limo rose up on its left side. The limo spun as it scraped down the road bed and stopped abruptly when the front end of the vehicle slammed into a vertical post.

So you know that the gas tank for a Volkswagen beetle is in the front of the car? Yes, that is true and when the limousine came fully on its left side, the beetle's gas tank was crushed under the driver's window. The scraping slide over concrete ruptured the gas tank and both of the front side windows were shattered by debris.

As you well know from the news, there was no explosion, but there was a fire. It was amazing that the driver was able to get out of the car. He climbed up through the passenger side window and was lifting himself out when the fire ignited. He was covered in gasoline and his suit erupted in flames as he jumped onto the road bed. He didn't stop there, however. The brave driver, now fully on fire, sprinted to the side of the bridge and vaulted into the river below. He was later found, but he had landed badly. He had been knocked out and he drowned.

Elizabeth was more lucky than the driver, if you can call it that. The chase vehicles were on the scene within ten seconds of the crash and the chasers all emptied from their cars with their on-board emergency equipment in tow. Six fire extinguishers did light work of the flames and the burn damage was only from the driver's compartment forward. A jaws-of-life tool opened Elizabeth's door within moments and she was pulled free without any burns at all.

Unfortunately for her however, she had broken her neck somewhere along the way and with all of the jostling around, she didn't make it. Princess Diana of America perhaps, no? <pause> I don't know if there is a moral to this story but I do know that I always wear my seat belt. Such a stupid way to go…

Anyway, my partners in crime and I stood there in the empty warehouse and listened to the whole incident. The phone call from the driver and his screams ended when he hit the water, but we listened to the police communications while the fire was being extinguished and while they recovered Elizabeth from the wreck. We eventually heard the words "I think she'd dead…" from one of the officers and we knew then and there that there would be no interview with the Secretary that day.

My partners in crime and I talked a bit about "what next?" and a few ideas emerged that didn't make sense to me. At some point in the heated discussion I finally said "Let's get this cleaned up and get out of here. There's nothing else left to do."

But as I explained earlier, that's when my partners in crime got weird and then, well, then their assignment changed. We have talked about this.

I left the scene to retrieve my car at the back of the warehouse and returned to the apartment to clean up and leave the USA, probably forever. But now we are back to the middle of the story.

Do you have any questions?

CHAPTER 12

The Caravan Riots - Interview with a Honduran mule

Interviewer: OK let's get started. Your name is Jorge Ramos, at least that is what you tell me. And you have an interesting profession that I would like to learn more about. Your business card says travel guide and your travel agency is in Honduras, correct?

Jorge: Yes, the business card also says Tagucigalpa, which is the capital, but I'm from San Pedro Sula, up in the northwest of the country.

Interviewer: I want you to talk to me about your travel guide business. And in exchange, I will give you five hundred dollars in American cash. That is that we discussed, correct?

Jorge: Yes, that is correct. An easy five hundred and then I disappear back across the border and return to Honduras. I might be back again; I might not. It all depends on the tourism business.

Interviewer: Then Jorge, you take it away. Tell me about your business and tell me about the last trip you made.

Jorge: Yes, no problem. My tourism company is an all-around travel service. Most of our customers are from Honduras, but we have a few from out of the country. My specialty is travel to America; specifically the southern border of America and more specifically budget travel packages. Most of my customers are poor local citizens who are looking for a better life someplace else other than Honduras. They have no money, just the clothes on their backs, really. And many of them are young single people or single mothers with their children;

families as well, yes. Most of the people I plan travel for come from close by to San Pedro Sula but sometimes there are people that join us from other places.

My name is very popular in the area. I used to be a very famous mariachi player, and I get plenty of music business when there is business to be had. But recently I have this new travel business and this new business is the one that is growing. Everyone wants to go to America in my country. Even with all the violence and terrible killings there, it is still better than Honduras. These days, you need to be careful and pick which side of America you want to be on, but that is mostly easy. Pick red if you lean to the right and pick blue if you lean to the left. And also avoid the hot spots. But everyone still wants to go to America, so I help them out.

The amount of time it takes to get from my country to America depends on a lot of things; how many people, how many children, how many other groups are traveling at the same time, and especially, how much money is available for transport. Many of my trips are business people and their families; as few as three people sometimes. No, let me fix that; I have had several trips for two people only, but I usually have two parents with at least one child.

Those trips are usually well funded, and they are very simple and very fast; typically under one week from a request to me to their entry into America. The people in those groups don't have to climb walls to get into America. They get to land at an airport and go through Customs with their fancy travel bags and their brand new passports and entry documents. They walk right into America with no customs hassles; that is my specialty. Within one hour of landing they are in their new country and then what do they do? I don't know. I don't care. I never see them again. My business does not have many repeat customers.

There are hundreds and hundreds of these little groups of Hondurans coming into America every month and this has been happening for years. So when you think about the big crowds that you see on the news, what you don't see on the news is all of these little families traveling by themselves and landing at international airports. But they have money to pay for transport and good documents, so it is fast and quiet and very, very easy to do. You know that America is easy to get into, right?

Sometimes I have other easy trips with groups of two or three, but for people not from Honduras. They always have the best funding and nicest clothes and they have their own documentation. And never any kids, so every step we take is fast and accurate. They show up on time and they leave me on time. And they pay well. But we don't use their documents to get into America, mine are always better. They can use whatever documents they want once they are in America. I don't care; I never see them again either.

My trade secret is to provide the best documents available so that American Customs is never a problem. And how do I do this, you ask? My solution is classic. I provide American-made originals; that is how. I know a cousin of my life long best friend that works in the Honduran consulate in Tegucigalpa and he makes them for me. I am his best customer he says, so we have a good relationship and my top paying customers land in airports with new passports and voila' - they get into America very easily. And I never see them again.

But for people with no money for transport? This is a much different story; a much different story and a much longer story. You must understand that I am not in the travel business to go broke. I am not a charity and I make my living by helping people achieve their dream of going to America. I am very good at what I do, but it takes a lot of money to get into America easily. Those families and those small groups of men that have the money - they move quickly and easily. Like I said, one week from start to finish can be done.

But for my countrymen who are leaving the villages and the towns for a better life in America - they have a different set of battles to fight. Imagine the conversation with me the first time I meet with them: "We want to go to America. The life is better there." "And how do you want to go there? Do you have money for plane tickets?" "No." "For trains?" "No." "For busses?" "No." "For hotels?" "No." "For food?" "No."

<pause>

"OK. Let me explain please. From our capital city it is a six hour flight to Texas; and over eight hours to California. Total distance to Texas is around 3000 km and 5000 km to California. If you walk to Texas it will take you over five hundred hours; that is more than two months of hiking ten hours a day when you count some down time for dealing with injuries and sickness. To California it is twice that long and most trips take more than six months on the calendar. So where in America do you want to go?" "California" "California, of course." "Of course."

Anyway, for many years only a very few small groups of poor Hondurans made the trip. It was just too hard and dangerous and way too long of a trip. But the desire to go to America was there. It is still there. As a result there are always a large number of Hondurans ready to go to America. Their decision had been made, but they have no money to reduce travel time and travel risk.

Until, that is, when Daniel Gump ran for President of the United States. When he came onto the political scene, suddenly there was money. Not all at once, but money started coming in. For food and for transport; and for marketing of all things. There was suddenly lots of money for advertisements and leaflets talking about America's open borders and America's land of opportunity. I didn't know where the money was coming from at first.

One day, a small American charity - I don't remember the name; "Freedom" something, I think - they came to me and asked if I would like to help them organize some travel. They let me know they would have many, many clients to send to me and they would be funding most of their expenses. I simply needed to tap into the local resources to help make this travel occur. I would be the middle man between the non-profit Freedom organization and the resources in Honduras and wherever the travelers went.

Certainly I was interested and I let them know that. The middle man is often where a lot of profit is to be taken. Honduras is not a rich country, so finding good paying clients for my business is difficult. If someone says "I have clients for you." I am all ears. And if they say "I have money to pay for these clients." I am more than all ears. So we talked a few details and I come to find out that these clients are all of the very poor people in Honduras that want to go to America. Then I find out that this organization has a budget of thirty-eight US dollars per person for a trip that starts in Honduras and goes to America. "Seriously?" I say? In Spanish, of course. "Seriously..." they say. In English, of course.

But they had their reasons for funding the travel this way. These, what did you Americans call them? Oh, yes, these caravans of thousands of poor peasants needed to be of meager resources. They do not have money in life, so they would have no money in travel. The people that would be travelling to America must arrive hungry, thirsty and in much need.

The first few caravans were a disaster in just about every way possible. Thirty-eight dollars was not enough money to start with, and the big line of people coming into every town between Honduras and America just saturated all the services and the space and the available food, water and whatever else people could negotiate for. The groups got spread out and even though we had experienced mules to guide most of them, there were hundreds and hundreds of unescorted Hondurans traveling through Guatemala and Mexico on their own.

When we got to international borders it was terrible; think of the fences across the southern Mexico bridges. The travelers were still strong then and there was lots of property breaking and law breaking those days; some riots even. When they got to America, it was bad as well. The walls were not stormed so much at that time, but America did not have the personnel to process thousands of Hondurans. So the wait time was long, long, long. And the thirty-eight dollars had run out weeks and weeks earlier, so we did not provide food or water or shelter or transportation any more.

Everyone was tired by the time they got to America, so there was not much rioting; except for the young men that joined the caravan in the very last days before reaching America. There were hundreds of them it seemed; coming out of the woodwork in northern Mexico. They had plenty of energy when they got to America and they caused some trouble, but that changed after a short while. I have no idea where these men were from. They were of all colored skins and stayed to themselves mostly. Some did not speak either English <u>or</u> Spanish, I know that for a fact.

We're in our fourth year of organizing caravans and it is a good business for us. We quickly negotiated the funding up with the Freedom organization to what was really needed to make it good business and we put in good people and some good processes to make things work. My company is making a tidy profit at this time and while this informal war of yours is going on, we are fueling your economy with lots and lots of eager workers. It's a good situation really. Well, for the Hondurans that make it all the way into America at least.

Interviewer: At the time of those first caravans, there were lots of rumors about violence and sex crimes and human trafficking in the caravans. It sounded like a lot of people were getting hurt.

Jorge: Yes, yes. I can tell you all about that. But people will be people, so these sort of things happen everywhere, and not just in caravans. Honduras is rampant with bad people doing bad things and I think the caravans are an extension of this culture of violence. Your caravans to America did not invent the idea of the powerful people taking advantage of the powerless people. And there are bad people in every country, so when you have so many people going through so many villages and towns and cities, then they are exposed over and over again to street scum.

This was another thing your media focused on poorly; just enough facts to make it look terrible, but not enough detail to truly understand what was going on.

Most of the violence like fights and stabbings and a few shootings were almost all due to the street scum in the local towns. They see these defenseless strangers streaming through and well, some people just like to hurt other people.

For God's sake, there certainly wasn't any money to go after. So the bored locals would pick some fights and sometimes it got serious. The good news is that this has gotten better over the years. The locals have found out that providing things like food and water for the caravans can be quite profitable if you plan well. So it is better to make some dinero with the travelers than to vent some steam and maybe end up in jail.

The sex crimes like rape and trafficking, that was another matter altogether. Sometimes, yes, the local street scum would pick a caravan senorita and she would get kidnapped or raped or murdered or all three, maybe. And again as with the violence reporting, the sex crime and sex trafficking reporting was a disgrace. I don't mean to say that sex trafficking did not occur. It did occur, and sometimes it still does and that it is very, very bad. And the rapes still occur occasionally, but things have gotten better here as well.

Your media reported during the early caravans that 30% of the women, and maybe the younger girls too, were sexually assaulted while traveling to America. I think this was over-reported. Don't get me wrong, I do think that 30% of the women were having sex while in a caravan, but it wasn't all assault. The smart women really understood how long and challenging a trip to America would be. And how risky it would be for them personally; especially single mothers with vulnerable children. They were very clearly targeted by some of our more, how should I say, "aggressive" mules.

So many of the smart travelers realized that having a good relationship with a person in charge of the caravan was a good thing and for most of them, the relationship involved sex. But the sex was consensual, and there was clear understanding in these cases: "You provide me and my family safety from others, food when available, shelter in the same way and in exchange, we have good times and I sleep with you."

You may think that my approval of situations like this is sick but it is really just an observation of how humans coexist. This has been going on since we were kicked out of the Garden of Eden and it has just continued from there.

Some of the mules would pick up maybe five relationships like this in each caravan and they would have their own little harem along the way. Most of the women in these harems would arrive to America in very good condition and there was very little enslavement of harem women into the sex trade. The benefit to a woman from Honduras of arriving at the border with protection was immeasurable. Arrive by yourself, and the pretty women have to fight off the pimps that are waiting at every border crossing. So it was very easy to decide to have a boyfriend on their travels and enjoy the company of others in similar situations. Just don't forget the birth control.

As with everything else caravan, the sex issues were worst in the beginning and have settled down over the years. I am an honest businessman and a husband and a father and I get nausea when I hear of the worst stories. You can remember the horrible things that were reported on the news and since this news was graphic, it was reported very accurately. But the worst of the atrocities were never made public and I have lit many candles over the years.

It took a little over a year plus one half to go from one-point-two horrible sex crimes every month to zero-point-one-four horrible sex crimes during the same period of time. That's almost a ten to one reduction in sex crimes. We're not done with this effort, but we feel good about what we have accomplished here.

Do you know how we accomplished these criminal reductions? <pause> Yes? No? OK, I will tell you that most of the bad people in these stories are the mules; the people we put in charge of hosting a caravan from Honduras to America. We find them and train them and give them lots of cash and send them on their way. We have made plenty of mistakes with hiring mules. But since business was good, we had to get more and more mules all the time and at the same time we didn't want any bad mules. A dilemma, no?

So we sent security people from our company inside these caravans, like your air marshalls I think. Their assignment was to lay low and watch for specific types of crimes, like rape, like child abuse, like assault; those things that come out of basic cruel human nature. And if our caravan marshalls find out about these crimes going on? There was immediate investigation, sentencing, and probably execution. And I do mean execution. Behind a warehouse, in an open field or a nearby forest; whatever worked quickly.

These security men would travel with the caravan and when something went wrong, they would pounce and clean up the mess and then take over the caravan as the new mule. They would get the funding money, whatever other resources the mule had in place and they would get the harem. So you can see that our security people were very diligent in their "quality assurance", so to speak. After a few years of cleaning out these cruel mules, I think that Honduras and most of

Central America have run out of bad apples to offer to the trade and that is a good thing.

The bad mules are mostly all gone and we really have a decent group now. We have changed their title from "mules" to "travel guides" and after three successful trips to the USA, they get rewarded with a free vacation to Hawaii. This caravan business is a nice business now.

CHAPTER 13

The First Rural Raids - Interview with a raid driver

Interviewer: OK, the recorder is set, so tell me your story and pretend I'm not even in the room. Talk as if you were having beers with your buddies back at the pool hall.

Grumman: I can do that, and then you're going to pay me right? You said an even grand for an hour of drama, right?

Interviewer: Yes, cash on the barrel head. Start with your name and a bit of your life history if you don't mind. I might ask a question or two, but just get started and tell me mostly about your recent recreational activities in as much detail as you can.

Grumman: No problem, my friend, I can always use and extra thousand bucks in my life; especially nowadays. The cost of everything is going way-way up now that winter has set in.

My name is Robert Grumman and I am a truck driver for a Denver based grocery store chain. I grew up in Fort Collins, went to high school there, and did a few years at Colorado State, but I never graduated with anything but a huge pile of student debt. I moved later into the Denver area for work, met my wife and we got married pretty quickly. We have three kids in grade school and a little house in Green Valley Ranch out near the airport. My wife is an accounting manager with the company, so between us we make a decent living. I'm on the road much of the time and she's a great single mom when I'm not around.

For years now, I've met with my buddies to shoot pool and listen to football at some of the local beer joints. We have a good time and are all of pretty like minds. Sometimes we go fishing or hunting together; John has a cabin in the hills above Boulder and we go there every year. But mostly we just shoot pool and drink beer and cuss our way through life. We have fun and it's all pretty harmless.

One thing we have in common for sure is that we all hate Gump. The guy is a total loser, a liar, a cheater and a modern day pirate. He tears things apart and then piles up his booty in all of those Gump Towers he owns and now he's our President? That's as good as we could do? America should be ashamed. Heck, America is ashamed. Gump was a deadbeat and a criminal and I can't believe we gave him the keys to our country.

A couple of years ago, this was before the 2020 elections, three of my buddies and I had a few beers and we were taking down some whiskey shots as well. Saturday afternoon, I remember, and my wife was visiting grandma with the kids so I was a bachelor that weekend. There was some big Gump rally down in Colorado Springs that day and it was all over the news on the TVs in the bar. Gump had just rolled out their new "Keep America Great" campaign with hats and shirts and coats and whatever and they were hollerin' and yelpin' like this was the best thing since sliced bread. God, they're all idiots.

My buddies and I, and everyone at the bar really, just got mad. The four letter words were flying that day; I can tell you that! Jordan, the youngest of our group, all of the sudden he lit up like a Christmas tree and gathered us in a huddle all serious like and started a joke.

Well, we thought it was a joke in the beginning, but he was definitely not joking and it got really scary, really quickly. He wanted to drive down right then to Colorado Springs and pop a few of those Gumpers while they were all gathered at the rally at Memorial Park. And when I say "pop", I don't mean beat up; he wanted to shoot a few. "Put the fear of God in them" is what he said.

Jordan is a big talker and a big jokester, so we all got caught up in his fairytale and went along with him; a good Saturday afternoon road trip with purpose! I thought for sure we would get down there and chicken out. Or better yet, find another bar in Colorado Springs to hang out at, so all of us acted the part and jumped into high speed prep mode.

We each headed home to dress for the road trip and gather our gear. Everyone came to my house and then we loaded up my 2003 F150 four door pickup with the four of us and four duffle bags of who knows what. Everyone had opted for the urban cowboy look; you know, jeans and jackets.

Except for Jordan; he decided that full camouflage was the ticket, including camo boots and a camo safari hat. What an idiot. We're not going into the forest, Jordan, we're going to downtown Colorado Springs. Anyway, it wouldn't matter. He can drink beer in Colorado Springs with camo gear on if he wants.

By the time we got to Colorado Springs it was getting dark and we had no plan really, so I just drove around the event site and Ed pulled out his camera and started taking pictures.

My God, the crowd was big. Not only was the event arena full of people, but a crowd in the thousands was outside of the building and every parking lot within a mile was packed. We drove around for half an hour deciding what to do. Every street around was lined with folks waving "Keep America Great!" posters and every intersection had its chanters shouting some slogan or another. Boy oh boy; that made us even madder than the TV coverage.

We quickly decided that we needed another beer and wound up at a local bar that used to be a feed store. We must've been quite a sight; three urban cowboys and one decked out hunter all hunkered down at a table in a corner hunched over a pitcher of Coors and four mugs. We fit right in really and as the TV coverage once again zeroed in on the rally, the entire bar went berserk.

Berserk on the positive side, meaning we hand landed in a nest of Gump-lovers and they were actually excited about the rally and Gump and everything. Oh my God! The screaming and yelling was pretty aggravating and loud and the people in the crowd who weren't as excited about the rally fell quiet and left the bar in quick fashion.

We were pretty tough in our corner over our beers and we talked about a half dozen plans to pop someone. Liquid courage is what it was. Jordan was epic. He'd lay out an idea to pursue and we'd all listen to it and then add our own flavor and then "Nah!, that won't work." And then another idea would get thrown out and we'd push that around the table until "Nah! That won't work." And so on and so forth for about an hour. I thought this was all in fun and jest and thought that soon we'd get tired and drunk and then roll back north; which is basically what happened.

After a final round of beers and two more shots for Jordan, we hopped into the truck and headed home. Everybody was pretty tipsy and happy by then; but happy with an underlying seething from all the rally coverage. Jordan suggested that we go back by the rally on the way home and we thought that was a dandy idea. I turned the radio to some country music while we drove and we just sat there and soaked in the beer and the whiskey and the music and the Gump idiocy.

The rally was starting to break up when we arrived a few minutes later and we got caught up in a heck of a traffic jam. It's bad enough to be in traffic during rush hour on a weekday, but on Saturday night? And in the middle of a sea of cars that were honking and blinking their lights and shouting Gump support out the windows. That was too much; I had to get us out of there.

So when another pickup that looked an awful lot like mine made a quick right turn into an empty alley, I followed it hoping that they knew a local shortcut to the freeway. Which they did, and after a few more turns down though an industrial park, we came to a freeway overpass. But we were over the freeway on a road that had no access and no ramps north or south were within eyesight as we passed over.

Crap, just where were we anyway? Ed had put his camera away and had his phone out and was booting Google Maps to get us some routing for Denver. Everyone was helping him figure it out when we came to a stop and Jordan said "Now lookie there."

Right in front of us was our rescue pickup truck at the stop light and clearly in my headlights we could see the bumper stickers: "Gump-Benz 2016" and "Make America Great Again" and "Gump 2020". And the best of all, or the worst of all was "Keep America Great" which was the theme for the rally and we could even hear rally music echoing from their radio.

John was usually the quiet one in the group and most of the stuff he says we don't even hear in a bar, but sitting there at a standstill behind the Gump truck with the faint rally music, it was silent for us. John said one thing: "Follow them." Which we all took as a command decision; so we followed them.

Long story short - the Gump truck headed out of town and eventually came to a small residential area, one of those neighborhoods of like fifty homes or something. The neighborhood must've been there a long time, because the trees and shrubs were grown up and provided some decent cover as we followed our new friends home.

This was crazy! There had been enough traffic along the way and enough other trucks to blend in while we were driving around Colorado Springs, but here there were only two all but identical trucks and in the suburbs, no less. I kept a good distance and took a few side routes, and we were yelling whispers to each other along with some rounds of "What the hell are we doing?"

It was getting late for the rural neighborhood and almost all the lights were out completely or maybe a lit room or two in the back of the houses. The streets were totally empty; no activity was around and no one was even walking a dog. When the Gump truck pulled into a driveway, I pulled over maybe fifty yards back with the lights out and we watched. Jordan and Ed rolled down their windows to see more clearly; quiet, quiet all around. Well, except for the hum of the truck, a few whispers from us and Jordan getting his flask out of his camo duffle - again.

The driver got out of the car first and even in the dark you could tell it was the father; a bit heavy set and wearing a big jacket. He shut his door and before he could turn, he suddenly stumbled and clutched his heart and fell. My first thought was "Heart attack - just desserts, you Gump lover." But then I heard the soft thunk, or was it a pffft? Was that after he fell? Or at the same time? Before? It was all moving really quickly.

Within a second of the man going down, the other doors opened and three others got out. The wife from the passenger side had seen her husband fall and rushed around the front of the truck. The back doors came open a moment later and two teens, not sure if boys or girls at the time, jumped to the rescue as well.

Then three times more...pffft, pffft, pffft. I spun around towards the sound and realized it was Jordan, not with his flask now, but with his target rifle he used for state competitions in high school. He is a crack shot, but where the hell did he get a silencer? A bit of smoke drifted over and into the truck and John, Ed and I were in equal state of surprise, anger, excitement and fear all rolled into three pairs of wide-open eyes.

I spun back to the Gump truck and the mother was already down, flat on her back and not moving. One of the teens was still dropping, first onto one knee and then onto both and then face first into the concrete drive. The second teen had fallen backwards against the vehicle and then sideways into the driver's mirror, and slid to the ground leaving a dark patch all the way down the white door. Jordan is a crack shot.

We just stared and gasped for a few moments, not even breathing. Except for Jordan, who was hyperventilating and whispering "Goddam Gump-lovers. Goddam Gump lovers." I didn't know what to do. There wasn't anyone around and we hadn't made any noise to speak of. The family had not been alive long enough to make any ruckus. I sat there for two more minutes, listening for any sign of other people, or any movement or anything. Nothing.

We were lucky that all four doors of the Gump truck had been closed, so there were no lights on inside. And it was a moonless night and some clouds were around, so all-in-all dark in the driveway. I put the truck into gear, took the next quick left, and then another left before turning the truck lights back on. We didn't say anything to each other for the whole drive back. Ed put some music on the radio. Jordan hummed to the tunes he recognized.

We got back to my house just shy of midnight. Everyone grabbed their gear and headed to their own rides. Before they split, I left them with one clear instruction: "Not a word. From no one. To no one."

CHAPTER 14

The First Rural Raids (Part Two) - Interview with a raid driver - the aftermath

Grumman: We didn't talk about it for weeks. Not one word that I know of. The family's murder was all over the news of course. For two days on CNN and for two months on Fox News. Three shots through the heart and one to the forehead. I told you Jordan was a crack shot; four bullets, four deaths.

We came and went with no witnesses, no leads; nothing but four dead Gump lovers. Social media went nuts and you saw the worst of both sides there. I knew we had dodged a bullet and after a few days my stomach cramps went away.

Eventually, I reached out to the guys and set up a pool game, not at our normal place, but in a little village east of here. I had been there previously, not so much as to be a known customer, but enough to not be a stranger. My compadres arrived off and on over the course of a half hour as instructed. Just as the lunch hour rush calmed down, we started a game of eight ball and shared a pitcher, something from Black Bottle Brewery; seemed fitting.

I told them I thought it was a good time to review our situation and felt safe enough to meet privately in a public place. More in code words than like I just said, but they got it and agreed. We beat around the bush for a while about what to do and leave it up to Jordan, he jumped right in and said "I want to do it again. I hate Gump lovers." We all stood still for a moment, not sure what to say. It was Jordan's turn to shoot pool and he continued "Seven ball in the side pocket." <thunk> "Two ball in the corner over there." <thunk> And then he stood up and looked to all of us. "Not all the time and not a lot. Just when I get really, really angry about Gump and his shit."

That was the end of discussion that day, but we continued to get together and things developed. Ed came to one meeting with a list of names and addresses. “Where'd you get that?” “It was pretty simple actually. Remember those pictures I took at the rally? There were a lot of cars in those pictures. I entered each license plate number into the DMV database and there you go, public domain information. This list is from just one of those pictures. I have pictures of twelve parking lots with like twenty cars in each lot.” “Instant target list.” “Yeah.” “And if that doesn't work, we can always look for bumper stickers.” “Yeah.”

Jordan got us all silencers for our favorite firearms. I got one for my Glock. Ed got a silencer for a shotgun of all things. I didn't even know they made those; if they even work, that is. We went on a couple of practice runs, taking road trips to find out where some of these Gump lovers live. Mostly nice homes and mostly way too exposed for anything serious. But it was fun and we drank a lot of Black Bottle, so it helped us manage Jordan's anger.

We hadn't gotten together for a few weeks, so we met again at the new bar and Jordan had an update for us; he couldn't even wait until we sat down. “I did it. I did it again!” “Did what?” “Took a family of Gump lovers down.” “Oh Shit.” “It was one on the list, one we visited; the one out in the country past Florence.” “When was this?” “Three days ago, late evening after their son's basketball game.” “I heard about that on the news.”

“How'd you do it?” “Same MO as in Colorado Springs. But instead of following, I had the home address, so I parked two farms over, hiked in, and waited in the woods until they got home. Pffft. Pffft. Pffft. <pause> Then Pffft. Pffft. Mom and Dad were still moving. I decided that we have to take out whole family units, not just individuals.” “Why do you say that?”

“Dude, think about it. It's like pulling a weed. You got to take out the roots or it just grows back. You leave Mom or Dad around and they're still gonna love Gump. You leave the kids around and they will start to breed little Gump lovers of their own. We've got to clean up the gene pool as we move along. Sabe?” “You're sick.” “Yes I am." <pause>

"The ground was dry, so no tracks.” “That's good.” “And no one was around anywhere that I know of, so no witnesses.” “That you know of.” “Yes.” “That's good I think.” “I think so.” “Me too.” “Me three.”

It was a months later when we ventured out again. There had been a few copycat shootings along the way; in other cities and in other states as well. People harassing Gump trucks and cars and mostly starting fights that ended up with shootings. But there was no planning, no organization to speak of.

That all changed when the red vigilantes broke loose. Three separate attacks in two Kansas towns; fourteen innocents died in one night because they had Elizabeth or Barney bumper stickers on their cars. The news was confusing as usual, of course, but when it settled down, these attacks had been planned and coordinated.

The local law enforcement could find no leads, so no one was held to account. Goddam red states. Don't they understand that they're pushing the corporate fat cat agenda and killing the planet along the way?

Anyway, all the politics aside, there was a huge ground swell in Denver to "Squash the red tide!" We found out that we weren't the only group in our bar drinking network that had ideas on what to do. Our pool shooting conversations turned into our own mini-rallies and soon there were karaoke machine soap box speeches about "standing by idly" and "we must lean into what we believe." It was mostly the beer talking.

There were a handful of us, high school and college buddies, that didn't soap box our message, but were angry and frustrated all the same. We had whispered conversations during the impotent soap box speeches and eventually came to share a common view of something actionable. It's bad and getting worse and intentional red/blue killings were growing at an astounding rate. Law enforcement, even though active, was very overloaded and out of ten of these shootings, less than half of the investigations went anywhere. Even when suspects were brought to indictment, most led to dismissal.

Unless the shooters were in the wrong place. Blue suspects arrested in blue places walked. Red suspects arrested in red places walked. But blue suspects in red places and red suspects in blue places were pursued to the full extent of the law. There was a 90% conviction rate for these unlucky bastards and one such trial handed three criminals their death sentences in a blue zone that had outlawed death sentences a year prior. The statistics for law enforcement looked OK - rising crime rate - rising arrest rates - rising indictments - rising judgments - "Hey, we're doing our job."

But the net effect of this law enforcement filter was to distill and concentrate the anger. As the overall bumper sticker murder rate continued to climb, the red places got redder and blue places got bluer. This was the case for all over the United States; especially severe at the seams between blue urban neighborhoods and red rural countryside. In between were the suburbs. That's where most of the shootings were. Soon there were no political bumper stickers to be found in the suburbs. It was too dangerous to stand with your hand in the air and call out a color.

With the victim count rising and the all but obvious failure of the legal system to keep up, all of America was feeling like Chicago in the two thousand teens; way too many events, way too few cops, and a legal system that treated suspects with more dignity than victims.

One of our bar chats shed interesting light for us. Mark was a friend of mine from third grade way back in Ft Collins days. He was a brainy quiet type with a degree from MIT in game theory or something crazy like that. He worked in a large consulting company in downtown Denver, end even though he had to wear suits on weekdays, on the weekends he wore ragged jeans and drank beer with us. Our conversation was in our typical "should do", "how to do", "can't do" death spiral and suddenly he piped up.

"We need bigger guns." "What?"

"I said, we need bigger guns…" "No, I heard what you said, but what are you talking about?"

"You know where this is all going to, right?" "Now what <u>are</u> you talking about, Mark?" "It's a question: You know where all this is going to, right?" <mumbles> "No, Mark, these shootings could go a hundred different ways in my mind. But why don't you enlighten us. We're out of ideas."

"I'll make it quick. State of the art now is vigilantes shooting innocents. Wrong place, wrong time - you die. But soon people will start focusing not on the Gump trucks, but on the people who shoot the people in the Gump trucks. We'll all get angry at the perpetrators as the deaths hit closer to home. And closer to home is a key, because everyone has a right to defend themselves, right? So for every ten vigilante squads that spring up, there will be double that in "defense teams", or whatever you want to call them.

We'll start seeing volunteer patrols of loyal gun toting Americans roaming the suburbs in the spirit of "protecting" their neighbors. It is difficult to organize and pull off a bumper sticker shooting, well, because it's illegal and there are real dangers of getting caught. But it'll be easy to form a roaming security team. And it will be supported by law enforcement, because they're super overloaded and they'll welcome the help."

“Mark, we’ve talked about forming up some groups like this before, you’ve been here.” “Plus, we’ve heard about some in other places already. No news there I think.”

“Yeah, our conversations - that’s what got me thinking. So when this plays out and you have red security trucks all over the countryside and blue security trucks all over the cities, what happens when one of these blue security teams runs into a red vigilante squad, or better yet, they run into another security team, but a red security team? What do you think might happen?”

“Hopefully nothing.”

“Nice try, but I don’t think so. They might drive away from each other a few times, but when you get enough red-blue confrontations? There’s going to be some hothead somewhere that starts shooting.”

“I can see that happening.” “Me too.” “Me three.” “Me four.”

“And what are they going to be shooting at the other guys?” “I don’t know...pistols? A few hunting rifles?” “And what will we be shooting back with? <pause> “Pistols, hunting rifles and a stupid shotgun with a silencer.” <pause>

“I told you. We need bigger guns.”

CHAPTER 15

Vigilante Recruiting - Interview with a Soviet agent

Interviewer: For the record, I am interviewing Douglas Chapman of Los Angeles. Hello Douglas. Or do you go by Doug?

Douglas: I prefer Douglas. Thank you for asking.

Interviewer: Douglas' LinkedIn account says he is an insurance salesman, but I understand from his dossier here...let me make sure I have the right one. Yes, this is it. This dossier says that you are also working for the Soviet Union. You have been made available to me by the Federal Bureau of Investigation and are willing to talk to me voluntarily.

Douglas: Yes, yes. I've been told that cooperating with all arms of the US Government is potentially good for my case, so yes. And I believe that the topic of our conversation will not at all be connected to my other reasons for being friends with the FBI, so we don't need my lawyer in the room; at least not yet.

Interviewer: OK, good. Let me set this up and then I'll hand it off to you. According to my information your side profession took you to a meeting in Boulder, Colorado with a few of the local people. And during that meeting you discussed weaponry that may or may not be available for purchase on the black market. You were connected to them by resources in Moscow and it was a generally successful meeting from your perspective. Please pick it up from there and tell us more about this day.

Douglas: Sure, but let's start a few weeks prior. The first contact information I received was pretty non-descript. Someone from an IP address in Denver was searching for "heavy weapons". This is one of our tag phrases and my friends in Moscow have a trapdoor set for this type of inquiry.

It's a clever trap really, basically a Google intercept virus. The search results you type in are tampered with and the top three returns lead to websites in a secure Russian server. As soon as the searcher selects one of these target sites, two things happen. First, the searcher begins communicating through a secure and encrypted channel to our "Sales Website" and from there we can observe the searcher's entire internet session while they are discovering their "heavy weapons". The other thing is that a communication protocol is put in place with the original search engine so that it does not keep a record of the user's choices; the search engine knows only about the initial jump vector and then later, only when a return is accomplished. None of the searcher's tracks in between are known beyond our Russian server.

When the searcher decides to return out of their research, say by hitting back arrows or picking another tab, then our Russian server again does two things. The original search engine is informed that the searcher has returned. And in order to cover tracks, we manipulate the original search term to something less innocuous than say, well, in this case "heavy weapons". With these words we sometimes use the words "heavy women" as the alternate.

So the original search engine thinks the searcher went looking for heavy women and the user's history is edited to remember this as well. Even though it may make no sense to the searcher if they find it, we think it easiest to keep our security high by making these changes. Since computers are famous for doing stupid things, it is soon forgotten by people anyway.

Oh, yes, I forgot. We do three things at the exit, not two things. The last thing we do is to plant another sophisticated virus deep into the searcher's operating system. It is a very clever piece of software and acts like a cookie for the most part, so it can send and receive information as it pleases as the searcher goes about their day. We will come back to this capability later on I think, so that is enough for now.

Once our heavy weapons searcher gets into the Russian server they learn all about things they were interested in. At the same time, we learn all about our heavy weapons searcher. The whole event is very passive from our side. Lots of people in America have visited our server, but mostly they lead to nothing; no repeat visits or maybe two visits total. But if they come back a few times? Then things can get interesting.

This is what happened one week before the meeting you speak of; a return visit from the same IP address as before and a longer session at that. Two more returns in two more days, and then a different IP address from the same zip code came on line and also had multiple visits. Perhaps a friend or a neighbor? This second person was physically about a half mile away, but that is next door on global terms.

We have protocols in place for determining our next actions built on years and years of internet espionage experience. Suffice it to say that if enough of the right interactions occur, we end up with a candidate that qualifies for a telephone conversation and then a follow-up call and eventually a face to face meeting. These are all gradual escalations of the relationship.

So one week later, I fly to Denver and drive to Boulder to meet with two new friends that were interested in buying "heavy weapons". They had a budget and we always insist that they pay a large amount of money so that things are more official. But heavy weapons are very, very, very expensive which would keep many customers from buying. So we find that it is better to subsidize these purchases to get more weapons out there, than to make a profit and starve the customer, so to speak.

Weapons importing and distribution into the US was one of the major incursion methods we used to help drive America's violence. My government wanted a big fire, and a big fire requires lots of fuel.

In this Boulder, Colorado case, the fuel we provided was four cases of American M16 rifles - both of the A2 and A4 varieties, four Remington sniper rifles, four SAW automatic rifles, and sixteen cases of hand grenades and smoke grenades. It was also the first of seven orders they eventually placed and after that they must've gotten their equipment through some other channel. Or maybe they no longer existed? No? That happens often enough as we know.

These Boulder, Colorado customers were one of many groups we met through our trapdoor on the internet. There were several people in the USA doing my same role, you know; regional sales would be a good name. Each of us had good business with multiple deliveries monthly. I myself managed twenty-two orders in one year for all over the west coast. My smallest order was for two rifles. My biggest order took a parade of flatbeds to deliver and had a count of over one thousand individual pieces and forty pallets of ammunition. This order included a lot of the normal things, but also fifty caliber machine guns and sniper rifles, H&K MP5s, M79 grenade launchers, M72 light antitank weapons, and an entire flatbed full of Claymore mines. We had one order delivered to the state of Tennessee for seventy-five old fashioned mortars, Vietnam era style. There were many fires lit with this delivery. Ultimately, my friends and I delivered nearly one million pieces of equipment to America. Not bad for something that doesn't exist, yes?

We did not care if we sold to the blue marauders or the red marauders or the blue defense teams or the red defense teams. We just knew that if we can get enough flammable material into America, it would catch on fire eventually. And it has as you know.

We can talk more if you wish and I can answer questions, but is it possible to have a break? I need a cup of coffee.

CHAPTER 16

The First Rural Raids (Part Three) - Interview with a raid driver - continued

Grumman: So we followed Mark's advice and got bigger guns. A few of the guys in the group went online and after a while they were having meetings with some shady character that could connect them to an arms dealer. I stayed away from all those shenanigans; who knew that these guys weren't Feds? We scraped up a ton of cash from everyone we could tap. We placed a small order, and what do you think happened? Heavy weapons delivered to directly to the shed on Mark's lot. Unbelievable; buy them on the internet? Not quite, but is it really that easy?

I guess so, because we weren't the only people with this idea. We started hearing about folks back east that have had some pretty lively encounters. When TV clips of these events were shown it was obvious that they were not using hunting rifles. A bunch of people with jeans and jackets walking down a street with M16s; it looked like an Army unit on home leave.

Those videos were inspiring and frightening at the same time. Inspiring because we were discovering that as individuals we can actually do something to affect the course of American history. And frightening in that we were also finding out that <u>everybody</u> was going up in arms counts and arms potency and <u>everybody</u> was angry at everybody.

At the time when the heavy weapons count just started going up, a small team like ours could be big men on campus. It is quite a feeling to have a few folks with military grade weapons driving around with enough armament to fend off a small town police department.

When we would run some drills on the weekend and there were like thirty or forty of us around, it was sight to behold; like a small militia actually. I've never had the same feeling of exhilaration and pride and fear and power all mixed together with a little adrenaline sprinkled in. It was intoxicating.

Mind you, it took a long time to bring in enough weapons to build our militia and so the early periods were squads and teams with consumer weapons and a few heavy items tossed in. But that was enough to make people bold and brash on both sides. And Mark was right about "Where this was going to..." Nobody with any moral compass really wanted to drive around and shoot families for bumper stickers.

But when the bad guys built more and more squads and teams and they started getting more powerful with their new gear, well, that was a different moral calling. "We must defend ourselves!" and "If they get too strong, what's to keep them from just driving over here and killing us all?" These became the new centers of the bar room debates.

So defense team fire fights started to grow. At first it was just random chance that sparked the conflicts; two trucks or SUV's getting too close to each other for comfort. But soon they ventured out further and started to travel in pairs and groups and to observe and report and set traps and plan ambushes.

It grew from once a month to once a week in our town. By the time the official militias were formed it was a daily thing. And both sides all over the country were doing it. The red teams invading the suburbs from the countryside and the blue teams invading the suburbs from the city-side. It was not a pretty picture.

As the team count went up, and as the heavy weapon count went up and as the boldness of leadership went up, so did the body count.

Total marauder and defense team casualties on both sides during the first phase of the civil war surpassed military losses from Korea, Viet Nam, and all the Middle East conflicts combined. Add in all of the bumper sticker innocents that died during that time and America became quite a mess.

CHAPTER 17

The Caravan Riots (Part Two) - Interview with a Honduran mule - continued

Jorge: OK, now where were we. Oh, yes I was telling you that my travel business is going gang busters and that we have been very successful at converting our mules into travel guides. So all in all, a good result, no? I mean we started with some disorganized ramblings of waves of people going through strange places, being hurt and abused and starving and getting sick, to a well-oiled network of funded transportation, food and shelter, with most of the mule riff-raff issues at modest levels.

Interviewer: So you are feeling good about your contributions to the immigration issue?

Jorge: My side of it, yes. But at the same time we were cleaning out the bad mules and balancing our financials and making good business deals, American immigration systems remain stalled. America's Congress is in charge of lawmaking, but instead of progressively addressing the situation across the southern border, they spent most of their time in hot air speeches and on TV with lawyers and lawsuits. So while we improved our ability to bring people to America's border, America was still operating with mid-20th century immigration policy. This policy was designed to filter and qualify and limit the inflow of people, not process them en masse in legal ways. No matter how many people were in line to get into America, there was only a trickle of those that got processed and moved onto their dream life in America.

Remember I told you that when the caravans were young and disorganized, people were tired and hungry when they got to America. This helped keep energy levels down as they faced weeks and months of wait time for America to meet with them. But with our improving transportation, food and housing, our caravans started off-loading more people faster and these people were in good health, high energy, and eager to get their new start. The net result? Many big piles of healthy, high-energy people all stacked up on the south side of the border with nowhere to go.

In our contracts with our sponsors, we provided transportation, food and housing services. It started at our local countries and stopped at the border of America. Also by our contracts, when our travel guides departed, they placed a two week supply of necessary materials with the travelers. This was like a few pallets of food and water and medicine for every hundred people or so. And it worked well to keep things in order; for two to three more weeks.

Our travel guides are well trained in taking people cross country and were the official leaders of these groups. They made the decisions; when to get up, when to eat, when to stop, when to pee, when to sleep. This helped keep the caravans running smoothly and in orderly fashion. But the travel guides left the groups at the border with a few pallets of goods and then what? I'll tell you what. Human nature is what.

The leadership gap left by the travel guide's departure usually remained unfilled for a week or more. People would form smaller groups and hang out waiting for their turn to talk to America. Then the food would start running out and as typical, the loudest or the biggest of the travelers would emerge as the de facto leader. It was never the smartest traveler, not that I know of. Many times it would take a few fights or a few deaths to clear up the pecking order, and this intimidation factor was a key factor in what would happen next.

Which of course was to climb the wall...

Or go around it. Or under it. Or just walk north if the travelers landed in a place where there was no wall. Our travel guides would return to a wall-less place where they had left a caravan six weeks before to find nothing but a bunch of trash spread across the ground and a bunch of empty boxes and pallets. All of the people would be gone.

When there was a wall to climb? Well, it was not very simple for a large group to do this. Most of the places where there were walls, there were also people behind the walls; people with badges and guns and patrol vehicles and backup support and jails and all the other border things. In these places with walls the new leaders - actually I should call them the new mules, because that is what they became - the new mules intimidated their whole group to storm the wall at once and we all heard about the crossing riots. Lots of people would get hurt, sometimes killed as well, but in almost every case, a handful or sometimes even maybe half the group would overrun the border officials and disappear into this great place called America.

During these times, America could not build a wall fast enough. There were seven by twenty-four construction projects going on in dozens of locations, but the funding was always being withdrawn and the construction resources were in high demand across America as internal security issues climbed. But eventually the wall became long enough and the behind the border resources big enough to turn almost every wall crossing into a news event.

No more was America tracking the number of illegal aliens disappearing into the country. The reporting changed over to Viet Nam War era body counts. At the height of the wall crossing period, there was an average of twenty-four travelers dying on the border every day. The highest month was over one thousand two hundred souls lost on the border alone.

But that wasn't the worst of it. The worst of it came when the vigilante squads and the neighborhood defense teams became popular. No, popular is a bad word; when they became operationally widespread. There, that is better. Nobody wanted the outcomes that resulted. There were simply too many catastrophic things happening in America at the same time and well, we got what we got.

You see, in the beginning, America was used to a constant influx of Mexican and Central American travelers; the undocumented workers, illegal aliens, what have you. But as tensions rose across America and the vigilante squads and defense teams practiced their trades, the net effect was huge on my customers. In the beginning, if a traveler could get across the border in any form or fashion, they would find clear sailing to almost anywhere in America. No one really seemed to care, or at least they didn't care enough to deal with it in their neighborhood.

After the squads and teams launched, my travelers faced a huge network of highly armed and energetic but unofficial law enforcers. The red and blue marauders, the ones that were leading the bumper sticker raids, they rarely targeted my travelers. After all, the travelers were apolitical. They mostly did not even know who was in charge in Washington. Yes, there were random attacks on the smaller traveling groups, but marauders were focused on killing Americans of the other color, not illegals.

The neighborhood defense teams were something altogether different. There were more of them for one thing. And they were officially sanctioned with street patrolling to ensure there were no dangers coming into their locale. As the piling up of travelers at the border grew and the rage of the replacement mules took over, the ones and twos and family units migrating through town become dozens and dozens and hundreds and hundreds and, well, we know what happened.

Some of the defense teams identified my innocent travelers as security threats and violence ensued. Most times there was verbal positioning and some minor fights and the group would be turned around to "go back south"; back across the border, I guess. But in many cases and we have all heard about these cases, there were weapons on both sides; but many more weapons were with the defense teams.

Waves of people were murdered. Almost all of them were my customers. With these defense teams, it did not matter whether they were a red defense team or a blue defense team. They were both commissioned with defending their soil. When any size group of immigrant looking people stumbled into a defense team, it was bad. When a wall storming horde of clearly illegals confronted a squadron of defense teams, it was atrocity.

Most recently, we have been able to better target drop off points to reduce these atrocities. And it has really helped as the blue enclaves have opened their borders to all that will come. The defense team deaths are but a fraction of what they were at one time.

I have reviewed a few documents provided by my sponsors - all reports marked "top secret" by the way - and they provided estimates of those killed in the interior of America during these terrible two years. Remember I said that one thousand two hundred people were killed at the border in one month? The equivalent number for the travelers lost in America's interiors was ten times this at its worst. Those reports estimated that perhaps as many as one hundred seventy-five thousand people met their fate in this way. That's not much compared to America's overall losses, but it's still a lot of people.

I light candles for them every day.

And for me.

CHAPTER 18

Gun Control - Recording of a Congressional Committee meeting

Interviewer: I must be honest with my sponsors that the original source of the following recorded conversation is not known. It is possible to share the name of the source that provided the recording to me and the name of the person that provided it to her if necessary. However, in my attempts to ascertain the ultimate source and corroborate the information in some fashion, I found at least eight layers of hand-offs. At least half of those are only suspected and not provable. In the course of these detection efforts, I burned at least two of my closest government contacts and received bodily threats from two non-government contacts, so I abandoned this line of pursuit.

I would prefer not to follow this trail any longer, but I can change that stance at the direction of the institute. Please don't make me do this. I believe it will hamper future research efforts. But, if I must? You will have to instruct me explicitly on this if required. I believe that 90% or more of the useful information can be garnered simply by listening to the recording, so the return for additional investment is small and the risk is high.

Let me get into details of how this recording came to be before I share the meeting content. I believe that the method of making the recording was with a cell phone in a jacket pocket as we have seen happen before. The recording itself has file headers that indicate that the recording was made with an I-phone XI, but there is no information useful to trace it to a single phone that someone owns. That tracking information was removed from the file before I obtained a copy. At least one person in the chain of ownership of this recording has access to someone who is savvy enough to defeat the I-phone's internal operating system protocols and render the recording device-generic.

I believe also that the person who made the recording was a high ranking official member of this Congressional committee based on the proximity of other high ranking voices. The voices you hear clearly and loudly are those that are nearer to the person with the I-phone. You will recognize some of the voices and it is clear who is speaking in many cases. Those voices that are recognizable but faint are further away from the phone and are all from junior members of the committee. This leads me to conclude that whoever made the recording was sitting at the head of the table, so to speak, and well in the midst of the committee leadership.

An important note is that I do not think that the voice of the individual who made the recording is on the copy that I obtained. It would be the loudest and clearest voice, but there is nothing like this present. Either that individual was very careful not to make comment, or their verbiage was removed during editing after the meeting ended. Both scenarios are possible.

I have listened to the recording over seventeen times and as you will hear as well, there are probably six to eight separate speaking individuals in the meeting. I have no estimate as to how many non-speaking people were in the meeting. The difference in my headcount estimate comes from people that had nothing of unique value to add - just side conversations, words of acknowledgement, random chatter, really the background noises. Given all of this setup, I believe there were five members of Congress that drove this meeting and the outcome. Please play the recording at this point, and I have included a transcript for your convenience.

Member of Congress #1 (MOC1): Let us privately convene on this matter of gun control, please, and let us subside our social side discussions and proceed to business. < pause> OK, good. Can we please have our standard report on firearm death rates?

MOC#2: Yes Bob, I'm prepared with an updated report as of the end of last month, so this information is only about ten days old. If you look at the screen, you can see the lower, red line that we've been watching and displays total body count on a weekly basis over the past eighteen months. There are four takeaways from this update and I will connect them to various elements on the screen.

First, this report reconfirms what we've observed in all of our meetings and deaths from guns are up again month-on-month. Whereas a year ago the monthly death count was cycling up and down, over the past eleven months straight we have seen the number of deaths climb each and every month. Over the last thirty days, we report that another 1158 people were killed across the USA due to resident violence and this is up from the 1032 people killed in the prior month.

If you look at the dotted red line below the solid red line, this is the weekly death count. You can see that it is a lot more volatile than the monthly rate, dipping in quiet weeks and jumping typically in the third and fourth week of the month. The second takeaway from this report is that we used to have weeks where there were zero resident deaths, but for the last six months, there have been people killed every week. The lowest weekly count during this period was eighteen not quite four months ago, and the lowest weekly count over this past month was one hundred and six.

We added a new line to this report, and this is the wounded count. This is the data you asked to be added, Bob, and your thinking was insightful indeed. "Wounded" is the orange line at the top of the graph and it shows that last month alone we had over three thousand injuries requiring hospitalization on top of the eleven hundred plus deaths that occurred. I don't think I can do the math anymore, but I was told coming in to this meeting that whereas last month's deaths were about a quarter of the total casualty count, that is twenty-five percent, more typically they run at about sixteen percent. This means that on average, for every person that dies, five more are injured.

The third takeaway from this is that people that are being seriously impacted, meaning killed <u>or</u> injured, this impact is about five times as large as we have been discussing in prior meetings where we had been talking deaths only. This new data goes a long way to connecting us with discussions we've had with the Department of Health. They've shared that America's health systems are straining at the gills and running over capacity and these new wounded numbers really show more clearly what our medical institutions are grappling with.

The fourth takeaway is on this new graph that I had prepared. It follows up another action item from our last meeting. Next slide, please. This is a display that is similar to the solid red line on the prior slide, but expanded underneath to show some of the specific numbers that make up our total death count. In particular, you'll see two lines below the red one. The blue line is the death count of US citizens for each month, and the green line is the death count for non-citizens, meaning illegal aliens coming across the border.

That's right, ladies and gentlemen, approximately 70% of last month's deaths were illegals and just 30% are United States citizens. In using the words "just 30%" I don't mean to trivialize the nearly four hundred Americans that died last month. But I do mean to emphasize that almost eight hundred deaths were along the Texas, New Mexico and Arizona borders with Mexico. California still refuses to give us their body count by nationality, so this eight hundred is probably understated a bit. The conclusions remain the same in any event.

<surprise by the members, hushed comments, and a few oh my god's>

Take a look at this green line since the beginning of this calendar period. Last year at this time, only about 10% of the deaths were from illegals, but this number has skyrocketed to last month's 70%. I know we don't like to use the word "war", but about six months ago, someone started a war with the people crossing our border and that factor more than any other is driving our overall death count.

OK, that's all I have, Bob. You can take the meeting back.

MOC#1: Thanks, Andy. Does anyone have any questions before we get back to reviewing our action platform?

MOC#3: Bob, I don't have a question, but I do want to share a summary to see if I have this all straight.

MOC#1: Sure, Candace, that would be useful for everyone I think. Go ahead.

MOC#3: Andy, if I'm not catching everything correctly, please chime in. #1 - we are facing a steady increase in death counts all across the country and a bunch of people are getting seriously hurt on top of this. Plus, this is a regular occurrence. No more on and off; no more violence coming and going. It is violent out there and it seems to be here to stay for the time being. Are we agreed?

MOC#4: And the undocumented visitor deaths are way up. I think that is a significant development and signals a change of attitude out there on the streets.

MOC#5: I say we need to quit analyzing this damn problem and start to do something about it. I've been just as hopeful as any of you that this violence would be temporary and cure itself over time. But it isn't and instead of feeling hopeful and having our fingers crossed, I'm afraid we're being ignorant and naive and I'm feeling more and more like the proverbial ostrich with its head buried in the sand. We need to do something...anything.

MOC#2: I agree with doing something, but not just anything. We need changes that will get to root causes, not just symptoms.

MOC#3: Agreed.

MOC#4: I agree as well.

MOC#5: OK, agreed as modified.

MOC#1: OK, great presentation Andy, and great discussion. I'm going to move us over to our platform now. Any objections? "No, sir." "None." "Please, yes."

What I'd like to do then is to spend just a very few moments reviewing the three platform items that we have agreed to and then come to a clear decision on the fourth platform item that Candace introduced last meeting, but we couldn't close on. Agreed? <agreement all around>

OK, good then, here goes. Remember that these clauses will be released over time, essentially about three months apart. Announce, deal with the clamor, implement, clean up the issues, then announce the next change and repeat. There will be no previews of future changes. The people will deal with one set of new rules at a time.

Platform Item #1: Elimination of sales of all firearms with a barrel length of greater than twelve inches. This includes all automatic weapons currently banned, but also adds AR style weapons, hunting rifles and shotguns of all natures, plus abnormal pistols of extremely large sizes. This also includes banning the sale of ammunition and accessories for these weapons as well.

Platform Item #2: Elimination of sales of all pistols and other firearms with barrels of lengths of under twelve inches, along with ammunition and accessories.

Platform Item #3: Elimination of non-military firearms, ammunition and accessories production throughout the United States of America in addition to substantially hiking penalties for violating import bans on firearms of all makes and models.

Now, these are the bi-partisan solution elements that we've all agreed to. We understand that these are barking up the second amendment tree and several of us in this room will face severe repercussions from our constituencies by even introducing these measures. However, we've talked and talked and talked, and have agreed that it is time to take some sort of action, or face more and more violence like we're seeing now. Or worse yet, we'll see even greater violence and get seriously bogged down in a civil insurrection of unknown magnitude.

We've convinced ourselves that these measures don't violate the second amendment because they are restricted to firearm sales and firearm production, not the right to bear arms that are already in people's hands. We predict that maybe half of the country will disagree with our stance on this and we have one hell of a policy marketing job in front of us. But we also believe that these are reasonable steps in removing a lot of fuel from future fires and are appropriate actions to usher forward at this time.

We also believe that the President will veto this legislation and we also believe that we will be able to garner the numbers across Congress to override those vetoes and pass the legislation into law. Agreed?

"Yes, we've talked this to death." "Yes." "Agreed." "Yes, sir." "Yes, sir."

MOC #1: OK. Let's move onto our fourth platform item, and we all know that this is even more controversial than our first three items, and by no means have we come to agreement on this. Today we decide. We decide today that we <u>do</u> agree to this platform item and add it to our action platform, or we decide that we <u>don't</u> agree to this item and we bury it under the table to be resurrected at some other time by some other team. Agreed?

"Yes." "Yes." "Agreed." "Yes, sir." "Yes, sir.

MOC #1: OK, fantastic. Andy, at the last meeting you and your compatriots were clearly on the "Don't do this..." side of the table. I asked you to go off and talk among yourselves and see if there is any change to that stance, or any accommodation or some sort of compromise that might allow us to move forward with platform item #4. Were you able to do this? Please tell me you have some good news for us.

MOC #2: Bob, and the rest of you as well, since our last meeting, I have met individually with each of the committee's GOP members and each of us had an hour or more of discussion as pairs. I also convened the entire group twice and each of these meetings lasted approximately ninety minutes. After much important discussion on issues and alternatives and much soul searching by each of us, I have learned something important.

That important piece is that as the senior member of the GOP representation on this committee, the other GOP members have been deferring to my stance on this platform item #4. They have been very supportive in towing party lines and standing behind me echoing my commentary on the right to bear arms and states' rights and whatever else we could piece together to keep us from going down this road.

But what I learned is that even though my compatriots are clearly in support of the conservative agenda, their hearts are not into standing in the way of this item #4 approach. Their heads are into supporting me and deferring to my leadership on this topic. But their hearts melt with every new story where people are killed. If I were not here on this committee - if any one of them was the senior member - this discussion would have been already completed and we would have been moving forward with platform item #4 weeks ago; maybe even months ago.

So to my fellow GOP members, I appreciate your support and I appreciate your loyalty and I appreciate your honesty with me over the past week as we met individually and together. Thank you for this and yet, this country of ours is in deep trouble and it's time to take bold stances. Plus, there is a new dimension to this discussion that none of you know about yet. Not you, Bob. Not my GOP counterparts. Not anyone here. Not anyone anywhere in Washington DC; at least not yet.

Yesterday I received news of yet another death in my home state of South Carolina. That raises our death toll to seven hundred and sixty two souls that have passed due to our civil violence. In this case, the young man got involved in one of those red marauder raids into Charleston and he unfortunately was on the receiving end of a blue urban defender's bullet. Clean head shot and instant death. It was an easy way to go for him, but not for his family.

My sister will never see her only son again. My parents will never see their only grandson again. And I will not ever see my only nephew again. He is gone forever and we miss this un-replaceable part of our family already; so unnecessary...so devastating...so permanent.

<quiet sorrys>

Thank you for your kind words. I share this development with you as it bears directly on our discussion. As I lay crying with my wife in bed last night, I came to a realization. If we don't stop this, more Tommys will die and more mothers will weep and more grandparents will wail and more uncles will lie ashamed at where we have arrived.

It's time, Bob. I can no longer support policies that are killing our Tommys. I can speak for myself and I know I can speak for my compatriots here. It is time to end this insanity. We agree to item #4 and want it added to our action platform.

It is time to confiscate firearms from across America. We may be too late, but we have to change our ways or fade slowly into the sunset of history. You have our full support.

CHAPTER 19

The Magic Dozen - News report on city attacks

CNN Anchor: "Today, the United States of America witnessed its worse mass shootings in the history of this country. In twelve separate, but highly coordinated attacks, Americans fell upon Americans. Five cites were involved: Austin, Cleveland, Denver, Olympia, and Sacramento. Two attacks came to each of Austin, Cleveland, and Denver. Olympia sustained one attack and Sacramento was besieged with five separate attacks in two waves.

The casualty count has yet to be finalized, but currently stands at two hundred and twenty-three dead, seven hundred and twenty-two injured, and as of one hour ago, another four hundred and thirty-one people are unaccounted for. Of those injured or dead, 78% were members of local law enforcement, first responders and members of various neighborhood defense teams. The remaining 22% were innocent bystanders. Some of the innocent bystanders were collateral damage during fire fights, but over 35% of the civilians were targeted by the marauders. There were six marauder bodies left behind, but final casualty count of the attacking elements is unknown.

The attacks were time coordinated with a synchronized start time:10:00 AM local time in Olympia and Sacramento, 11:00 AM in Denver, 12:00 noon in Austin, and 1:00 PM in Cleveland. Each of the attacks was carried out by a marauding force of between three to five civilian vehicles, typically pickup trucks or SUVs. In each city, the attackers descended on a shopping area and began shooting. The initial targets were the unlucky shoppers going to and from their cars. Within minutes, law enforcement was on these scenes and in some of the attacks short firefights ensued. The longest of these was less than twenty minutes long; that was in Olympia, Washington.

At the end of each attack, the marauders fled in an uncoordinated retreat to the suburbs and rural areas nearby. Two vehicles were rendered inoperable in Cleveland and the same for a single vehicle in Austin, but the people in these vehicles jumped into other attacking vehicles and all escaped the scenes.

Let's go now to Jane Manuel at Park Meadows Mall in Lone Tree, Colorado, which is just south of Denver. Jane, bring us up to date if you can. Can you hear me?"

Jane: "Yes, I can here you, Bob. It's a sad day in America. In Lone Tree, Colorado and four other American cities, flags are dropping to half-mast. The Governor of Colorado has called for a state of emergency and as you can see behind me, elements of the local Army National Guard are on station providing security.

At 11:00 AM local time, a group of four pickup trucks which might be best called a truck squadron came speeding in from East County Line Road and pulled into the covered parking lot here at the mall. They stopped in some sort of chevron formation where there were empty parking spaces and jumped out of their trucks armed to the teeth. Some of them appeared to be wearing body armor and once they got lined up behind their trucks, they started shooting shoppers at random. Panic ensued and in this case the mall security force halted people from going into the parking lot in time to save a lot of lives.

One mall security officer forced a confrontation with the marauders, and was unfortunately killed as he attempted to get close enough to the trucks for effective pistol fire. Out gunned and out-manned, the two other security personnel contacted authorities, remained in constant communication with them during transit, and provided line of sight observations regarding the attackers.

Three minutes after they entered, the marauders ceased fire, re-entered their trucks and fled in formation to I-25 heading south. Local authorities arrived on the scene four minutes later and by this time the panic had spread from the parking lot to the streets. It was traffic grid-lock in every direction and access to the freeway was blocked. A short pursuit was attempted by rerouting police to freeway entrances to the south, but by then the attackers had simply disappeared into the countryside.

The entire parking structure is cordoned off now and there are at least three medical examiners on site. We do not have reliable casualty numbers to share, but one first responder said the word "dozens" as they passed by our film crew. Let us hope we heard the wrong thing. There will be a press conference at 7:30 PM and we don't expect any more information until then."

Bob: "Jane, I understand the incident at Park Meadows Mall is just one of many today. What do you know about the other events?"

Jane: "Here is what I know now, Bob, but realize that this information changes every minute. The latest summary report indicated very close to what you described earlier: there were twelve separate attacks; two in Austin, Cleveland, and Denver, one in Olympia, and five separate attacks in Sacramento, California. Currents deaths are tallied above two hundred people spread among police, firefighters, security people and civilians.

We're here in Lone Tree where one of the Denver attacks occurred. The second attack in the Denver area was at the Orchard Town Center, thirty two miles north of here in Broomfield, Colorado where Northwest Parkway crosses Interstate 25. We will show interviews from Orchard Town Center later on and you will see that Park Meadows Mall, where I am, is an indoor shopping mall. The parking structure where the attack occurred is at the edge of the property. Orchard Town Center is an outdoor shopping area with roads going through the islands of stores separated by huge expanses of parking lots.

The marauders took these layout differences into consideration when planning for their attacks. Up north in Orchard Town Center the attack was again carried out by a squadron of pickup trucks and the attack started precisely at 11:00 AM, the exact same time as the attack here in Lone Tree. A key difference between what happened here and what happened there was that in Orchard Town Center, the attack was a moving attack. The pickup trucks never stopped during their rampage which lasted maybe six long minutes.

Early details indicate that four pickups came from the north and exited at West 144th Avenue heading west. They turned immediately right which brought them into the shopping center. Eye witness reports indicate that three to four people in the back of each pickup had evidently been lying down and as they drove in front of the Starbucks coffee shop, these passengers came to an upright sitting position with weapons ready and started firing into crowds and store fronts.

Witnesses also say that the squadron split up at the next intersection with two trucks going left and two going straight. These half squadrons eventually met up again at the east side of the shopping center, swung back south on the road closest to the freeway and then exited back onto West 144th Avenue, this time going east.

As they sped up on the overpass over I-25, they began shooting into the cars they were passing on both sides of them. We understand that there were at least twelve vehicles hit, but luckily there were no fatalities or even injuries from this phase of the attack.

They encountered a line of cars waiting to turn right, so they were forced to jump into oncoming traffic for a block and bypass the traffic jam. The squadron then turned right on Lincoln Street, still going the wrong way into traffic and entered a second shopping center.

Here they performed another shooting pass into the cars and crowds there. With all of the confusion and less traffic congestion in the parking lots, the trucks began travelling as fast as sixty miles per hour. This made for less effective shooting, and as far as we know, only three people were hit on the east side of the freeway with one fatality.

After that, the similarity with Park Meadows resumes again with the trucks jumping back onto I-25, heading out of town and disappearing into the countryside. The total casualty count from Orchard Town Center is in excess of thirty civilians, but final numbers are not in and that estimate is expected to rise."

Bob: "Are there any ideas on the motivation for these attacks? We know that the street violence has been climbing over the past year, but why this time? Why these places? Why this big?"

Jane: "Bob, it is way too early to be placing blames and finding whys.The authorities are still picking up bodies and those that were lucky enough to make it to a hospital? Many of them are fighting for their lives at this very minute.

I can only point to one witness that may shed light. A gentleman I talked to earlier here in Lone Tree was shot at as the trucks here exited the covered parking lot. He was not hit, thank goodness, but he says he heard the marauder that shot at him yell "Keep America Great!" as they sped off to the freeway.

This is Jane Manuel from CNN News."

CHAPTER 20

Passing of a Firearms Ban - Interview with the mother of a victim

Interviewer: I'm here in Cleveland, Ohio with Pam Swanson. We are meeting at her home in East Cleveland and Pam's son was killed during one of the first mass attacks that occurred six months ago. She was quite vocal in local news coverage about the event.

I had reached out to her then, but she declined to meet for a variety of reasons. Maybe you can join in with me now, Pam. What led up to your calling me yesterday and our scheduling of this meeting today?

Pam: Well, to tell you the truth, I have been thinking about sitting down with you and talking more over the past weeks. When you first called me, the death of my son was too raw and the publicity from the few local interviews I had was very unpleasant. I think I just needed some space and time to grieve and get my head on straight.

But yesterday, when they finally passed the American Security Act, I... <pause> Well, let's just say I wanted to get my experiences and thoughts into your research. We've needed total overhaul of our Wild West gun laws for decades. It's finally happened, and it's about frigging time.

Interviewer: Pam, let me jump in with some info for the recording on the American Security Act, or ASA as it is being called. Yesterday, on the floor of the Senate, there was bipartisan celebration of the veto override and enactment of the first clauses of the ASA. The legislation had originally passed both the House and the Senate almost two weeks earlier, but had sat on the President's desk for the allowed ten days, the so-called veto window. Congress was supposed to adjourn on day six of those ten days, but stayed in session over the long holiday weekend.

By law, if Congress adjourns before the ten days passes, and the legislation goes unsigned, it then dies and does not become law. With the ASA on the President's desk and the Congress still in session, the President was forced to issue a veto over the legislation on day ten. On day eleven, which was yesterday, Congress overturned the veto with near unanimous votes from both houses.

Pam: <interrupting> Yeah, and those idiots in Congress are celebrating with at least half of the country as well. But I'm not celebrating. I'm furious. My son is dead because our government would not agree to any real restrictions on guns for years and years and years. And now they celebrate?

Sure, they will tell you that this is bipartisan, that it's a great change and that we can finally start to address the violence across America. But I will tell you that all of them should go to jail for manslaughter - dereliction of their duty that led directly to the deaths of many, many Americans.

How long has it been since any meaningful firearms restrictions were issued? Four years? I'll give them bump stocks, but really, is that all they've got? My son and a lot of other sons and daughters are dead because they, the "theys" in Washington DC, they did not do their job. For that I will never forgive them.

Interviewer: I understand your point of view and I am truly sorry for your loss. My sponsors recognize the trauma America has already received and fear for even more trauma if we don't deal with root causes and not symptoms. And we believe that if something drastic is not accomplished, many, many more people will die.

Pam: You'll get no argument from me on that point. Just look at the statistics. I tell people I'm from the United States of Baltimore. It's already a war out there; it just hasn't been announced.

Interviewer: Tell me your thoughts on the specifics of the ASA. Not everything, but some of the key points, like the immediate outlawing sales of long barrel semi-automatic weapons, hunting rifles, and shotguns. They can be owned by individuals, but cannot be sold. Nor can accessories or ammunition for these weapons be sold. This round of legislation puts a damper on some really big issues. Do you agree?

Pam: Oh, I like all the things that were done, but they don't go far enough. My son was killed with a .22 caliber pistol for Christ's sake. <starting to cry> Too little, too late. But that's only part of my anger. We've had laws before, but they weren't enforced. Too many bad guys; too little law enforcement, and way, way too many lawyers. So what's changed? Who's going to enforce the new laws?

My God, there are marauders out there with military grade weapons - American military grade weapons! Where did those weapons come from? How many of them are out there already?

So the fat cats in Washington issue a memo saying "I know there's a lot of violence out there. But really, we're going to stop selling them in stores now, OK?" Congress is a bunch of useless bags of flesh all safe and sound in that big Capitol building of theirs. While out here in the trenches, we get mowed down. <pause>

Do you want to know what really makes me sad? I mean beyond my son and all of the other innocents? I'm afraid for America. We've been driving in this direction for a decade and the road is getting rough. We're coming unglued at the seams. And I truly fear that the only effect of this now famous bipartisan agreement to finally deal with the issue of the century will be to simply drive us over the edge.

I fear we've reached the tipping point.

CHAPTER 21

Enclaving of America - Interview with an FBI department head

FBI: As the amount of violence across the United Stated increased, there were quite a few population factors that became important to understand. The FBI segmented our interests into a few major areas: local government, communications and social media, economic alterations, corporate accommodations and methods, technology adoption and advancement, things like that.

One entire FBI division was added to the Bureau of Alcohol, Tobacco, Firearms and Explosives to understand weapons and military strength; that was a really big area of focus. I was assigned a team to investigate two of the social topics: family migration and leadership evolution.

It was obvious to everyone that the amount of families moving around the country was on the rise. At the peak of this period, we estimated that one percent of America was moving themselves or their families continuously. That is one out of every one-hundred Americans with their bags packed and in transit at any one time. It doesn't sound very big, but look at the math.

Let's say a move takes two weeks; that means that there can be twenty six "move periods" per year. So one percent times twenty six means that over one quarter of the population was moving every year. Factor in the total population and America had three million people on the move at any one time; seventy five million people were moving every year. Normal pre-war move stats were one fifth of that; moves went up by 500% in the early phases!

As a result of moving that much of the population around, there were a significant amount of new personalities going out of and coming into every neighborhood, village, town and city. Local leadership evolved with the new population at all levels of decision making; PTAs, school boards, city councils, business management, law enforcement, county agencies and so on and so forth. The FBI coupled our studies of family migration along with emergent leadership so that we could best understand how the local leadership was changing and model how the new geographical personalities were developing. In a situation like ours, ultimately it gets down to "Who's in charge?" and "What is their agenda?"

My assignment was to spend a few months at most to develop a theory, or a model, or a tool that could be used by the FBI to focus resources. "An ounce of prevention is worth a pound of cure…" is just as valid now as it was when Benjamin Franklin first printed it in 1736. If we could do anything to be able to help us concentrate our few resources on important things and at the same time be accurate in knowing which areas to ignore, that would amplify the effectiveness of our efforts.

The ongoing assumption at that time was that the violence was random and driven by local lunatics and that the key abatement strategy should be to put out the fires. If we could predict where the fires would start, we could solve America's violence problem by putting out a lot of small fires, not ever having to deal with a really big one.

Two things were wrong with this thinking and we'll come back to that. I will tell you, however, that we did a good job in building our understanding of family migration and we developed some useful theories about local leadership. The theories helped a lot, but like many of other aspects of the war, too little, too late.

Three of the questions we pursued with our team were "Why are people moving?" and "Where are they moving from?" and "Where are they going to?" We could spend hours diving into all of the statistics, but there are just a few key points to pull out for your research.

The number one factor for moving prior to the war was "jobs & economic opportunity", followed by "life changes". During the pre-war violent period the number one move motivation became "safety & security". When innocent deaths started to rise, people moved away from the hot zones and moved to where they felt more protected. So instead of jobs #1 and life changes #2, it become safety, then jobs, then life changes.

That wasn't the end of it though. As the civilian death rate increased, "life changes" took over the #2 motivation. A lot of families were losing people. The most likely outcome of the early violence was that the husband and/or father didn't come home. For the family, this meant loss of companion, loss of parent, and loss of income - all good reasons to move back home. And it showed in the statistics. So at the peak of things, people were moving for #1 – safety, #2 – life changes, and #3 jobs.

Another side note - moving for job purposes was almost constant during normal times, pre-war times as well as early war times. There was a noticeable shift in the reasons positions were open, however. In normal times, job availability was driven mostly by growth, followed by employment changes like a retirement or someone would take a new job and leave a hole in the company. During the war, the number one reason for job availability was life changes - people were getting killed and their jobs needed to be filled.

The pre-war period was the time in which hiring went from fueling growth to filling holes, no pun intended. More and more people were moving to jobs where someone had died. Not retired, not even died from old age. These were holes in the organizations where young, strong, vibrant people simply disappeared; they never came home alive. The holes in the organization needed to be filled. This societal change - from hiring for growth to hiring because of dying - was a huge factor in the morale of America.

As security and life changes became #1 and #2 motivations for a move, there was a substantial change in the distances people moved as well. During normal times, short moves dominated relocation as people sought better housing as a result of success and stability of a regular job; "I'll move to a better neighborhood plus or minus my tolerance for commuting."

As security became the dominant driver for relocation, moves became longer distance-wise and this was for two reasons. The first reason is simple, if security is an issue and you want to find a safer place, you have to find different neighbors. The new neighbors you want don't live across the street; that's why you want to move in the first place. So as security concerns rise and the job is still there, people will drive farther to work to put the family in a better situation. This is "finding a better neighborhood for us, but I'm keeping my job..." thinking and it drove the average move distance from under twenty miles to over forty miles.

The second reason for increasing move distances was "We're going home..." thinking. This typically was a couple that followed their careers and moved far away from their family roots for economic purposes. This type of behavior was rare in the mid-20th century - people tended to live where they grew up. As farming and other rural jobs decreased in numbers, and transportation and communication technology made living away from family more possible, lots of people moved across the country for great jobs and careers.

A "rootless" and mobile society was actively growing by the beginning of the 21st century and many, many people would follow their careers to unfamiliar places and develop new friends when they got there. But they typically did not find family in these new places. Plenty of friends, plus we can have children and raise our own family, but parents and siblings were many times half a country away.

Bottom line? When faced with a substantial security threat, more and more family units began packing up their households and moving back home. The 500% increase in moves during this time was made up of people that were keeping their job and moving to better neighborhoods nearby, or they were walking away from a job and moving cross-country into closer-to-home neighborhoods and reconnecting to their roots.

To summarize this family migration topic: when violence started going up, people made decisions to increase their security in two major ways; moving to a new neighborhood within commuting distance or moving home no matter how far. Wherever they were going, the families that were moving were looking for greater security.

From a human psychological perspective, that means finding a place where people "think like us". If people think like you, they are more understandable; you get where they are coming from. Their values and motivations are similar to yours and there is more agreement than argument. People that think like you are more predictable, more comfortable to be with and the complicated topic of trust moves positively.

From an FBI investigation perspective, this family migration was a horrible development and exactly the opposite of what would be best for the country. Let's just use one simple example of two families moving and I will color them for clarity. A red leaning family has a job in the outskirts of a big city. They like their jobs for sure, and the location is just fine. Recently there have been too many blue protests and local regulations are tightening down on red thinking, so they decide to go home. They uproot, pack their bags, drive across the country and settle down near their home town. They fit right into the location where they learned their red leaning ways in the first place. So the red color at home just got a little bit redder.

Meanwhile, the people that buy the home from the red family are most likely a blue family. After all, this is a blue leaning neighborhood and blue leaning people are looking for blue leaning places to live. There have been some nice protests nearby about the evils of red living and the regulations put in place by local governments seem appropriate restrictions on the backwards thinking of the red leaners. So a blue family moves into where the red family once lived, and net-net, the blue color got a little bit bluer.

We can talk this blue-red thing until we're sick of it, but in reality, America has always been purple. Its strength has come from the melting pot of many "colors." As these new colors came to the United States, they typically integrate, not concentrate from a geographical perspective. Sure there are cultural neighborhoods, but think about a Little Italy in Boston or wherever compared to Italy itself. Or consider Chinatown vs. the People's Republic of China. The concentrations are in no way as intense, nor are they large in the scheme of things. America works well when you have a purple society. Even if the purple is made from tiny dots of red and tiny dots of blue, it still looks and acts like a purple society. This is the political melting pot.

Now multiply this little bit redder and little bit bluer by a 500% increase in moves, add to it a series of violent episodes, and smother it with a political dialogue that is clearly not looking for purple. What do you get in return? Where does this lead to?

The technical term is that you get enclaving; a small, distinct area or group enclosed and isolated within a larger one. In America's case we formed distinct groups within distinct areas; social and physical enclaving at the same time if you will.

I've tried using bubbles to describe it, and you can think about blue bubbles next to red bubbles. But bubbles actually have liquid, defined boundaries. Most of America's neighborhoods typically don't end in fixed and defined edges. Where does Hollywood start? Where does farm land end? Sometimes there are rivers or mountains that help define a fixed boundary, but these are rare in America's scheme of things. Plus bubbles are way too happy and fun to describe enclaving in America. You have bubbles at birthday parties; you don't serve up bubbles at funerals. So bubbles are out.

I like to talk instead about stains; red stains and blue stains. But these stains don't mix with other stains and change colors. These stains are always going to be blue leaning or red leaning stains. And these stains don't dry out and get fixed, so to speak. With our red and blue stains, you can pick up the individual stain drops and move them around. In normal America, there was lots of purple, but only because you had red and blue living in proximity. Step back, see the forest from the trees, and you see purple. But look closely and you actually see the individual blue and red stains.

Let's go back ten years and look at America's stained weave. Like I said, it looks purple for the most part, but some of it is bluish purple and some of it is reddish purple. Now take your stain vacuum and suck up blue stains from the mostly red countryside and drop them into the blue purple cities. Then vacuum red stains out of those same cities and drop them into the red countryside. The net effect is that the blue gets bluer and the red gets redder. And it's worse than that because the blue stains and the red stains don't like each other; especially after the killing started. The red and blue stains are not only not mixing and not making purple, but they are effectively pulling back from each other and leaving white weave in between. "Don't touch me!"

Now stand back and look at America. A sea of red that goes from ocean to ocean with large areas of blue centered on the urban strongholds, the immigrant edges and the southern poverty arc. In between the blue stains and the red stains all across America there are now not-colored spaces. These were the interfacing suburbs. They used to be purple, but too many people died and the rest of them left. Not many stains are left in those suburbs.

I had a person argue with me once that the not-stained areas between the colors is actually a red space, "...colored with the blood of many great Americans. This is the battlefield," she said, "the boundaries between good and evil. And that it is fitting to call it a red space as the red thinkers are the ones who have caused all of this!"

"Sorry, Speaker Perotti," I said, "you're not getting the point. The moral of the story is that there is no bloodshed if you have a purple weave and a sane dialog. Distill and concentrate the blue and the red and you get polarized stains and the <u>potential</u> for violence. Cover it with a dysfunctional government and media coverage that amplifies red-blue political dialogue and a few people get hurt? Then you get mass bloodshed. This war is not the fault of the red people or the blue people. The war is the fault of the people who <u>lead</u> the red people and those who <u>lead</u> the blue people. People like you and Gump and Benz and the Squad and everyone else that stands in front of a camera and drives division and uses hate as a tool. That's who caused this war and it's time we take responsibility for what we have wrought."

CHAPTER 22

Fortification of Cities - Interview with an MI-5 agent

MI-5: The United Kingdom has spent considerable time and talent studying what is going on in the United States. We have our own versions of disagreements among our own countrymen and especially with the European Union. Think of Brexit in the immediate past and Lord knows we've been at war with ourselves for centuries. We are all in new territory when it comes to the civil unrest we are seeing across the globe over the past few years, but America has developed this unrest to a new level of issue.

The UK is lucky in that we haven't seen the violence that is going on in your country. Gun control and other British factors probably have helped there. Certainly mainland EU has had their share of internal strife and every day we are learning from them how not to do things.

What is going on in America is a new beast for the world. We've seen hostile countries invade and take over - think of Crimea and the Ukraine and most recently the Baltics. We've seen countries that are smaller and more tribe-like develop rampant civil violence and some have escalated into full-scale, but local wars - think of Rwanda/Burundi and Afghanistan after the American invasion ended. We've also seen the influx of immigrants lead to street violence in the EU, but again this is a local issue and usually constrained to one city. Well, at least one city at a time. Paris is able to do this once or twice each year it seems.

But what is going on in America is a new beast for the world. Think of it. America has a land size that is 2700 miles wide by 1600 miles tall and I'm only including the mainland. That is as big as Australia, and almost as big as China. It is as big as all of Europe combined. The UK covers ninety thousand square miles. The lower forty-eight US states cover three million square miles; that is over thirty times as large as the UK.

There is violence across the entire face of America. There are over three hundred and fifty million people in that land area and it is estimated that at times, over one-quarter of them have been directly engaged in the war efforts. That's eighty-five million people or more connected to the violence. The entire population of the UK is just above sixty-five million. America has more people connected to their war than we have people. The scale is astounding.

America's situation is like World War Two happening all inside of one country. That is the problem they face. But in World War Two, there were typically distinct fronts between the warring forces on the ground. The front was to the east or the west or the north or the south and behind the front, yes there was war support, but the violence on the ground was between large armies who faced each other across a line of battle.

Not in America. The gathering of the blue leaning areas into nine zones sets the macro-stage, but the real story of what people in America are doing is driven by the enclaving at the micro level. Think of a city like Denver. Denver is clearly a blue urban stronghold and the major metropolitan area within five hundred miles in all directions. To the west and north and south is more blue territory where it is reasonably safe for blue-leaners to travel and conduct business and live from day to day. But to the east of Denver is red territory. Traveling east from Denver is not safe for blue-leaners, and traveling into Denver is not safe for eastern red Coloradans.

So what exactly is going on in America at the interface of deep blue Denver and the red countryside to the east?

Or take Austin, another blue city, but this time it is totally surrounded by red territory. Austin lives with three hundred and sixty degrees of hostile neighbors. How do they exist? Where do they get food or fuel or building materials, or even office supplies for God's sake? How do they defend Austin against angry intrusions of red marauders? Even in Austin's mostly red countryside there are blue leaning communities. There are many of them close to the city limits and they diminish at longer distances.

Within the city there are red-leaning neighborhoods where the conservatives have not yet departed for areas more red. How do these people live from day to day? How has their environment changed and how have their behaviors changed as the violence has risen to new heights?

The coalescing of blues and reds at the macro levels gives you the nine blue zones we all know of and it is useful to look at an overall map. But people act on what is going on with them locally. What if a pickup truck or worse yet, a line of pick-up trucks comes flying into your village or near the place you do business or the place you shop? What do you do? At that time, when you are confronted with a life or death situation, you are not concerned about blue and red policy. You are not concerned about successes occurring in far-away places like San Francisco or Washington DC. You are concerned about getting home from the grocery store with your family safely in tow.

The human behavior at the edges of the blue zones and at the edges of the larger enclaves are of great interest to the MI5; as are the methods of protection adopted within the micro-enclaves surrounded by their opposites. These are the places where most deaths are occurring. These are the places that the MI-5 studied, and we have studied them in detail. And we studied them in private; we did not broadcast our studies to your Congress nor ask for your permission to study you.

Our reports go to no place but the highest levels of the UK government. What I am telling you now is known to very few people. If you live where we studied, then our stories will be familiar. But if you live in the middle of a blue zone or in the middle of the countryside, these habits and institutions and clever inventions are not well known.

Let me share a few of our more interesting findings and then we can - what is it you Americans say? Yes, that's it; we can circle your wagons and see where we want to go from there. I'll start with comparing and contrasting blue and red responses when it comes to travel control and weapons policy; all of this centered on the blue-red interface areas.

Denver displayed the most immediate innovations around travel control. They were one of the cities that were first impacted by the truck squadrons and there were no existing solutions to the new problems they were facing. Many of their solutions to these new problems were developed incrementally; a problem surfaced and it was solved. And then another problem surfaced and it was solved, and so on and so forth. Step back to when the red marauder raids began - one of the first raids occurred at Park Meadows Mall and all of the marauders escaped simply, easily and quickly by using the large freeways nearby; Interstate 25 runs north and south and Colorado Hwy 470, which runs east and west.

The immediate Denver response after the first raids was aimed to prevent the escape of red marauding forces. Denver did not want to establish a martial law environment and impede their people from going about their lives. Instead they wanted to detain the marauders and remove them from circulation. The idea was that if you remove the bad red apples, then certainly law and order will be restored. I think they did not know just how many bad red apples there were out there in the countryside, but that's another story. This story describes Denver's attempts to control traffic to prevent marauders from escaping: "If you bring a squadron of pickup trucks to our city, you will be caught and you will be removed from circulation."

Denver was not blind to this challenge as they are the major transportation hub in Colorado. If you look at a road map and count the roads coming in from the east, you will find that Denver has five or six major freeways entering their zone, counting I-25 to the north and south as two of those. Plus, each of those freeways intersects with several ring roads and other connecting highways, so controlling escapes from a web of this nature is difficult at best. The amount of land that is threaded with these roads is approximately thirty miles north to south and fifteen miles to the east from downtown Denver proper; that makes more than three hundred square miles of territory to control.

This dilemma of size is not atypical of the issues faced at all of the blue zone interfaces. America has roads that go everywhere and a freeway system that has been designed to assist traffic in going from A to B. In order to be able to arrest traffic at a moment's notice - remember, many of the marauder raids last less than ten minutes - you can't have a SWAT team stationed in the middle of the zone and expect any sort of apprehension.

If you follow that thinking, then any mobile deterring force would have to be distributed around the city and each force would need to have instant access and be of a size large enough to deter a squadron. Calculations indicated that Denver would need a fleet of at least fifty fully staffed and heavily armed chase vehicles operating in teams on a seven by twenty-four basis and this idea was quickly tabled for practical reasons.

Without going into all of the iterations that Denver went through to perfect their traffic control, let us jump to their current system. Today's Denver has automated "instant barriers" at more than thirty of their major freeway intersections on the east side of the city. All entrance and exit ramps to freeways and freeway to freeway connectors can be shut off at a moment's notice, either locally by law enforcement or emergency responders. Additionally, remote closure is possible from a new control center in downtown Denver. An excited call to 911 can close a freeway intersection within thirty seconds; telephone call to escalation to verification to decision to pushing a button...all within thirty seconds.

These barriers are constructed with a dozen each eighteen inch diameter pop-up steel posts across the road bed, complemented with tall and thick concrete walls on either side of the road to prevent drive-arounds. There are also video feeds coming from each barrier to provide intelligence to authorities and in some of the later versions, tear gas dispensers were added to help subdue the marauders once stopped.

Soon they found that marauder squadrons would evade the barriers by traveling side streets and then jumping curbs to gain access to the freeways. This led to a secondary measure installed on the freeways themselves. Denver was very clever with this innovation and now there are over two hundred remotely activated tire-spike systems installed once every mile or so on the major roads. It took a while for the locals to get used to it, but now, when the red lights flash on the "tire-spike" alert system, you pull over and wait for the all-clear signal or risk replacing an entire set of tires and spending some quality time with the police discussing just exactly why it was that you didn't pull over as required by law.

Both of these traffic control systems have gained popularity in the urban blue zones and there are now over one thousand instant barrier systems installed across America. The exact number of remote tire-spike systems is not known, but at MI5 we estimate that over 2200 miles of blue zone freeways are controlled in this manner and they are being added at a rate of around three miles per day. Freeway access and control is a booming business in the blue zones of America and there are at least four major companies that provide these solutions on a commercial basis. The barriers have become extremely popular to install at government buildings and other large corporate locations and even a few affluent neighborhoods have seen fit to purchase barriers and also the tire-spike systems to deter visits from strangers.

The red territory response to traffic control was just the opposite for the most part. Their thinking was driven by the huge number of road miles and massive size of the territory that would need control. The overwhelming thought process was "if you can't control all of the traffic, why try to control any of it?" I don't mean normal traffic control like stop signs and lights at busy intersections; these all continue. But the countryside population had no stomach for telling people when and where they can and can't drive on the roads and since the problem was so huge, they simply chose other protection schemes.

When you drive across red territory these days, you find no barriers or tire-spike systems for the most part. There are some towns that have installed a few of the systems, especially red enclaves that find themselves a little too far inside a blue zone boundary. In fact, installing these systems makes the neighborhood feel very "bluish" so it also serves as a bit of camouflage for the stranded conservatives.

What you do find in red territory is lots and lots of video cameras. Video cameras connected to a modern day version of a volunteer fire department that is electronically activated when trouble occurs. Red traffic control strategy is to observe and report a blue incursion into red territory and to inform the closest mobile deterrent forces available.

As a result, a blue marauding force can easily access its target, but it is quickly identified as an enemy incursion. Electronic alerts are all but instantly sent out and tracking reports are provided in real time. Red targets are usually deeper inside a red territory than similar blue targets. You have to drive cross-country to a town to find a crowd of red citizens to attack. Compare this to Denver's malls on the edge of the city where red neighborhoods are just a few scant miles away.

So when a blue marauding force completes their mission, it becomes a sprint for them to return to their zone. They know that the alarms have been tripped and there may be as many as a dozen defense teams trying to overtake them, or just as likely, taking alternate roads and shortcuts to intercept them.

It is very thought provoking that when faced with the same issue - marauding forces intending to do harm to your populace - the blue response and the red response are all but opposites. The blue zones want to control the roads and stop the marauders in their tracks so that they can kill them. The red territories want to use location information to increase their ability to find the escaping marauders so they can kill them. Same problem, same end goal, but going at it in different ways. Fascinating, isn't it?

Weapons policy is another area where the response between blue zones and red areas differs significantly. An obvious response to increased violence carried out with guns is to restrict access to weapons. This is what the UK does and our gun crime rates are low and this is what is done in many places of the world. Blue zone weapons policy is based on the philosophy that citizens do not need guns. Eliminate the guns among the populace and you eliminate the violence. Authorities and defense officials are the only ones that need weapons and they will protect the people.

Red territory weapons policy is managed in an opposite way. The overriding red philosophy is that the reason there are deaths from guns is that the bad guys got to shoot first. Additionally, since rural areas are so spread out, the closest law enforcement authorities may be thirty minutes or more away. It is unrealistic for a person in red territory to expect seven by twenty-four hour protection from a sheriff or a city cop or whomever. As a result, in red territory it is expected that each family has the ability to protect itself; gun ownership is not only encouraged - in many cases, it is required.

In 2017, 42% of all American households - red, blue and purple combined - reported owning guns and the average number of weapons per gun-toting home was just above eight guns per family. A frightening number of weapons all things considered, even if the vast majority of them are owned by law abiding citizens. As America divided itself between blue and red preferences and voted with their feet, the majority of these 42% of households landed in red territory. A little known fact is that at the beginning of serious red/blue hostilities, the number of red households having guns had risen to over 70%. The equivalent blue number hovered just above 15%.

It is hard to assess the current situation as neither side reports gun statistics any longer. Blue zone governments collect statistics and have the information, but they feel that gun ownership statistics are confidential information and are not shared without a clear need-to-know requirement. We actually believe that the blue numbers continue to be considerably lower than red gun ownership statistics and that releasing this information to the public would create clamor for more gun ownership. This is counter to their weapons policy of restricting blue gun ownership to authorities. No statistics, no clamor.

Several of the blue zones attempted to confiscate all guns owned by individuals as American violence began to rise. The public message was "We need to arm the authorities as rapidly as possible and we need your gun to do it." The private message was closer to their belief structure; that is that individuals need not own guns - there is no reason for this. Let trained authorities fight your battles.

These confiscation efforts failed after a many unwelcome protests and especially after a few blue gun owners helped thwart marauders and saved lives in the process. Blue zones now continue to allow guns, but there is no effort to arm the populace. Arm the police, not the people. Guns are not easy to buy in a blue zone, but they are available at a price. Over the years blue household gun ownership has doubled, we think, to nearly 30%.

Compare that number to today's red territories. Red weapon philosophy is to encourage gun ownership: "We are not going to be able to help you when you need to defend yourself." Guns are readily available and easy to purchase. Currently, nearly 100% of red households have weapons and we estimate that the average number of guns per household has risen by 50% to a whopping twelve guns per family. That is multiple deadly weapons per person in each and every average red home.

These are only estimates as well because red territories also quit reporting guns statistics. Their spoken reason was that "it's none of your damn business..."

CHAPTER 23

Resources - Interviewer commentary

One of the things that has simultaneously helped and plagued mankind during its history is access to resources. We can discuss resources on many, many topics and we can discuss resources across eras. If a society has access to important and valuable resources, it tends to flourish and the opposite is true as well; no resources and life is not easy.

Take for example, oil & gas; these natural resources from inside the earth have shaped the course of human events. The people and the countries that have been able to exploit this energy source became rich and powerful. Those that did not have this gift from Mother Nature had to find other paths to prosperity.

Take food as another example. People and societies that reside in desolate areas of the planet struggle from day to day simply with getting enough to eat. Those that live in fertile regions can not only feed themselves, but their excess supply can be bartered and sold to generate income and wealth.

Or how about fresh water? If you are lucky enough to live where fresh water is plentiful, then hydration and cleanliness become foundational elements of your existence. You assume water, you don't worry over water. If you are unlucky enough to not have plenty of clean water, then you invest huge amounts of time and energy acquiring it. Plus you get the added non-benefit impacts of dealing with sanitation and disease control issues that come along when there is too little water.

The list of resources that impact people and societies is long indeed, but before we get comprehensive on resource implications during the war, let's boot a mental model that will help describe things in a more thorough fashion and help us understand how the violence in America morphed over time.

Maslow's hierarchy of needs tells us that people have a lot of needs and desires, but they are stratified according to tiers. People aspire for love and self-esteem and status and to quote advertising, "to be all that you can be..." But if you are starving to death, dying of thirst or struggling to breathe, then things like respect and recognition pale in comparison to getting food, water and air. Similarly, if your health and personal security is threatened, things like friendship and respect can go out the window pretty quickly.

America before the war had a pretty sweet deal from a Maslow's hierarchy of needs perspective. The access for everyday people to physiological and safety needs was among the highest in the world. Opportunities for employment and wealth building were commonplace.

People focused on growing their families and communities and for those lucky enough, i.e. for those that had ample resources, they were able to engage in activities that grew their self-esteem and garnered recognition and respect.

Even a chosen few, with all of their other needs well covered, were able to pontificate broadly and focus on high and flighty concepts like philosophy, politics and policy.

As America moved from violence in conversation to violence on the streets, the distribution of people across Maslow's hierarchy changed dramatically. When things are going well, we are happy to attend our PTA meetings and our sporting events and plan our vacations. When individual and family's lives are threatened, we shift gears and grapple with more basic concerns. When issues of food and shelter rear their ugly heads, well, then people may also rear their ugly heads as they pursue putting their basics back into place again.

When people are experiencing their Maslow's hierarchy, they do not live on one plane at a time; "I have a home and a family and a job, but the water went off and now I need to fix a basic physiological need." In pre-war times, you might solve this by staying home from work for a day to be able to let the plumber in to fix the leak.

As the war progressed and the water went off here and there, there may not have been phone service to call the plumber, or perhaps there were no plumbers that would come service your neighborhood. Later, it got terribly bad and the water failed on larger and larger scales because of things like marauders smashing trucks into fire hydrants. Sometimes the utility company would fix the problem, but maybe not today...or tomorrow...or this month...and sometimes not ever, depending.

If you follow this water story a bit further, let's think how the water-less homeowner might solve the problem. The best solution would be to restore the city water supply, but since that is not happening, let's find a source for bulk containers of clean water, say big drums that we can bring home and access by hand. If that's not available, then any clean, bottled water will do. If that's not available, and if we're lucky, we may have a resource available in the form of a creek or a pond that we can draw water from and filter on our own.

But if eventually the water problem cannot be solved and I mean literally - there is no water to be had - then drastic actions are required. People and communities have to leave a place if physiological needs cannot be met, whether that be water, or food, or shelter from the elements; "We are abandoning our home and our community to meet a life requirement. We must have..." whatever the issue that is being faced.

And, oh by the way, in these dramatic conditions, there is no buyer standing by to give you money for the privilege of moving into your house with no water. You get to take the financial gut punch and simply walk away.

Hopefully there will be some housing with water available nearby that you can afford. But maybe not, especially if an entire neighborhood goes waterless at the same time and the housing magnates become overloaded with new customers. Some of these customers may be faster than you or perhaps have more money than you. If that happens and housing competition is too much, then you have to go further and further away to solve the water problem.

In Maslow's world, the family that abandons their home in search of water is trading off higher levels of the hierarchy to achieve access to the lower levels. If your Maslow foundation is disrupted, it can bring down your entire life experience as you struggle to keep you and your family alive. America is not used to these trade-offs. America did not respond well to these trade-offs.

Let's move on to another hierarchy and return to Maslow later. Let's call this the hierarchy of resources; and this means that there are multiple solutions possible to get what you need. We discussed city water, then bottled water, then creek water then no water. The easiest and best is the "whole solution" - clean water coming out of a tap at unlimited quantities at the turn of a handle. But if the pipes are broken, then bringing in bottles of clean water will work. As the situation worsens, it can devolve to having to carry dirty water home by hand and filtering it to make it potable. Much of the world lives this way day-to-day.

Let's talk about a food hierarchy. It's easiest to go out to a restaurant for meals, but a grocery store and fixing your own meals will do. And if something is not available at the grocery store, or perhaps there are no grocery stores anymore because they were all burned to the ground, then maybe we need to learn to grow our own food.

There is more than one way to skin cats they say, so as resources come and go, people creatively find solutions to make things work. If we can't buy a meal, then we'll buy packaged food to make a meal. If bread is not available, then we'll buy flour and sugar and salt and yeast and bake bread. If we can't find flour, then maybe we'll have to buy wheat and grind it up. If wheat is not available, then we may have to grow wheat first if we want to bake bread.

The protein side of food is more complicated. A cooked steak is easier to eat than a package of raw steak that requires cooking, which is easier than a side of beef that needs to be butchered, which is easier than a cow that is running around in a field. If there are no cows, then we'll have to find other sources of protein. This is where knowing how to skin cats may be a literal skill required in America's future protein resource hierarchy because skinning cats may be easier than crunching grubs.

These resource hierarchies exist on all fronts. As you move up and down and over and across your personal Maslow's hierarchy, the resources you need and what it takes to obtain then varies dramatically. Let's move to safety and security. This is a good next topic, especially for a country breaking out in war with itself: "OK family, we're watered, fed and we have air to breathe and a place to sleep." These needs covered, other questions follow. "Are we safe here? Will we live through the night?"

As our Maslow hierarchies present issues and priorities, we jump to our resource hierarchies to find solutions. Those resource needs will vary with urgency. If the security issues are far away and of future concern, then eventually relocating to a safer place might be in order. What resources are required for moving our household? We have time to think and plan these things thoroughly and move resources can be obtained gradually over time.

But if security issues are imminent, e.g. "one of those damn truck squadrons just drove down our street...", then there is little time for thinking and planning. Resources must be readily available. And what resource is America's favorite choice when it comes to safety and security?

Firearms, of course. We all know that.

Well, that is not true actually. People improve their security differently than just going out and buying a gun. After we have solved food, water, air and shelter from the elements, security-wise we first want an upgrade to a shelter where we can lock the doors. Locked doors keep the riff-raff away.

But not all of the riff-raff. There are desperate and clever scum out there, so once we have locking doors, we may need to have a tool to intervene should an aggressor gain entry in spite of the locks.

There are common multi-use items for this that will serve in a pinch; think of a baseball bat or a golf club or a butcher knife. These are good self-defense items that are often in homes with locking doors.

But a non-trained defender with a bat is not going to succeed against a goon squad. There might be a lucky hit or two, but for the most part it probably won't end well. And knives are messy; you actually have to touch your enemy to do damage and you had better have technique against someone that knows what they are doing. Plus, the thought of being on the receiving end in a knife fight turns our stomachs. This is a last resort for most of us.

Now if you can throw your knife... Then you can avoid the close encounters and some of the mess and put some space between you and your target. You can defend yourself from a distance and not get any on you, so to speak, which is much easier physically and less intense mentally.

But knife throwing is hard. Which brings us back to firearms, America's #1 choice in home security. We all know that.

As America moved from violence in conversation to violence on the streets, demand for firearms of all types grew and grew. More and more people were being killed by random acts in public and targeted home invasions. Many reasonable and sane families who felt they might need to defend themselves invested in a pistol, or a shotgun, or a rifle, or all three, and maybe even more than one of some types.

There were millions of guns in America's households and millions more on the way. Simply go to your neighborhood gun store and buy one and get some ammunition as well. But what happens if there are no more guns in the stores? What if there is no more ammunition to purchase?

This happened; the US government outlawed gun sales and people did what sane people do. They looked up and down their security resource hierarchy and sought out alternatives. Stores are out, so who else has guns? Where are the warehouses that sold guns to the gun stores? Where are guns being made? Where is ammunition being made? Where can we get parts to build our own guns? Where can we get brass casings and primers and powder and lead to make our own bullets?

The connection between Maslow's hierarchy and the security resource hierarchy is easy to see. And there are many, many Maslow's needs that need to be resourced.

Think clothing. If there are no more clothes in the stores, where do we get fabric?

Think transportation. If our car breaks down and we can't get parts? Where can we get bicycles?

Think communication. If the mail stops coming and going and cell phones go offline? What next?

Think building supplies. Think tools. Think income. Think education. Think. Think. Think.

America's Second Civil War started with random acts of violence that killed people and caused untold personal hurt. These are the stories that filled the airwaves, saddened our hearts and brought us to tears. This is what polarized our society and made us scream for justice. But unless we were directly impacted - "we lost our bread-winner..." - these isolated incidents did not impact America's Maslow's hierarchy. There was still bread and water and shelter from the storm.

As Civil War Two organized and increased in intensity, Maslow interruptions affected more and more people and these interruptions become more and more dire. This in turn sent people scrambling for resources in competition with others and created a whole new reality. No longer was there bread and water and shelter from the storm. No longer was there safety.

Maslow's hierarchy interruptions and resource non-availabilities are what pitted neighbor against neighbor in America's second civil war.

CHAPTER 24

Completion of the Southern Wall - Interview with a red Senator

Interviewer: Senator, I want to thank you very much for taking time out of your busy day to talk to me about your most recent success, the completion of the border wall across the southern United States. It has been years in the making and you must be very happy that it has finally been completed.

Senator: Yes, Yes, but before we start, I want to make a statement. I know you told me all about your research and your sponsors' objectives, but I want it entered into your recording. Is that a reasonable request on my part?

Interviewer: Of course, yes. Go right ahead.

Senator: OK. Ready? You can start recording now. <pause> At the request of some of my friends and acquaintances, I am having this discussion with you. I think these friends and acquaintances are some of your sponsors and they are important people to me, so we are meeting as a result of their requests. You and they also have told me that while all of this material is very, very important, it is also very hush-hush, will only go to fuel your research, and that my name as well will not be part of that record. This is correct, is it not?

Interviewer: Yes, yes. My sponsors are very serious about my research being completed, but they also want facts; pure and unadulterated information not tainted by politics and headlines. As such, they provide anonymity. I will use your title of Senator, but I will not use your name and there is an electronic filter in the recording system to disguise your voice as well. If you would like, I can provide a transcript for you or your staff to review and will integrate your comments before I send in my reports. Is this all acceptable?

Senator: My turn to say "Yes, yes." Those safeguards are adequate. And yes, I would like a transcript for review prior to your report being completed. I don't know if I will tell you anything today that is not available in public records, but I understand the need for honest commentary about goings on in our country. With all this on the record, I will begin, is that OK?

Interviewer: Certainly, Senator.

Senator: OK, perfect. Now we can talk content; back to your opening question.

Yes, we are happy about completing the southern border wall. Well, I should be more accurate and say that some of us are very happy. My conservative friends are very happy and the people who live on the border are ecstatic. But as you know, half of America thinks that the border wall is useless, expensive, and a very bad decision. It is not their decision to make, so they can think and say what they want. Between the far left of our government and the media coverage, you would also think we have under-aged children serving drinks and meals at our GOP luncheons.

When most people think of "the wall", they think of this fifty foot high concrete barrier that stretches from the Pacific Ocean to the Gulf of Mexico. They think that it has destroyed the environment, ruined scenic areas, fouled rivers and killed people. They see videos on YouTube and view only the scenes from Berlin decades ago when that wall came down and wonder why we are making that mistake all over again. This is what they are teaching in college and it is a shame that true history is distorted or not taught at all. <u>That</u> Berlin Wall view of barriers is very far from the truth of our wall. Berlin is very different from our situation, but you cannot tell that from news coverage and speeches from idiots.

The United States has just completed one of the largest construction projects in history. Our southern border with Mexico is one thousand nine hundred and fifty-four miles long and this is a big problem to solve. We have been very smart with this project and we have had excellent results for our efforts. Illegal immigration into the United States from Mexico is down by 87% while legal immigration is at record levels. Deaths of illegals at the border or after entering our border is also down by over 73% and remember that these are pre-wall completion statistics. The numbers will improve even more rapidly now that the wall is finished.

Remember also that every Congress for the past thirty years has voted for and provided funding for barriers on the border. Most of the negative coverage on this topic is simply because so many people hate the President. Given the upsurge in illegal immigrants coming into the US from Mexico over the past years, we had to do something that would more effectively manage the influx. It's not that we don't want people from other countries coming to America, it's just that we want to know who these people are and give them a helping hand with their integration into American society.

We want immigration, but it needs to be legal immigration, not rampant border abuse. Immigration needed to move from highly dangerous, highly random and driven by foreign interests to something that is managed by America, reduces the numbers of people entering illegally by a factor of ten, and accomplishes this in the most cost effective way possible. We believe we are on the right track for this result.

When we started this most recent barrier building, only six hundred and fifty-four miles of the two thousand mile problem had any barrier at all. Three hundred miles of that six hundred and fifty-four were simply vehicle barriers and people on foot could walk right through them. When we started this latest round of upgrades we only had eighteen percent border coverage by walls that stop people from simply walking into our country. In this project, we didn't simply build sixteen hundred miles of wall and put armed guards behind it. We have constructed the most elaborate and effective port of entry system in the history of the world.

It must be noted that the US/Mexico border is the busiest border on Earth; over three hundred and fifty million people cross the border each year. It is not possible to simply close the border and not tremendously impact the economies of both Mexico and the United States. People don't generally know this, but along the border there were already forty-eight legal crossing points and a total of three hundred and thirty ports of entry where people have to submit paperwork and are subject to possible inspection.

A major complaint by everyone is the amount of time it takes to legally gain entry into the USA, both from an everyday commuting perspective as well as the amount of time it takes to get work visas, manage asylum requests, and gain citizenship in general. These sorts of activities are not "fixed" by putting in a wall. To achieve the illegal immigration reduction goals we sought, our efforts included changing immigration law, expanding the number of ports of entry, construction of staging and detention housing suitable to humanely manage large numbers of people and families, relocation of immigration courts to directly on the border, etc., etc. We added staffing to every department of government that impacts immigration, as well as dramatically increasing connected budgets. A lot of things had to change to make the border work better.

The average automobile wait-time to get into the USA hovered at seventy five minutes two years ago and now it is a scant fifteen minutes and continuing to shrink. Green cards can be issued at the border as required and many more people are coming to America already in possession of the documents they need to help this happen. Even the time to become a citizen has been reduced and the situation for integrating the twelve million plus illegals we had at one time is 46% complete and schedule to reach 83% by the end of the year. These are phenomenal results in any measurement system.

Oh yes, and we did build a wall... People who disagree with the wall think it was built to keep innocent women and children and families and future productive Americans out of our country because of the color of their skin or their religion or their economic status. That is not what our wall provides.

America's new southern wall funnels everyone wanting to come to our wonderful country into well managed and adequately staffed welcoming facilities that bring them on board and on their way quickly and easily. Plus we are able to sort the wheat from the chaff, so to speak, so that we can turn away people of questionable intent. Lord knows we have enough issue in our society today without inviting yet more bad players onto our streets.

The wall was the final immigration element that allowed all of these improvements to work together. The wall is the backbone of our southern border security system, which by the way has become the envy of many, many countries around the globe.

CHAPTER 25

Suburban Cleansing - Interview with a gang leader

Gang Leader: You know, we used to be able to go out and enjoy the countryside. Just for fun; Sunday morning drives just to see the beautiful world. Me and my wife. Not a care. Not a care. <pause>

But now, the countryside is such a dangerous place. We never go there anymore. Lone drivers just disappear. Groups get chased and shot at. It sucks; I loved the countryside.

Sometimes the countryside seems so far away. Yet between where we are standing and the countryside are the suburbs. We live in the city and we are all blue liberals. In the countryside it is deep red, especially now. But the suburbs are purple; all made up from our nice blue spots and some ugly red stains.

Sometimes in the suburbs there are neighborhoods that feel and act like they are a lot more red than purple. These are the stains that have set into the fabric of that area. These stains must be eliminated so that the red purple changes to a blue purple and then to blue and then maybe someday we can go into the countryside again.

This dream is compelling. So on some Sundays - well, now almost all Sundays - we leave our blue city and enter the purple suburbs and find a red stain. Then we, well, you know, convince the people there to go away.

It's not that we hate our red stained friends. I've met them many times and they are often honorable people. But their ideas are wrong in their heads. The world does not work the way they think that it does and they have succumbed to the seduction of the corporate fat cats.

They have no place in my America, so we start by pushing them away from close by. Just go away. Then we hope someday they will get the hint and totally disappear? I don't know. I don't care. They just need to move away to where I can't see them or smell them. Damn Gump-lovers.

I remember one time we were out on a red stain removal drive-around. We were not more than five miles from our house and we find these really nice homes in a gated community. They have one of those security entrances with the steel posts and such, but I just waited for a car to come by and I followed it in.

We turned our music off and rolled down the windows to see if we could hear anything going on. Before too long we drove past a house that had country western music playing in the backyard and they were having a picnic or a barbecue with some friends over.

We parked the car a few houses away and two of us walked into the barbecue house through the garage. We knew that almost everyone would be outside in the back yard and when we ran into guests, we shot them dead; double-tap just to be sure. We cleared the house of six people in like fifteen seconds and then we high tailed it out of there.

When we got back to the car and out of the neighborhood, I told my shooting partner that I really liked the silencers he got for us from some guy called Jordan. "We could hear a pin drop with those babies. Good job, my friend."

Can you imagine the next guests that came inside from the back yard? They must've just shit in their pants. No clues, no witnesses, no nothing; just six dead red stains.

Of course it was in the news. And we worried a bit about being identified. But there were three other events like this that day and that's just in our state.

Plus, I'm a blue leaner and I live in a blue place, so if I go before a blue judge I'll plead self-defense and by noon I'll be eating a nice lunch from a blue restaurant being served by a blue waitress who's also serving two blue cops sitting at the counter.

<pause> We drove back by that neighborhood and the house a few weeks later to see if there was anything new. And there it was! A real estate sign that read "Home For Sale. Price Reduced. Motivated Seller."

Bingo! Another one bites the dust.

CHAPTER 26

Bomb Shelter Communities - Interview with a resident

Interviewer: Heather, as we have discussed, I have started a recording of our interview and you have agreed to answer some questions for me. Even though you said I could use your real name, I am calling you Heather to provide at least modest anonymity. I am researching people's responses to the increased levels of violence across America and you have a unique perspective that I would like you to share. Ready to go?

Heather: Sure, Bob, or whatever <u>your</u> name is. This project you're working on seems really interesting. And the violence across the county is unreal. Everything we're doing in our neighborhood here is according to code and by-the-books, for the record, so really, you can call me Janice, my real name.

Interviewer: Janice? I've been calling you...

Heather: <interrupting> Whoa there mister, I'm just joshing you. Heather is good. <long pause> OK, so ask me a question to get me started; that would be helpful.

Interviewer: That's fine, but I don't want to lead you in the interview, so after you answer it, just keep talking about whatever comes into your mind.

Heather: Super.

Interviewer: OK, how about this: Heather, please tell us about your latest home improvement and what led you decide to make the investment.

Heather: That's actually not a question, but it will do for starting. <pause> Bottom line? We put in a defense shelter. Call it a bomb shelter is that's more familiar. But we're not worried about nukes; at least not now. Maybe they'll be a problem someday, but it's the street violence that has us in a twist. I mean there were three people in our neighborhood killed during one of those marauder things and it scared the crap out of the rest of us.

So we decided to remodel and add a place that can protect us like a panic room, but not just for a few hours. We want to be able to hide for a couple of weeks, maybe a few months even. When you think about the three of us in an enclosed place for that long, well, the numbers are mind numbing; really mind numbing.

Take water. The recommended consumption of water is a half-gallon a day; times three of us, times thirty days in a month. That's forty-five gallons of water per month; just for drinking. Showers cost two gallons a minute. Toilets take a gallon and a half per flush. Cooking? Dish washing? Hand washing for goodness sake. So how many gallons of water is enough and when you open that next barrel is it even going to be fresh enough to drink?

Take food. Two thousand calories a day; times three people; time thirty days per month; that's one hundred and eighty thousand calories per month; the same as one hundred and eighty pounds of beef. I mean you eat different types of things, but for us, we need to consume the calorie equivalent of a side of beef per month. Of course, we have to figure out exactly what to eat to get those calories and then again, how do you prepare for an uncertain event? How much food can you really store? How do you provide variety? What is the real storage time limit for cans, MRE's, dehydrated foods and all the rest?

You can research and learn these things, or at least find people's opinions on this stuff, but in the end, you pick a number and plan for it. We picked ninety days and we have our shelter packed full and ready to go.

One of our neighbors picked ninety days of storage space, just like us. But they only filled one month of inventory to save on spoilage and start up inventory costs. If things get worse, then they'll buy some more to fill up their warehouse. If it gets really bad, really fast, then they have one third of what we've got. We'd share with them and such, but it just points to the choices you have to make.

We were lucky to find three really cheap shipping containers to use for our construction. Big heavy steel beasts and they sealed just fine, so good enough for a couple of thousand dollars each. This approach fixes your total floor space, but it's so quick and easy, we just did it. So that gave us not quite a thousand square feet for everything.

We wanted it to be more secure and much less visible than simply another building on our lot, so we buried the containers in the ground, covered them in concrete and voila' - instant panic home. Not quite instant, but better than starting with some two-by-fours and having to make a buried basement from scratch.

There was actually a ton of planning that went into building our shelter. We had these amazing big cans that are really strong and durable but they have doors on one end only. Useful doors for trucks I think, but not so useful for connecting multiple units underground. We basically dropped the containers into a big hole in the ground and then added custom doors where they were needed and pipes where they were needed and air ducts and electrical and plumbing. To get it right, you know. We were doing construction for about a year; from planning and purchasing to being able to start loading things in.

We weren't the only people doing this sort of work. There were four families in our neighborhood that were all building shelters and there were rumors of a ton of neighborhoods in Lincoln County that were doing the same thing. All with different strategies and construction techniques, but the same exact endpoint. If violence comes knocking on your door, find some place to go and go quick.

Seriously, what would you do if you woke up at like three in the morning and there was one of those squadrons parked on your street; right outside your house maybe? Are you going to sneak away? Are you going to negotiate? Are you going to fight?

We chose our response; we're going to run and hide. We'll drop down our hidey-hole in the back of our closet, close and lock, and go have a cup of coffee. If they enter our house anyway, they might take some stuff, but they won't find us. We'll be watching them on video from every room and we have outside views as well. If they go away, we come out. If they stay, we start our new underground life. We figure we get ninety days for the situation to change and things to clear, so why put ourselves in harm's way while there are idiots about?

It takes a lot of moving parts to make your shelter work this way if that's your vision; run and hide and disappear. And everything in our shelter isn't fail-safe either. It all works best for us if our home remains standing and the power and water stays on. We set up a separate bank account and an auto-pay system for the utilities so they won't get turned off, even if we're "missing" for six months or more. It will simply be an empty house. We figure that if it gets bad enough to send us underground, there are going to be plenty of empty houses around, so it really won't stand out from the crowd.

A worst case scenario is if some idiot decides to torch the house; then we lose our utilities. No more grid power, no more city water, no more internet and cable, no video feeds. Plus our closet access would be blocked with debris probably, so we would have to use the emergency exit to leave the shelter. That's not so easy, and it's certainly not invisible.

We have lots of batteries, and several solar panels stuck up in trees in the forest to the south. We put in our own underground well, so water is not an issue. We have an exercise bike connected to a generator and can run a ventilation fan that will keep the air fresh while you exercise. All in all not perfect, but there are a few redundancies, so that makes us sleep better.

One other thing we can do if we get into trouble is to use our tunnels. This may be a unique feature to us, but it's so obvious that I can't believe other people haven't thought about this. I told you a minute ago that there were four families that were building our shelters all at once. There was a lot of construction going on all around.

We live in one of those neighborhoods where the properties all back up to each other and it makes a nice green space. Most neighborhoods fence this space up, but not in Chantilly Meadows; we actually do have a meadow still.

And tunnels. Our four shelters are attached by a ring of galvanized steel pipe; roughly a circle, but a little oblong in one area to get around a big tree. It's only three feet in diameter, so not practical for day to day going to your neighbor's home, but usable in a pinch. It's kind of dirty too; a few small leaks to keep it damp and we've found a few rats in there at times, so not for playing around in. And it is really dark. Headlamps and flashlights required. Plus, for security reasons, we never leave the doors open; at least two families must be in contact so that at least two doors will be open when needed.

My husband hard-wired some mics and speakers through the tunnels and now, all four families can talk together if we need to. He also had an app written for our phones so that we can use them instead. Just plug in a micro USB or one of those fancy Iphone cables and we have an instant private communications system that can't be listened in on or hacked. Isn't he a sweetheart? I love him to death.

To go between shelters, you basically lay down on your back on one of those trolleys that mechanics use under cars and then push yourself down the track head first and backwards. We installed some flooring to make this work well. For access, we put the tunnel deeper beneath the floor of our shelters.

To get into them, you open a steel plate, drop your cart down, climb in, lie down and go. We've moved two people at once stacked on each other, and we're also tied a couple of carts together to test moving things back and forth. Any cart over fifty pounds is hard for me to pull around down there. But we can do it if we have to.

The access door opens up in different areas of the shelter depending on whose home you are at; that's neat. Warner and Sylvia's access is through one of their bedrooms. Their access door is covered by a rug and some plywood. Pull the rug, pull the plywood, open the access door and you're in business. But Warner and Sylvia's shelter is made with two containers and they didn't want to consume storage space to put in tunnel access; hence their bedroom design.

We have three containers arranged in a special way. Our "front door" from our above-ground home drops into container number one. This is for bulk storage, the underground well, and where we put the exercise bike, some tools, and things like that. If someone finds this then they'll think it is a storage basement. And this is where the tunnel access is, about halfway into the container.

Way in the back corner, there is a slide away shelf that gives you access to the next container, which is our living area; sleeping, cooking, sitting, working, bathroom, and toilet. All that is in one container and it's tight. The last container is food and water storage and critical systems like lighting, electrical, internet, video, air control, all that stuff.

We designed our layout so that if we were breached, the bad guys would be in bulk storage and maybe just take some things and leave. If the intruders come in further and find the next container, it would be our living spaces and we would retreat to the third container with all the critical storage. So no one gets to our critical storage without going through two other containers that have heavy duty metal and lockable doors.

If we do have to retreat behind door number three, then we're stuck with no emergency exit, but we'd have plenty to eat and drink. Crappy sleeping, but we wouldn't starve; at least not for a while.

One of our neighbors texted me a news article link recently that talked about family shelters. It said there have been over a quarter million shelter installations over the last two years. Think about it; enough air and water and food for maybe a million people to go underground for a month or more. That tells you how bad it is out there. There are a quarter million families investing their life savings into an artificial cave with no windows.

So, yes, our expensive and crazy remodel was to add an underground panic house to our normal above ground house. Now that we've spent all the crazy money and crazy time and crazy effort to make it happen - we hope we never have to use it. Now that's crazy.

CHAPTER 27

Georgia Killing Spree - Confidential presentation to the President

DOJ Official: Mr. President and other distinguished members of the audience, I've been tasked to study in detail and in turn, provide to you a report regarding last week's multi-front attack in Georgia. Although there have been many marauder raids occurring all across the United States, this particular series of attacks were coordinated across a one hundred mile zone stretching between Atlanta and Augusta. These attacks mark the largest escalation of violence we have seen to date, involving at least sixteen truck squadrons. Two of the squadrons were composed only of two trucks, but six of them were composed of least eight vehicles each. The others were composed of four vehicles. All in all, these attacks involved between seventy five and eighty five trucks and SUVs.

Additionally, each of the large squadrons was accompanied by one and sometimes two full size vans that carried five to seven "soldiers" - and I use this term deliberately - in body armor and helmets and carrying military grade assault weapons. Two of the squadrons, the smaller ones, were accompanied by four to six each two-passenger motorcycles providing escort and flanking interference during their raids.

All in all, there were over two hundred blue zone combatants involved in the attacks. Casualties from these raids were abnormally low given the firepower dragged along, and the most recent count stands at thirty six dead and another twenty one wounded. Four of the dead and six of the wounded were local law enforcement officials; the remaining were innocent civilians.

We believe that due to the extreme coordination between the attacks and the blitzkrieg style of the attacks themselves, casualties among the attackers were exceptionally low, with probably zero deaths and two confirmed injuries.

If you look at the map on the screen, you can see that all of the attacks were along a corridor that stretches between Atlanta and Augusta. Eight different towns along I-20 were attacked simultaneously; Rutledge, Madison, Buckhead, Greensboro, Union Point, Siloam, Crawfordville and Warrenton. This is essentially every population center in the red countryside between the Atlanta and Augusta blue zones.

The attacks were coordinated to start precisely at 3:00 PM in all locations. To accomplish this, the drive start times of the squadrons were staggered over a ninety minute window; this indicates the presence of closely coordinated premeditated intent. The six attacks closest to Atlanta were hit by Atlanta squadrons and the ones furthest to the east were hit by squadrons from Augusta. It is these last two squadrons that had the flanking motorcycle escort teams.

Most of the attacks displayed a similar sequence of events. Each truck in a squadron would drive by itself from, say, Atlanta but would arrive at the correct freeway exit at pre-planned times. After exiting the freeway, the single trucks would then start gathering together on their way to their destinations. By the time of their arrival at their target, the squadrons were fully assembled and in formation.

The destinations seemed to be chosen ahead of time and not just random strike points. Upon arrival, approximately half of the squadron would park and the other half would hover, most of the time driving slowly around in sight of the parked vehicles. There were two destinations in each city, typically family homes, typically very close by, and even a few next-door targets were chosen. This is where the storm troopers came in. While the pickups set up a perimeter and did some roaming, the vans with the armed soldiers would stage.

In each attack, the goons would break down the front door of a target home with no warning; just a smash-and-grab style entry. The first family would be dragged out and paraded onto the street. Then each family member was executed in gangland fashion; dropped to the ground in a line down the sidewalk or in the gutter.

After that, the second target family would be paraded out and brought within eye shot of the prior murder, evidently for terror building. But these second families didn't get murdered, only their kids were shot. Shot in the knees, no less. No more field sports for these children.

Immediately after the second family had been assaulted, the attackers packed up and left; in a hurry and in a dozen different directions back to their blue zones. In a few cases there was some random shooting into homes and store fronts on the way out; most times there was not.

In all cases, there were streams of leaflets left all over the city that basically said: "If you are a registered Republican, you are no longer welcome here. Pack your bags and leave. You have seventy-two hours. We have the voter registration rosters and we know who you are. Please don't make us use you and your family as another example. Just leave. You have seventy-two hours before we start helping again."

They left dead and injured people in every town with a message that was crystal clear: "We can get to you and yours at any time." Comply or die. But they were also very surgical and in some cases even compassionate. One second family had a single little girl that was in leg braces for some reason. Those goons didn't shoot her in the knees, they just cussed out the dad, pistol-whipped him to the ground and then left. On at least three occasions, we believe the raiders actually called 911 on the way out of town to summon emergency vehicles to their victims. It's like some of them were saying "We really don't want to hurt you, but we have to send a clear message for you to leave town. Sorry."

In this last week after the raids, we have seen over five hundred families vacate from these eight towns to points elsewhere. I met with a few of these families and most are not planning on coming back any time soon, if at all. As indicated in the leaflets, these moving families are almost 100% Republicans. They are heading away from the cities and going home or going to where red friends are. Who knows where you go when you decide to drop your entire life and everything you own and simply pick up and vacate?

The attackers are being kind with their deadline as well. At seventy-two hours, they did come back in to the zone. But there was no violence; they just spewed out another round of leaflets, this time in the middle of the night. They gave the locals an additional week proclaiming "We don't want you dead, we just want you gone..." They also expanded the leaflet drop zone north to Athens and south to Macon. That makes maybe a forty/fifty mile wide blue space if it works out that way.

That week long deadline ends in forty-eight hours. We expect another couple of hundred families to be gone by then and we can provide some intense protection for a while for those that haven't yet left, but the attackers want their two sad little blue zones to become one big happy blue zone and they have put their money and their action where their mouth is.

That's the update for the most part, but there were a few interesting sidebars that emerged along the way. The biggest of these were the motorcycle flankers. We haven't seen these before, especially not this configuration and somebody has been thinking about this - a lot.

The flankers are fast bikes; crotch-rockets, not big hogs. Everything about them is sleek and speed. A driver and a passenger; the passenger is armed with a pair of Uzi-style submachine guns - left and right - that tuck into quick-release holsters for driving. Each Uzi had duct taped flip clips to provide a double load of ammunition for each gun.

The passengers also had backpacks we've never seen before. A little bit larger than normal, but by no means huge, these packs have a pair of launch tubes from the bottom of them that point down and backward behind the bike. With the press of a button, either the passenger <u>or</u> the driver can drop one or two canisters out of the pack. The pack itself can hold six, maybe eight munitions. The canisters they were dropping were tear gas; standard off the shelf stuff.

But what was really new here was that the tear gas canisters were dropped with some sort of high tech glue on them; almost a gel coating. When it hits the ground - no bounces mostly, one bounce every now and then - it sticks fast to the ground and can't be picked up without tools. They literally have to be cut away from the road bed.

When they plant their tear gas, it stays planted. No picking it up and throwing it back. They zoom in, drop a few of these stickies to cover an area with an optimum placement pattern, and the bikes can be out of sight before smoke even flies.

But that's not what has us thinking. What scares us is what if they figure out how to place pipe-bombs or hand grenades in these packs? Then you have a high speed ground unit with precision bombing capability while on the move. Can you imagine a dozen bikes with sticky pipe-bombs each flying through a town or a neighborhood or a shopping center or an industrial district? A hundred bombs placed by streaks of color. In and out in thirty seconds. Frightening. If they figure that out, it's going to create a lot of havoc...

One final note: this was the first time that we've seen this, but we're pretty sure it won't be the last. Look at the screen...a fully blue and white American flag was flown on a couple of the attack vehicles. No more red, white and blue for these folks.

CHAPTER 28

KGB & NYC - Interview with a Russian operative

KGB Operative: My name is Boris Radminivich. Just call me Brad, please.

I am a retired aerospace engineer and now a landlord. I have lived in this country for eighteen years and I have a home in Culver City, California and an apartment here in New York. I go back and forth between these places, taking care of my investments. It provides plenty of time for me to work on all of my jobs during my travels. This is my American life. Yes, and I am also an American citizen as of four years ago. I love living in America.

In my Russian life, I control a communications node in our network of contacts across California. Mostly I forward pieces of mail that have been sent to me in bulk. I also hand carry many packages back and forth from coast to coast. There is email to manage and text messages as well, but my role is sufficiently low level to leave me plenty of free time. The people at the airports know that I have business interests and I have seen them every week for many, many years. Some I even send Christmas cards and gifts to. They make my travel happy.

I have diplomatic identification and state-secret travel pouches and all of those things, but I have never had to use that shield with the Americans. My talking is very convincing, no? So I am one of those people that move special information into and out of the US. And the US government knows that I do this. And I know that they know that I do this and they know that I know that they know. And so on and so forth. And they still let me become an American citizen? You American's are crazy. I get to vote in your elections!

I tell you this easily as most of my espionage life has been dull and not motivating. No trouble caused and none received. I just do messaging. I run my real estate businesses and perform glorified postman duties. I only need to know how to route zip codes and nothing more really. But I have led a good life and have a family and some children and no debt, so my life is better than most I think.

That changed around a year ago. I was in LA alone and stopping along my normal round of post office destinations. I was in Redondo Beach at the time and a small paper wrapped package from Utah dropped out of my P.O. Box and into my hand. I took a photo of the return address and dropped it into the Post Office trash bin after spraying the label with some disappearing ink concoction from Moscow. Of my next six pickups, five had similar small packages that were all photographed, sprayed and tossed.

I returned to my home in Culver City and loaded the photo files of the boxes to an app on my phone. This app in particular is not available in the Apple Store or the Play Store. After a second or two, the program screen went blank, and then an error message displayed "insufficient information".

Over the next week, I received four more packages and these photos were also loaded into the special app on my phone. Four downloads later and after the final photo upload of the group, the app did something different than before. It congratulated me on winning some sort of sweepstakes with flashing colors and a few buzzes and beeps. It also sent me an email that I read later that day.

The email itself contained another round of congratulations and gave me a lucky number. I also received two texts on my phone from two different numbers that had apparently garbled messages.

When I forwarded both of the text messages to the app, the display once again faded but returned with an empty data entry field and a flashing question mark. I hastily entered my lucky number. The screen faded again and the app quit again, but only after starting up iTunes and selecting a Russian folk song I had not heard in eighteen years. I went to bed knowing that I had done my part.

Two days later, the app came alive once again in the form of something like Google Maps. There was a location pinned across town, so after my rounds of pick-ups and drop-offs, I headed over there only to find an apartment complex I have never been to with a huge row of mail boxes out front along the main drive. And then I remembered.

I pulled my St Christopher necklace out of my shirt and untangled the amulet from my mother's wedding ring which had been handed down to me when I was fourteen years old. I also separated a very old looking, but very unused key and read the number once again; three-eight-six.

It had all came back. I drove up to the mail box with the only three-eight-six address and used the never before used key to open the box quickly. I removed a stuffed envelope package, shut and locked the box once again, and then I drove away. This was the most fun I have ever had in my espionage life, so pardon me if I relive it a bit. <sigh>

It was very exciting for me that day, especially after I got once again back to my home and after dinner I was able to retire to my meager office. I retrieved the stuffed envelope, opened it and began reading the instructions. That was just the first of what I call my period of ultimate excitement, and it was an amazing journey.

After three months of this amazing excitement, I was apped to come to another Google Maps location where they gave me another stuffed envelope and a really wonderful duffle bag stuffed with clothes and new identities and cash and tickets and weapons so that their new super-agent might disappear and have a bit of a life until called again into action. Just like the movies.

Interviewer: Ok, back up for a second if you please. What happened during the three months?

Brad: Hmmm. So you want to know more about our operation? I can tell you but then I have to kill you. Just kidding. You are paying me for this information, no? <pause> OK, I have been told to cooperate. No one wants to see America bleed from the seams.

Well, except maybe Iran and Saudi Arabia and another dozen countries that feel they have been traumatized by US colonial policy and its military out-lashes over the past hundred years. Oh yes, and me and most of my countrymen. But I digress.

Back to our story, my friend. Of those twelve weeks, eleven weeks were for planning and provisioning; week twelve was execution week. Our mission was to create a series of violent episodes across New York City to let all the citizenry know that "you are not safe!"

My eleven week job was to figure out how to create some huge injustice onto the American blue citizens, and in particular, my neighbors around me on Manhattan. I was instructed to leave a message: "We are in the biggest city in America. New York has the most experience dealing with people like us and you can't do a damn thing about it. We can go anywhere we want in your blue zones and create havoc at any time. Perhaps soon we will come to a neighborhood near you." Signed by the red marauders. Blah, blah, blah.

I know for fact that there was another operation being planned to create huge injustice as well, this time onto the American red citizens instead. We find that a balance between red and blue atrocities does best at keeping hostilities alive and growing.

And so we did just that; I mean we created our huge injustices and put them in motion. We put together a series of seven events to occur over seven sequential days. Even on Sabbath Day with the not so subtle message of "Red evil does not rest on the Sabbath; oh, contraire." We spread our daily events across time of day, location in the city, venue, intensity, and savagery.

Monday was an attack on a school with a small team of attackers, not an individual. More like Breslan, not Parkland. Trained and focused, not random and unprepared. Result: two dozen students and faculty dead, forty-one injured and zero, repeat zero perpetrators injured or captured.

Tuesday was a subway platform bomb during morning rush hour. Result: fourteen commuters killed, thirty two injured. One train car derailed and out of commission for months with track and station damage as well. Zero, I repeat zero perpetrators injured or captured.

Wednesday was a multi-gunman shooting at a shopping area in the Bronx. This event was designed to maim and not kill, so the damage was over forty people with mostly superficial gunshot wounds. One person under blood thinner therapy died of excessive blood loss and one gunman was killed by return fire from a security guard.

Thursday was an autonomous vehicle bomb on Fifth Avenue that left a dozen dead and nineteen injured with no incriminating evidence ever recovered and no attackers charged.

Friday was happy hour, where four pre-planted pipe bombs exploded in four different venues in four different boroughs at 4:44:44 PM with a result of nine dead and 33 injured.

Saturday was game day and six snipers shot sixteen parents dead as they watched their children try to score goals. Snipers are cruel; sixteen instantly dead with only one bystander injury to the unlucky bastard that was behind the poor lady near midfield. When she fell I then knew that there was a second victim and he fell as well, but more slowly and in control. The lady dropped like a rock; the man just looked scared and was covered in splashed blood along his left side. Anyway, he was shot in the arm and he is OK now.

Sunday - day seven. This assault was planned to be predictable with blue Manhattan security expecting churches or synagogues or mosques to be attacked. But instead of religious institutions, the religion of money was brought to example and sixteen different motorcycle attacks were unleashed on Wall Street pedestrians across the span of three minutes. Police responded and tried to control the situation, but by the time a call was made to detain motorcycles in the city, the assault was over.

These were the first, real motorcycle squadrons. The ones in Georgia were a model for this attack. The individual bikes appeared to be acting on their own to the pedestrians, but there was choreography to the three minute assault. A solo motorcycle with a driver and an armed passenger would pop up at random times and locations. They would pick their moment and then perform a high speed bullet spitting pass before disappearing into the city. There were eight bikes and each did two passes through the crowds.

Results of these attacks were low human caualties, but there are a lot of new bullet holes in buildings and windows all down Wall Street and other streets as well. The actual count was four dead and twelve injured pedestrians; two of the injured later died. There was some random gunfire from a security guard or two and one quick chase by mounted police, but to no avail. Again there were zero apprehensions of the attackers.

I am happy for the contributions that we made toward destabilizing America. Our efforts were covered in the news for weeks and the interviews with the victims and the victim families were compelling. I am proud that media coverage incorrectly blamed the red countryside for the seven days of attacks. And I am happy that I have been recalled to Mother Russia where I can recover and rest from my labors and eventually return to help America move forward in some other new and different way. Probably nearer to the elections I think. That would be a good guess.

CHAPTER 29

Fortification of Cities (Part Two) - Interview with an MI-5 agent - continued

MI-5: That was a nice lunch. Thank you for the break. You wanted me to now talk about some of the most recent innovations in your cities and blue zones. I can do that, no problem. I'll give you some examples across buildings and facilities, some cool new software, and even some policy innovations.

The people that lived in urban areas adjacent to red territory soon found that highway control was not enough to achieve total safety. The road system is just too porous to be able to stop all hostile traffic. The instant barriers and tire spike systems had been able to drive truck squadron attacks down, but not to zero. Raids peaked at four per month a year ago and are now down to around one-tenth of that. There has also been the apprehension and execution of over seventy five marauders, so there are many examples of how the traffic devices succeeded.

Marauder attacks by individuals still happen even with the highway controls and everyone hates the motorcycles. Several cities outlawed motorcycles for a while, but then quickly learned just how many of their own needed their bikes and how much positive impact two-wheelers have in their economy. So there are restrictions in some places, but motorcycles are still allowed in most.

The targets of the truck squadrons were initially citizens, but eventually moved to defense teams, law enforcement, and commercial establishments. As the number of the attacks that were stalled by barriers and spikes grew, the incursions became fewer, but more strategic in nature and less random. Lone attackers would pop out of nowhere and blow up a few electrical transformers that would cause a few city blocks of black out. Some others would fly drones and drop bags of nasty chemicals into water supplies. Warehouse centers were attacked at night and trucks were stolen. Others disrupted airports and bus stations and still others wreaked havoc on gas stations and innocents fueling their cars.

The choices the blue zones made regarding their next level of defenses were driven largely by resources and lack thereof. What did you need, but not have naturally where you lived? Perhaps you should make a special effort to keep your precious stocks of these things safe. What do you have a lot of that others have need of? You can trade your surpluses of these so that you can get more of the things you do not have. Perhaps you should make a special effort to also keep those things safe.

What things need to be kept intact in your infrastructure to even have basic existence - water, electricity, fuel for transportation, food to eat, coal or heating oil or natural gas or whatever else is required for heat in the wintertime? Perhaps you should make a special effort to keep these things safe as well.

So the blue zones, which were once as open and free to travel as the red countryside, began to harden their world against random attack. They built walls, restricted travel, added bunkers and then taxed their citizens for the increased security costs that jumped by leaps and bounds.

Critical water supplies began to have buffer space applied and there was more than one neighborhood that suffered from imminent domain as government took possession of key parcels and added them to security perimeters. Protective barriers were erected to surround industrial districts that produced cash yielding goods and products. Airports especially were subject to ever increasing security and a simple airplane trip, even within a single blue zone, began to feel more and more like international travel than ever before.

If you fly over a fortified blue zone today, you will see not only the instant barrier systems and the pods that are still used to deploy the tire spikes, but giant walls around industrial areas, electrical distribution, fuel storage facilities, food warehouses, and so on and so forth. Each of these areas has a manned guard station with bullet proof glass and their own instant barrier systems. Many, many attack destinations have been armored in such a manner and it has helped level off the destruction.

This integration of security forces and assets is scaled according to size and need. For a warehouse location, a single or a pair of guards in a hardened shack is adequate to deter incursion until help arrives. For big businesses and industrial parks, there might be a housed onsite team of maybe a dozen or more security guards.

For government facilities, the colocation of police and security forces grew to new records. The government of the State of California moved from Sacramento to the Presidio just south of the Golden Gate Bridge. The California State government is now living and working on a military base which has been there since the early nineteenth century. This "co-location" has led to many way-too-cozy relationships between the blue zone government and their security police/ military.

When challenged on these organization developments they are denied of course. There is even talk about establishing a Blue New Deal that solidifies these institutions as being innovative and would make them permanent for the sake of security.

There were lots of changes made inside the blue zones, but there are so many targets in each of them as well. As soon as you protect an area and make it hard to inflict damage, the red marauders simply re-target to another priority. Seal up the electrical grid and the attackers shift to communications towers. Protect the towers and the attackers shift to food distribution. Protect the food warehouses and then the attackers shift to government offices. Protect the offices and they shift to grocery stores. There is an endless number of targets so there is something always uncovered; something always available for attack.

What is unfortunate in all of this is while the authorities try to second guess the marauders and what they will do next, people are getting killed. The death rates have come down as the raids have re-targeted from people in the streets to assets of the community, but still they die. No more crowds gunned down, but always - everyday - there are blue zone citizens that lose their lives.

There is a fifty-fifty ratio if you count deaths between authorities and defenders vs innocents in the line of fire. Last week across six of the blue urban zones there were one hundred eighty-six civilian deaths. We have no idea what the death rates are in the immigration zones, but rumors have it that the key targets remain the people on the streets. That is a shame. They all come to America for a better life and how many have lost their lives in the process? More than a hundred thousand it is said on the streets. Our MI-5 estimate stands at nearly twice that many, but we would not place bets on any number. <pause>

The red countryside has its own problems of course. It is as you know, very big and spread out and there are few blue stains left. Red towns and cities remain physically unchanged from what they looked like years ago if they are more than a hundred miles from a blue zone.

Contrast this to the populated border areas where we see lots of trends developing and we've studied that intensely. A few key things have been learned about the boundary areas between red and blue. There are at least three dominant trends.

The first of these is a drop in people count; families leave and no one moves back in. As the intensity of the marauder-defender hostilities grew, the people at the intersections of blue and red suffered most. It was hard to carry on your life with bullets flying around at times. Groceries became hard to come by; first monthly and then more like weekly shortages on something or the other.

There was also rampant inflation with the shortages. We all like blueberries and when a blueberry truck gets stolen, blueberries cost twice as much. Or ten times as much. Gasoline was always a mess with prices up and down and up and down and nobody ever really knew why. Except I know that somewhere there are many bank accounts that are full of the excess profits from the price gouging. This is all the nasty, non-violent war stuff that nobody talks much about.

Add to these shortages the level of people dying in violence, and well, it may not quite be Syria or Gaza, but still, it was very intense for Americans. Many of these border areas simply hollowed out - people left and no one moved back in. In these places the exit of, say, a red stain was probably not replaced by a blue stain. The apartment or the room or the house simply goes vacant. This is not every departure, but when you hold replacement in-moves down based on increasing life dangers, then the out-move numbers dominate and eventually there are fewer and fewer total people. These neighborhoods don't go from purple to red or blue, they go from purple to a pink or from purple to baby blue. There are somewhere between 40% and 85% fewer people living along the red/blue borders than before the war, depending on location.

There is one clear exception to this hollowing out effect. If there is something important in an area like big businesses, warehouse hubs, mining or other natural resources, you can't move them very easily, so even in the pink areas of the deleted blue-red borders, there were some pretty deep red targets that found themselves needing armor in their hostile situation. The same held for blue assets too close to the red countryside. They also became a nice shiny target and had to weather their remoteness in similar fashion - building walls, securing human protectors and keeping a low profile.

The second trend in red rural America was increased reliance on detections and rapid response with improved communications. We have already talked about the red response teams being summoned up to chase blue marauders and this strategy evolved dramatically over time. What began as walkie-talkies and cell phones and CB radios morphed into app driven updates issued in broadcast fashion and usable across a variety of communication and IT platforms.

Those that were members of the red volunteer defense forces usually had a laptop or tablet in their home always getting chase information. At the peak of the early clashes, there were chases going on somewhere in the USA literally all of the time; seven days a week and twenty four hours a day. It was too much data for anyone to follow. But it was also too much information for anyone to ignore.

These local info reports would be watched intensely and the app's reports for you were always focused on your own neighborhood. People were trained that after all, anyone, no, make that everyone, can see an intrusion when it is happening and respond in some way, even if it is simply to call someone. This is the culmination of See-Something-Say-Something which was invented in the post-911 terror period. All red citizens are coached to use their eyes and their ears and their mouths as well if something is fishy.

You can see these computer security stations across the red countryside in businesses and bars and restaurants, as well as homes. People need to know what is going on, so all red citizens keep up to speed on real time security information. And there are very few red citizens that will hesitate to place a call to 911. Or activate a standing chase squadron into pursuit. Or jump into their truck with their chase partner.

Time to interdiction of blue marauders - by this I mean the time from violence occurring to when a red chaser has full confirmation that they are in pursuit of a bon fide marauder - has dropped by 50%. The chase communications app had much to do with the improvement, but there was also city and county IT integrations that helped merge the chase brains into the fabric of smart city technology.

One of the most clever things done with smart city technology was to help defenders with traffic light control. This seems obvious, you know, to turn the lights all red and everyone including the bad guys will stop and wait to be arrested, right? That is not what happens. Bad guys panic and high speed chases in urban areas are hard to finish without exposing innocent civilians who live there to collateral damage. To use the lights without inducing panic, AI was employed to create only modest delays into the marauders escape time and also a modest shaping of the marauder's escape route.

At the instant a violent episode triggers the ChaseApp, all local cameras start feeding the smart city data records. Databases are created to track all vehicles in the video streams and categorize them with a threat level. As more information comes in, for example, we now have a license plate number, this information is added to the database and interrogated by the threat level determiner.

In practice, the data spread would start with maybe three hundred cars that are moving in the videos at an attack scene and they become part of the database. On a scale from zero to one hundred is "known enemy" status, and all of the cars start with threat level one hundred, that is they are assumed guilty. When new information is added the AI tries to prove innocence.

As an example, if a license plate is interrogated and is owned by a store manager in the mall, minus twenty-five threat points. If the video information points to a family inside, boom, subtract twenty more points from their threat level. If the car in the video feed is a small compact economy car, boom, subtract fifteen points. All of the cars being tracked and measured have threat scores assigned. When the smart city security environment finds any single car's threat sum below twenty-five points, it categorizes it as safe. And that's when, well, you know, that's when the little dots turn green on the display. <smile>

In a parallel AI process, another algorithm is focusing on the remaining high-threat vehicles and analyzing where they congregate on the city traffic light grid. The goal at this time is not to stop traffic because it will cause a panic. "Stopping" the high-threat vehicle is replaced by two other goals; 1) herd the threat towards more defensible exit points, and 2) slow the threat down just a bit.

You would think that the red defenders would want to stop the marauders immediately, very similar to the Blue Zone barrier systems. The goals are very similar, i.e. remove the intruding force from circulation, but the red defenders found that even one minute of exit delay increases interdiction success of their roving defense teams by over 65%. So instead of stopping the intruders, the red smart city would make the lights last just a bit longer or just a bit shorter or go just a bit out of order. Since the entire grid was coordinated, the net effect was to squeeze and push some of the impeded traffic in a general direction; fast enough to avoid panic, but presenting traffic decisions to the escapers that moved them to where the red herders wanted them to go.

The locals that were in their vehicles immediately after an attack would be caught up in all of this, of course. Everyday innocents were shot up and smashed up as marauders met defense teams and clashed in the city. Remember however, that the ChaseApp is broadcast to many people, so when drivers are informed that they are caught up in a chase, they do their best to get out of the way. They pull over, they get off the freeway, they pull into a parking lot, they park their car and go inside a store, whatever seems right. They "shelter in place", to use another American security term, even if they are moving around. Go to a place that is familiar and listen to your ChaseApp.

The AI grid control when squeezing and pushing is very subtle and very, let's say, sub-conscious. There is nothing visibly wrong to clue you in, but drivers find themselves going a different way than planned. The left turn lane is clogged, so go straight. This street is blocked, so take that right and go to the next light. If I go north, I hit every red light. If I go east, it's all green. People have related that it is like swimming in the ocean and hitting rip currents. You can't see it when you are in them, but you feel the pull. You just can't seem to get where you are going.

In the beginning, most exits from blue marauders were hit and run scenarios; attack and high tail it out. This worked for countryside targets and small towns, but as targets were selected in the more urban areas, this tactic caused traffic jams and traffic jams caused panic and marauders and innocents suffered alike. In result, blue marauders are now just as often trying to fit into traffic and sneak their way out of the city until they can get to some high speed path back to their territory.

As they blend into traffic and the hurried rush of red city life, smart city AI has pegged them as hostile and squeezes and pushes. Two blocks over another "probably hostile" vehicle is squeezed and pushed from the other way and perhaps soon they find themselves in sight of each other on their way out of town together. They might be delayed a bit from their original plan, but things are moving smoothly now, so relax.

They relax and feel good, yes, very good until they run smack into the face of a waiting defense squadron. And remember the ChaseApp that we have discussed? It is broadly available to red citizens. While all this pushing and squeezing brings the situation to a crescendo, the non-threat vehicles in formation with the marauders are instructed to gradually slow down and stop. The marauders come to find themselves face to face with a wall of waiting trucks, just to look around and find that everyone else has stopped back a hundred yards and they are pretty much alone with their chasers.

The ChaseApp and smart city integration doesn't work in every circumstance and there are still panics, even when the blue marauders find themselves in a hopeless situation. Humans are strange that way. But time to interdiction is down, interdiction efficiency is way up and civilian deaths from chases are down by 75%. These are good AI results from some very innovative people.

We also find ChaseApp-like software being used in the blue zone cities more recently and having the same effect on improving capture rates by the defending teams. We don't know if this software was a unique development that is now just coming into use, or whether it is stolen software from their red opponents, but it doesn't matter, software and AI is becoming a key strategy for improving the defense of both sides of America's war.

A third development within the red countryside is what they have called their Right-Place-Right-Time Strategic Defense doctrine. Given that their area of concerns are physically huge and building barriers doesn't work very well, the red engineers that integrated the ChaseApp with smart cities were re-commissioned to apply AI in another important area.

This focus has been trying to predict where the next attacks may occur, which is an exceedingly complex problem if you think about the land mass of the lower forty-eight states. Trying to assess threat probabilities along more than five thousand miles of red-blue border is a tall task. At first this seemed way too much to bite off and chew, but the red team dove right in and after a four month development period, they started showing progress.

The problem with trying to predict attacks is that you basically have to understand how decisions are being made on the other side. That involves knowing who the decision maker is, or worse, who the decision makers are. Even within a single blue zone there can be dozens of people engaged in battle planning and oversight. Now complicate that single decision node with a real-life system of nine blue zones total and hundreds of decision makers. Trying to understand who and where the decision makers are is nearly impossible.

You also have to predict what exactly is the question that is being asked of the decision makers. Trying to answer "What city to attack next?" is different than "Where can we cause the most damage and use the least amount of fuel in the process?" And you also have to understand the data and information that is flowing into the decision space. Even with identical decision systems, if you put data into it in a different order, you'll get different answers. If you find out about a family member's death before you are asked to approve a mission, you may take different paths than if you find out about the death after the mission has already been scrubbed.

There are many other areas of information needed to predict an attack location, but the AI process for attack prediction is similar to smart cities and understanding how urban areas work and how they can be controlled. First, build vast databases that cover every possible factor of concern. Next, test responses to stimulus so that outputs/decisions from the databases are reasonable considering test levels and test types. Later, connect these data bases together with software protocols and priorities through algorithms that describe observed or modeled behavior. Repeat testing at this higher, more comprehensive level and adjust variables to get outputs that make sense given the input.

AI systems start out being pretty crude and error-prone at the onset of the system development. Regularly new database models are added to consider yet other factors that affect decisions. Each of the database models are optimized individually and also as part of the overall system.

The red engineers titled their project "The World View Engine" and proceeded to build a system comprehensive enough to include twelve blue zone presidents, twenty-seven blue zone district commanders, seven teams of key administrators across all of the zones, economic tracking on forty two factors, health tracking on sixteen factors, historical records from six global sources, current news streams from fourteen global broadcasters, and many, many more important considerations.

The entire purpose of this enormous undertaking was to be able to feed in what happened today and be able to ask "What's going to happen tomorrow?"

Specifically, "What military escapades might we expect in the next twenty-four, forty-eight, or seventy-two hours? What might be in imminent danger?" After the World View Engine achieved a complexity of one hundred and seventy-two factors, it started to achieve modest results. Clear decisions were produced, and they made sense on the surface. But when the test teams described historical events with known historical outcomes, the predictions were seldom correct.

"OK, we hit their refinery today and did moderate damage along the east edge of the facility. Will they attack us tomorrow and where?"

WVE: Hmmmm. World View's answer is "Yes, tomorrow, 95% probability and yes, interdiction at an airport, 88% probability..."

Wrong. Real history showed a response attack three days later and with a motorcycle squadron raiding an industrial park. <buzzer>

So the red engineers continued to add complexity to their AI models and continued to tune the algorithms that tied the World View Engine together. Ultimately, the system reached a level of complexity that considered over three hundred factors for threat assessment and this new sophistication began to produce predictions that actually mimicked history. As soon as the historical decision accuracy rose above 50%, the information was shared with line commanders to be added to their list of considerations when planning defensive operations for the day.

Approximately three months after this informal sharing began, the World View Engine's decisions on historical events reached a whopping 82% correct based on an AI machine that considered four hundred and seventy-six factors. Given this extremely high level of historical prediction accuracy, the World View Engine reports become the lead story for each defensive planning session and the meetings evolved from "OK, this is what we've decided, what does World View say?" to "This is what the World View Engine gave us based on yesterday's events. Does anyone have a reason for us not to take action based on this prediction?"

The World View Engine was producing output that was correct four times out of five given tests with historical information. It wasn't quite as accurate when fed with current events, but it was still achieving accurate predictions two out of three times. Imagine that. Two out of three blue marauder incursions were met with immediate resistance and more than half of these raids were stopped dead in their tracks.

Well, most of the time the increased level of defense activity simply scared the attackers away. The attackers decided that it was too hot to proceed and simply turned around and went home. But every now and then some blue zealot would not pick up on the increased security, or simply didn't care and in those cases, well, they were literally stopped dead in their tracks. Idiots.

The blue zones were also innovating on the software side of things. After all, the tech companies in the Bay & Boston Areas lay fully within blue influence and their intellectual capacity for building great new things has been proven over and over.

Even though the platform of the blue party is descriptively peaceful and blue corporate leadership had actively disavowed connections to war machines, the blue zone tech community proved to be able to deliver in times of war as well.

Blue zone innovation reached its peak with their vision and delivery of AppLife. AppLife is much less an app and way more of an environment. Maybe best described as a community operating system, Applife surrounds client citizens with layers of digital assistants. Theses assistants take care of the regular and mundane, freeing the client citizen for other more critical activities.

Getting technology to do mankind's bidding is not a new concept; it has been happening since the invention of the wheel. But providing tech-connect to humans has always been limited by eyes and ears and hands and such things. Yes, those human things.

AppLife allows a client citizen to attach to any number of the hundreds of possible digital drones built into the AppLife environment. Early users are challenged with keeping up with a half dozen of even the most primitive drones. But now, the blues have hundreds of AppLife super-users that have digital assistance on many dozens of vectors.

The record for AppLife is Carly Preston from Bar Harbor, Maine who interfaced to sixty-two separate information processing applications at the same time. Carly was part of the early AppLife QA team and she saw the potential of wide band digital assistance in helping her play chess with her friends. She built up her app based chess world over a three year period while interning at the University. When she achieved her AppLife record, her sixty-two digital drones helped her win fourteen different chess games she played at the same time.

And not against lightweights; these opponents were pros and semi-pro's and computer opponents and neophytes and phonies, all lumped in together. Three of the games were those timed beasts where you have to respond in real time to your opponents move.

You don't get to walk around in these umpteen-on-one contests. Carly had to sit within an arm's reach of the three timed opponents and within eyeshot of the other eleven games. Sometimes she was able to get up and make a move on one of the game boards. Most times things moved too fast and she had to call out moves to others for the games to progress.

And Carly beat them all; all fourteen parallel champion chess games. The fastest win against the neophyte was under three minutes. The last win came in at one hour twelve minutes and six seconds. This match was against a Russian chess champion who holds the last four Olympic gold medals.

To have truth in advertising, Carly's AppLife environment would not pass the requirements for professional or Olympic chess play. My gosh, she was smart- matching every move made by her opponents with the best in class moves her digital drones acquired and she plagiarized as many response tactics as her drones could find.

The funny thing was that Carly didn't actually know how to play chess. She has never played without her AppLife connection and she would lose to everyone if she did not have digital support.

You see, Carly may not have known chess, but she did know how to operate her AppLife. Look, I know, this is heady stuff; but techies do what techies do.

The real impact of AppLife was near zero in Phase One of Civil War Two and things like the red's ChaseApp and World View Engine led the way. AppLife matured during Phase Two and kicked ass in Phase Three, but we'll save that for another time. <long pause>

Why don't we shift gears to policy changes. In this first case, it's really about policies that didn't change as the violence grew; at least not at first. This has to do with economics and basic commercial and consumer activity. People need to eat, and go to the doctor, and buy clothes and a hundred other things. When these get interrupted, life becomes inconvenient at least and downright impossible sometimes. Compare "I can't get the right size shoes" to "The lights went out and they have yet to come back on..."

Getting those shoes, turning on the power and the other life things take lots and lots of events to make things perform correctly. Many people have to do their jobs across broad swaths of connected things to make the daily stuff happen. It ends up that all of these things are tightly intertwined and none of these connections are organized by blue and red. Not the power grid. Not the communications companies. Not water utilities. Not grocery stores. Not, not, not... That makes it impossible to draw a line on a map and say "all the blue groceries come from here and all of the red groceries come from over there."

Think about business ownership. Thousands of store fronts, small businesses, and corporate entities spread around at random. Sure there may be some neighborhoods and business complexes where there is better alignment between politics and property, but it is way more mixed up than you might think.

What this gets us to is that if you want to provide as little interruption as possible into people and their lives, "you'd best be leaving stuff alone..." Supply lines for necessary goods and services are delicate and interconnected. Pillage a warehouse hub and you impact a hundred thousand residents for a few days until the owners get it back into business. Burn it down and all the destroyed inventory creates spot shortages that drive predatory pricing and other nasty results.

So the policies, more specifically, economic policies regarding commercial ventures and the basic consumer purchasing infrastructure stayed untouched by blue and red politicians and force leaders. There was always excessive blathering going on in governments all around about changing these "archaic conventions". But saner minds prevailed and calls for derailing this economic factor or that economic factor found themselves stuck in government committees forever.

It was business as usual for the most part. Seriously, everyone across any red-blue spectrum you might pick as an example all agreed that policies and practices that cause major disruption anywhere across the economy must be avoided at all costs. No one wants to be kept away from haircuts and groceries. People kept buying the things they needed. Businesses kept providing their value.

There was mental compartmentalization when it came to "supporting the economic machine" and reconciling that with increasing violence on the streets. It was easy to do this at first, keep them apart I mean, but as the body count rose, the impact on the economy was inevitable. The real economic issues did not develop to dangerous levels until the third phase of the war. All during the first phase, the economy was humming along and blue people were buying from red stores who got shipments with blue trucks full of brands from red companies that imported products through blue customs departments and so on and so forth. The economy worked for a long time; it was very strong to start with and people wanted it to sustain.

The economy was one area where blue and red were able to maintain agreement and support the status quo. In another area, however, red and blue policy responses were dramatically different approaches to solving very similar issues. This story has to do with the question: "How do you manage your property after dark?"

The issue is basically the same for reds and blues; humans are diurnal. They are active during the day and they sleep at night. 90% of all activity is during the day and most places pretty much shut down at night. There are critical things that are twenty-four hours a day and some industries run all of the time and places for food and drink are sometimes open all night, but it's a lot quieter and a lot slower after dark.

The blue approach to managing the night grew out of urban best practices. As violence rose, curfews were put into place and permits issued for those with a bona fide need to be out at night. Police forces and private security teams were beefed up or put into place as the case may be. Everyone else - stay inside! This is for your own protection as well as to help make law enforcement and defense teams more effective. Nobody likes curfews so there was some expected complaining, but blue urban people are accustomed to rules and the ruffled feathers soon relaxed.

The red response to managing after dark was markedly different. "Please, everyone that wants to be outside at night, we can use your help. There is no compensation associated with these roles, but your sheriffs and your police cannot be on every street corner in the country." People crawled out of the woodwork to become night helpers. The response was huge all across the country. It was as if there was a need to connect, but no way to engage until someone said "can you come out and play?"

At first, the red night helpers were not really organized. There were no instructions and no funding and no place to go. Each set of friends would make their own rules and do their own thing all aimed at this amorphous threat of nighttime raids. Eventually they settled down into groups or six to eight people in three or four vehicles, all armed and dangerous. Most of the groups would return night after night to a workable location – a park and ride, a movie theater parking lot, what have you. They would take three to four hour shifts and mostly sit still. Two or three times a night, one or more of the vehicles would go on a roving patrol of neighborhoods within a couple of miles. They would be gone for a twenty minute random route, then return back to hang out again.

The extra presence of people at night helped curtail the courage of lone blue attackers. For many people thinking about joining in the early bumper sticker shooting sprees, the extra heat in their target city was enough to send them home. Eventually, the first waves of lone gunmen grew into lone vehicle teams and then grew again into truck squadrons. When these truck squadrons ran into a team of night helpers, one thing led to another and eventually there was shooting and bleeding and dying, typically at high speed through a suburb or screeching through a shopping center parking lot.

A few of the night helper teams were caught flat footed at their camping spots when very organized and very intentional blue squadrons attacked then head-on. Many red night helper lives were lost over a six month period. That's when we started to see more and more military grade weapons on the scene and the firefights grew in intensity and duration.

Many of the red camping spots were ultimately armored through erecting a small building with thick concrete walls and a very few tiny windows. Most had nearby quick-launch parking structures also with walls where idling chase vehicles would stand ready. The common term for these now is a "quick response pillbox". There are hundreds and hundreds of these along the blue-red conflict front; many of them are fully staffed by volunteer defense teams seven days a week and twenty-four hours a day. It's all voluntary. We're not sure how they do that.

CHAPTER 30

Closure of All Firearms Production - CNN news report

"CNN is happy to announce to our viewers that tonight, right at 11:00 PM eastern time, the United States Congress signed into law new legislation that puts a ban on all firearm and ammunition production across the United States. House and Senate leadership were locked hand in hand when the final Senate vote came in to support this dramatic change in America's approach to gun control.

Speaker of the House Francine Perotti cheered the legislation with this statement: "For too long America has stood by and watched as our citizens have slaughtered themselves in the streets of our great country. For too long, we have held fundamental disagreement in how to solve this problem and Republicans and Democrats have failed to come to a solution that worked to everyone's satisfaction. Today we finally pushed the ball over the goal line and have issued comprehensive legislation that will ultimately reset gun violence across America!" <cheers>

Senate Majority Leader Marvin Connelly, one of the last holdouts in support of the 2nd Amendment protecting American citizen's right to bear arms put it this way: "After years and even decades of debate over how to simultaneously protect individual rights in balance with societal results, we are finally laser-focused on the issue of civilian death rates. Up until three days ago, we were still locked in heated debate about how to support gun rights and somehow deal with our ever increasing levels of open violence across America. Three days ago, both the House of Representatives and the Senate listened to pleas by a group of young widows whose husbands never returned from their recent civilian street fights.

These were not a group of Democrat widows or a group of Republican widows; these were widows from both sides of the conflict with children in tow that will never see their fathers again.

These brave women's speeches were emotionally dramatic and their challenge was clear: How can the USA prioritize any single Constitutional amendment over our fundamental rights as claimed in the Declaration of Independence? During the last seventy two hours since these widows spoke to us, we have been working in bipartisan fashion to enact this priority - that no individual, no group, no corporation, and no party has the right, nor should they have the ability to deprive the vast majority of our population from our God given rights of Life, Liberty and the Pursuit of Happiness..."

It is expected that this Firearms Production Ban legislation will sit on President Gump's desk for the legally allowed waiting period and when that window closes, he will veto the bill as he has stated in the past. By law, it takes a two thirds majority in both houses of Congress to overturn a veto.

Here is what Speaker Perotti had to say about that possibility: "We are confident that we will be able to override a Presidential veto and put this legislation into our written laws. I have been asking for an intervention to our mistake-of-a-President for years now and I thought it would have come from investigations into his illegal behavior or from compassionate members of his useless family. But now, both houses of Congress are marching in lock step and we are putting our foot down on the growth of firearm violence. We are the intervention that is needed and I am glad to be able to reach across the aisle and come to agreement on this with our Republican friends."

CHAPTER 31

Pillage of Gun Stores - Interview with a store owner

Interviewer: Elaine Marcos here has agreed to talk to us about some things she and her family went through over the first year of the war. She is the majority owner of a family owned business and her story is pertinent to the research I am doing. Thank you, Elaine.

Elaine: Yes, you're welcome; I am happy to help out. It has been very dramatic with all of the changes and I'm afraid that will continue, no?

Interviewer: I'm afraid you might be correct. <pause> What I'd like to hear about today is how all this unfolded around you. There you are, successful, growing, prospering, and then one day, well, it starts coming unglued. Tell us about those times if you don't mind.

Elaine: OK, yes. The history we are recording here needs to show that yes, indeed my businesses were succeeding, growing and prospering. My goodness, we were in the firearms business. Everybody in the firearms business was succeeding, growing and prospering. Business was booming to say the least. We had six stores open in towns across four Oklahoma counties, including two stores in Oklahoma City.

It was a fine Tuesday evening, a pretty normal one at that, and we closed up all the shops right on time. Many in my family work the various shops we have so we talk to each other all the time. After closing up, everyone went home to dinner and settled down into whatever they do after work. I remember watching the ten o'clock news and there was this big announcement about gun control legislation. The FPB - Firearms Production Ban - sounded pretty ominous, but we didn't have access to the legislation yet, so who knew what they had actually agreed upon? It was probably another thousand page bill that no one had ever read anyway.

Fast forward two hours and my phone ring tone for my sister wakes me up. She yells at me to turn on the TV. The scenes were alarming with a couple of burning buildings, but we've seen that before. "No", my sister says "the picture on the right is store #3 in Oklahoma City." "That isn't possible; that's not even the same building." "The shot is from the back of the building so it looks different. Bobby was coming home from a date and drove right past it on his way home. That's when I turned the TV on. And then I called you."

Over the next forty five minutes, we began realizing that there were hundreds of scenes like this happening all over Oklahoma. Later we found out it was all over not just Oklahoma, but the entire nation had exploded! An hour and a half after my sister called, Larry and I climbed into our Tahoe and took a really, really early morning tour of our shops.

Of which there were none left; not the ones we visited. All four stores we saw had been torched and were still burning. Two of them had a fireman or two trying to squelch flames, but two of them were abandoned to the fires. There were so many fires that night; they ran out of people to fight the fires and then they ran out of water.

We pieced things together and realized that each of the stores had been broken into and robbed before the fires were started. Robbed isn't the right word. Totally cleaned out is more accurate. Emptied of all inventory; pistols, rifles, shotguns, everything. They stole the ammo, accessories, supplies, cases, books, safes, shelves...everything! And then they torched the places. Same MO for each store: the Pillage of Gun Store America.

If the creeps would have left the buildings, then at least we could've opened up new businesses and survived. But we have many mortgages; firsts and seconds and sometimes a third on some properties. The income from those gun shops was paying for those mortgages and for salaries and for some of our children's college educations.

If a robber takes just the inventory, then we have a temporary setback that can be negotiated away given circumstances and friends at banks. In that case our corporation would be alive and well. It would just need something to do. So maybe we would open flower shops, no?

But when you burn down the real estate, you don't burn up the loans, unfortunately. Yes, there was insurance money and yes there were some things that make income not tied to the stores. But the hole left in our business capacity was devastating in the financial sense for sure, and in a mental sense as well for most of the family. We went from a vibrant family business to a burned out hulk in twenty four hours. I wanted to cry. I did cry.

No one knew how much pressure was in this cooker called America; it was continuously debated to no agreement. We, yes we all agree that violence was up, up, up. You can argue about changes in the climate, but you can't argue about stacks of bodies and funerals for friends. And we all knew that the fringes were heating up. No, make that, the fringes were already steaming at the gills.

One legislative announcement about disruption to firearms supply lines and these fringe people started staring at their livelihood and basic safety being threatened with extinction by government proclamation. No way, not on my watch. A few phone calls later and the chant became "Not on our watch; no way."

So the fringe went nuts and took what they could get. Which was just about everything that resembled a gun that happened to be in any gun store, sporting goods store, hardware store, general goods outlets, fancy chain stores, anywhere. Everything firearms was taken from everywhere.

It was a sad day for our family and for our industry. We were never able to keep the siblings together after that. Two of them moved back home closer to our parents. Others stayed, but faded into the woodwork of some other job that was at least good enough. Most of us have survived all of the raids and the fighting back.

Two of my half-crazy nephews got nailed in a marauder nighttime attack. That was sad; they were nice kids. Their moms were devastated; they still are.

But the rest of us are OK because of two things. Do you know what those are?

Interviewer: No, I don't think so. Please enlighten me.

Elaine: Two things. First, we all have street smarts. We know when to lay low with our heads down and when to get the hell outta there. How many people have you met that don't know when to shut up? They just keep blabbing and blabbing and well, they don't have street smarts. And many of them have gone to meet their Maker.

Interviewer: And second?

Elaine: Second, we're armed. We all have guns; and lots of them. And lots of ammo and supplies as well. We owned gun stores for goodness sake. Of course we're armed. We're armed and dangerous. Aren't you?

That's how we stay safe.

CHAPTER 32

Chattanooga Lockdown - Interview with local law enforcement

Bailey: Yes sir, my name is Lee Bailey and I'm the Hamilton County Sheriff here in Chattanooga. That's in Tennessee, in case you were wondering where you are. I imagine with the amount of traveling you do it is hard to keep track of all of the hotel rooms.

Interviewer: I've definitely seen my share of thin walls and noisy air conditioners. But we're here not to talk of my travels, but for you to share what happened here in Chattanooga not quite a year back. I was told you were one of the main law enforcement chiefs at the time of the twenty-four hour Chattanooga lockdown.

Bailey: Yes, yes, yes. I had the lucky opportunity to be the County Sheriff when our little tiny Tennessee world came collapsing down around our knees. It was after midnight when I received a phone call about a report of explosions. Yeah, right. More likely local yokels having fun, but in some unplaced sense of duty, I took it upon myself to finish waking up and investigate these "explosions" further.

Chattanooga has the luck of being on both sides of a river valley and all but surrounded by flat-top ridges and other interesting topography. It takes a while to truly experience it, but when a loud noise occurs anywhere around here, you cannot really tell where it actually comes from; too many echoes and reflections.

I would place a bet with you that I could go anywhere in the county and fire a pistol and you could not find where I was from the sound of the gun shot. I'd take that bet ten times and fire that pistol ten times and you still wouldn't be able to locate me by ear. The acoustics of this place are confusing if you don't know the patterns. Hell, even if you do know the patterns it's confusing. That day we were clearly victims of this natural feature and I call it a "feature" kindly.

I should've been more thoughtful in my response to the explosions. After all, it was only one week since the Congressional announcement on the Firearms Production Ban. We had gotten off lightly during the gun store pillage. Most of our gun stores in the area are owned by this single family, even though they have different store names; "Billy Bob's" and "Chattanooga Defender" and "Tennessee Weapons and Gear", they are all store fronts associated with the Sullivan family businesses. Don't tell anybody I told you that.

The Sullivan family has been around since before the first Civil War and they have some pretty deep roots in the local area and across Tennessee and Kentucky. They are also rumored to have some pretty sophisticated "get-the-hell-out-of-dodge" capabilities, if you know what I mean. Those don't really connect to our twenty-four hour lockdown story, so, you know, we don't need to confirm or deny those rumors to keep going.

A good side bar to the twenty-four hour lockdown was the Sullivan's response to the gun store pillage. Their Tennessee stores stay open way late and they have plenty of upgraded security since the unrest has been, well, unresting. The Sullivans saw the Congressional news announcements about the Firearms Production Ban while they were still at the stores and realized they were going to get hit. They <u>knew</u> that they were going to get hit; and hit big time. It wasn't just guessing or circumspection, it was a fact that hadn't quite yet occurred.

How did they know this? I told you the Sullivans are very successful and they are also very smart. They realized that they were going to lose their firearms inventory no matter what they decided to do. They could stand their ground and die if they wished. There would be plenty of angry neighbors from the fringes to see to that end if tested.

I tell you the Sullivans are amazing. They are getting ready to lose millions of dollars of inventory and wealth and who knows whatever else the crowd might have in mind. So what do they do? In the face of an angry mob they have a big firearms sale! No kidding. Instead of robbery and damage and possible death, they disposed of their entire firearms inventory at a whopping 90% discount. The Super-Sale of all Super-Sales. The buyers were happy as they got their guns. Law enforcement was happy as there wasn't any violence. And the Sullivans were happy… and alive. What a maneuver! Plus they had 10% of inventory value in cash and fresh credit card receipts to send to the banks, so not so bad for a bad day.

But let's get back to the strange explosion-noises that pre-shadowed the Chattanooga lockdown. I didn't personally hear the first three or four thuds of this big acoustic event as I had been inside and asleep for those. I emerged from my home to an echo of some nature, but too late; too faint. It was pitch dark. Lots of street lights around, but a thin layer of clouds above the city absorbed most of that light and most of the sound and all things were shades of grey.

Then another noise came to me that I had not heard in years, not since Desert Storm. Not an explosion, but an unmistakable "thunk" and then silence. A big, long, nasty period of silence and then if you are lucky, incoming shrieks and whistles. They say it's the shrieks and whistles that you don't hear that get you. I was lucky enough during my tours of duty to have never heard that particular silence. I'm sorry; my thoughts are wandering.

I began to realize that the city of my birth is undergoing hostile mortar fire from positions unknown, with force strength unknown and with intent unknown. Great; it's Tuesday morning for God's sake. It's bridge night tonight.

Then the math came back to me. Light flashes are instantaneous, but sound travels at five seconds per mile. If you hear a bang, that could have happened five seconds ago if it was one mile away or ten seconds ago if two miles away.

Mortars like I'm hearing have a three mile range and have a flight time of twenty seconds or so. If you are near the mortar target, heaven forbid, maybe you get to hear the thunk only five or ten seconds before incoming shells arrive. Horrifying. And to make things worse, mortar units are brought into an area accompanied by ground troops. The weapons are big and they need a crew and they need to be secured to the ground sitting still to hit a target effectively. So there will be a squad of goons somewhere guarding and patrolling and who knows what else. Great, great.

Thank God it was the middle of the night and most people were at home. They weren't going to be sleeping much longer, but most of them were out of harm's way as best possible for now.

I had counted three, maybe four launch thunks as I had exited my house. After twenty seconds, nothing. Twenty-five; thirty; nothing. There they were at forty-four seconds; three distinct bangs and some echoes. Probably from the west of us, I think. But it was hard to be sure with the echoes. My home is east out near the airport and my heart sank as I guessed that downtown Chattanooga may be taking mortar fire. Great, great, great.

I arrived in Chattanooga proper seven minutes later and there had been one more salvo during the transit time. I picked up the deputy that had called me and we could see the flashes from the explosions as we flew up McCallie Avenue towards the aquarium and the waterfront district. We could smell smoke and it wasn't a lot yet, but that would soon change, of course.

Long story short - we arrive downtown and there's nothing going on except a few night time runners and a few brave souls who heard the noises. We get to the waterfront to find that this is where the carnage occurred. Except that there was no carnage. There were holes in the ground, okay, but they were restricted to three target areas.

I use the word "target" very, very specifically; these were no random holes in the ground scattered over blocks and blocks. No buildings were hit. No cars blown up; no homes. These were precision mortar strikes and these guys were good.

There were a total of fifty-five rounds launched that night. The volleys died off after ninety minutes and we were safe to at least go survey the damage. That's when we realized there were pros out there that knew how to shoot. They had bigger guns than we had and we had no idea where they were or what they wanted. Great, great, great, great.

The bridges across the river were useless now, maimed by precision targeting of the roads leading to them. Highway 27 was pulverized right by the ball park. Market Street was gone at the base of the John Ross Bridge. And Georgia Avenue was swiss-cheesed, again at the base of the Veterans Bridge. The bridges weren't hit, just the roads leading up to them. That's hard to do in full daylight. It was darker than heck and all these attackers had were stars and a bit of streetlight. They were damn good at their job.

Each target zone was an ovoid set of maybe twenty craters that covered the roads from curb to curb and beyond the curbs to sidewalks and lawns. Each crater was three, maybe five feet across and a foot deep. Ground debris was everywhere, cast in star shaped patterns centered on the craters. Later we found two unexploded ordinances near the ball park. That slowed down cleanup.

Net effect? The bridges were intact, but the roads to the bridges were completely destroyed. There would be no traffic moving over these bridges for days, maybe even weeks. Repairs were going to blow the mayor's road repair budget. Unless we have insurance for it; can you even get mortar damage insurance?

Near each target zone, there was one lone crater. Two of them were maybe a hundred feet away from the rest of the craters and one was at least two hundred feet away. At first glance they look like misses and made the whole scene very messy. <pause> But they weren't misses; they were targeting rounds. These craters were smaller and burned out and dead center in each one was a metal spike stuck in the ground that had a bulge on the tail.

OK, these guys were serious pros. The targeting rounds come in first as normal, and there was just a single round per target zone mind you. These puppies land with a small explosion that sets off a bright phosphorous burn as well as some smoke, and then the GPS in the spike comes on and transmits satellite-based location information. With all this going on, a spotter can hear the impact, and either see the smoke, or the flare, or run the app that gets coordinates from the GPS transponder and superimposes the location on Google Maps. Adjust the aim of the mortars based on the visuals or the GPS info; then fire for effect.

We figured that since they blew up all the bridge access roads that whatever they wanted was across the river. I issued orders to send teams north to cross the river at the State Community College; there are two more bridges there. My scouts reported back fifteen minutes later that the bridges there were unusable as well. They had arrived to find two cars aflame on one of the onramps and a third one burned out on the second bridge.

They got close enough to see the dozens of canisters that were all over the roadbeds; two different types roughly organized into two wide rows. All of them were about the size of a twelve ounce soda can. All of them were stuck fast to the pavement with glue or something. And all of them had these ominous flashing LEDs; orange lights in the front band and red lights behind them.

For each of the burning vehicles, there was a swath of soda cans that no longer blinked. They had done their thing and then self-destructed. We smelled tear gas in the air and realized that was what the orange-lit canisters were. The cars had each driven over the tear gas warning belt, probably not even noticing anything except maybe a bunch of trash on the street.

But when they hit the red belt, well, they were stopped almost immediately to become an example for anyone that followed. Each of the cars had been taken out by a single no-longer-blinking-red soda can bomb. There were hundreds of them around; a damn mine field glued to the pavement. What the hell? Nobody is going over those bridges either for a while.

Just before dawn we received reports of two more mine fields having been placed during darkness; I-24 below the west flanks of Lookout Mountain, and east on Highway 58 just before Harrison. These were double sided fields of cans with two bands of orange blinking cans sandwiching a very wide and nasty looking red blinking patch in the middle. At the time we had no idea how these mine fields were getting placed, but later we found online information about motorcycle flankers and we put two and two together.

While the mortars were coming in, I was told that we received one 911 call from across the river with some information about soldiers in an apartment complex. But the call went dead and we never got a location. Maybe later we could use some cell phone information to find the attackers if the caller had their phone GPS system turned on, but that wasn't going to happen that night for sure.

The mortar attacks had been kind to the pedestrian bridges and the railways; they could still be used. They weren't very useful to transport any sort of real defense response, but we sent scouts across each with as much stealth as possible. "Find out what is happening on the other side of the river!"

In each and every transit case, and we tried multiple times, the scouts would be met by pairs of mortar rounds, exploding into the water on each side of the intact bridge we were using. The enemy was watching and they aimed well. Each of our scouts were turned back before making it halfway across and they were soaked when they did get back. Bastards.

Pinned down and outgunned, we contacted authorities in other nearby cities and requested law enforcement and first responder support. The additional resources started arriving as the red sunrise was replaced by a beautiful clear blue morning.

"I've been told to report to Sheriff Bailey and to offer our support in rescuing your city. We have six peace officers in three vehicles and they are armed and armored. We also have our two firetrucks with full crews to help wherever they are needed." "Thank you, Sergeant. Your assistance is appreciated. It's been very quiet here since we quit trying to cross the river. Please go over to the command station on the west side of Finley Stadium. We're trying to beef up that location." "To respond to what?" "That's it, we don't know, but we're thin there. We need you there just in case." "Yes, sir. We'll help in any way we can." "Thank you, Sergeant." "Yes, sir."

There never was any more mortar fire, or motorcycle flankers, or armored goons marching the streets or sneaking through yards. They simply disappeared. We found this out late morning when we started receiving phone calls from friendlies on the other side of the river. "There's no one here anymore..." We immediately sent in three squads of defenders; this time with no warning splashes. They spread out on the other side of the foot bridge and double-timed it up Cherokee Blvd.

Two miles later they infiltrated the CityGreen at Northshore apartment complex. We had finally figured out that this was where the 911 call had come from the night before and we needed to find out what was happening there. They single filed it up the winding driveway to rediscover just what the locals had told us: there were no hostile forces anymore. Oh, there had been some there overnight for sure, but they were gone now.

In four parking lot locations around the apartments, there was evidence of military presence. Empty wooden mortar round cases and packing materials were strewn about. Deep gouges were in the asphalt where the equipment had been set up. A handful of empty green MRE's were stuffed into trash cans. Cigarette butts were everywhere and some bushes had become a latrine. The residents said that the mortar forces started showing up in pickup and flatbed trucks around 10:00 PM and before long there were twenty or more soldiers in place. The mortars were manned and operated for about four hours, and then they all packed up in a hurry and left.

We found one body in the parking lot as well. This was the brave soul that called 911. The mortar team must've had some pretty sophisticated comms monitors, because within fifteen seconds of the call going out to 911, the line went dead. Interviews with residents described three goons that crashed into the caller's apartment and smashed his phone. The caller was dragged out into the middle of the complex and within two minutes there was a small crowd of residents that had been summoned by other goons to witness his interrogation under a parking lot street lamp.

There actually was no interrogation, just a short speech with instructions. "This person's name is Robert. You may or may not know him, but he lives in unit 377. He made a mistake tonight of trying to call 911 and report our presence here. We are not going to harm anyone here who cooperates with us fully. This cooperation can be shown by going back inside your home and going to bed. No telephones, no internet, no TV, no lights. Turn everything off and you'll be safe. We will be able to tell if you do not turn everything off and we will quickly find you. We found Robert here when he made his phone call and as a result we are going to make him an example to you."

At this point, one of the non-talking goons walked over to Robert and blew his brains all over the sidewalk with a silenced 9MM. Robert fell, and eventually stop twitching while the echos from the quiet gunshot faded away. The speaking goon gave instructions once again: "You will be safe if you do as you are told. Go home. Everything off. Go to bed. Get up tomorrow. Go to work. You will be safe. If you try to do anything to observe us or communicate to others or anything else than what we have told you, we will know and you will be asked to join Robert here, and join him for eternity. Now go to bed."

We found another mortar site at St Timothy's Episcopal Church up on Signal Hill about three miles north of the apartments. In this location there were no locals to harass and events passed by without incident for our town folk. We think there were four mortars at the apartment complex and there were at least two at the church. They must've had a mortar malfunction in this second location as they left a twisted, shattered mortar tube behind and there was a pretty decent bloodstain in the gravel parking area. No bodies were left behind and it wasn't really a big pool of red, so I think that that person lives to fight another day.

A third mortar site was found a week later on the side of Lookout Mountain. By the time we found it, it had rained a couple of times and any useful tracking evidence was gone, but there had definitely been another team in place. Probably just one mortar here and only two soldiers; definitely packed everything in and out on their backs. They were set up and ready to go, but no mortar rounds were loosed from here. Just watching - just ready - just in case - gone maybe six hours after arriving. What were they doing there? What were any of them doing here? <pause>

I'll tell you what they were doing here. They were robbing us blind. Not for money, not for jewels, not for food; nothing like that. Those bastards came in with a blitzkrieg, crippled our transportation routes, and scared everyone enough to make us all jump head first with eyes closed into the nearest proverbial foxhole. While we were all hunkered down trying to figure out what the hell was happening, at least a dozen eighteen wheelers came rolling in from Powell's Crossroads and made their way to the Komatsu's Heavy Equipment manufacturing operation on the north side of the river, which just happens to be right in between mortar site number one and mortar site number two.

While we were trying to get a few scouts across the river, those trucks pulled up one after the other to an old warehouse on the Komatsu property that had not been used in years. In fact, that building had been included in the property sale to Komatsu nearly three decades earlier, but it had been valued at zero dollars due to the condition of the building, the age of the equipment inside, and the rust on all of the materials around.

But a funny thing about fabrication machines is that their primary functions haven't really changed over the years. Cutters still cut, benders still bend, and drillers still drill. New machines are automated in these functions and operators watch the machines run their programs and shape their parts without human intervention. Not the machines in the Komatsu graveyard. These were all manual machines from an era long past when operators needed to know about the knobs and the guides and the speeds and the feeds and the sprays.

But still, these cutters would still cut and the benders would still bend and the drillers would still drill and that in itself has value. Especially when these machines were all purchased and setup and operated to make one particular product - firearms; specifically long barrel rifles. The now-defunct "Tennessee Rifle Corporation" had ceased operations in 1948 after they lost their World War Two contracts, and was being resurrected in the twenty-first century. Resurrected to build more long barrel rifles; big, honking, .50 caliber long barrel rifles that with the right type of ammunition can put a hole into a light armor tank.

Half of the equipment in the warehouse had been used to make barrels and mechanisms and gun stocks and springs and triggers and sights and, and, and... The other half of the equipment was used to make that right type of ammunition that can punch through steel. And a bunch of other types of ammo as well depending on what atrocity needed unleashing at the time.

At least six, and maybe as many as ten of the in-bound trucks were filled with the heavy metal fabrication equipment. At least another eight were filled with materials critical to production; hardened steel blanks, brass sheeting, specialized stocks of exotic metals, tools of the trade, and a room full of manufacturing instructions for building weapons that used to be mounted in Allied fighter planes and used in action to shoot down Axis bombers.

We later found out that back deep in one corner had been six dusty wooden crates, olive drab and with faded stencil lettering; eight feet long, two feet deep and high. Inside those crates were fully assembled, tested and packed, but never shipped, P-51 fighter machine guns from 1945. Some poor P-51 hulk is laying around the world somewhere without any teeth, and well, here were the teeth.

Those almost-cannons eventually ended up mounted on a half dozen dual-cab, double-wide Dodge Ram 4x4 pickup trucks. They made a hell of a dent early in the truck squadron battles; nothing with that fire power was around at that time. But later, when production was restarted and the kinks worked out, just about anyone with twenty-five grand could take one of these nasties home. That made the war fun.

It ends up that the father of one of the Komatsu production managers used to operate some of those machines that were taken that night. The father had been in a memory care facility for a few years and was not really all together most of the time. We know how that story goes. But when the violence started growing, the dad's war stories emerged once again. During a Sunday afternoon visit with his father, the stories rolled and rolled and the manager himself started remembering more and more of his father's tales from his childhood about when his dad had helped fuel the war effort.

The next day, this same manager went and visited the dark and dank warehouse on the back side of the property full of obsolete and useless artifacts of a bygone era. He wrote down some of the equipment numbers, took a few of the manuals and did some quiet internet research at home. Now convinced of what Komatsu owned and did not care about, he contacted his blue and red compatriots and started a bidding war for the ex-gun factory. Someone won the bidding, and we really aren't sure where the equipment is now. But the manager, who was never seen again after the mortar attack, was rumored to have been paid over two million dollars cash for a set of keys to the warehouse and an ID badge to get onto the property.

Further rumors of Costa Rica and sometimes other exotic locations abound and the manager and his family have become somewhat of a local legend. I hope the manager sleeps well knowing that hundreds and hundreds of his fellow citizens were shredded by the weapons he unleashed. Bastard.

CHAPTER 33

The First Urban-Rural Battle - Fox News report

Fox News commentator: Hi. My name is Sam Parker and I am here with Detective Harper Downing of the Georgetown police department. We are standing in a field northeast of the Georgetown Municipal Airport. Georgetown is a thriving suburb of Round Rock which is a thriving suburb of Austin, Texas and we are about thirty miles north of downtown Austin proper. Georgetown is the home to this very vibrant small town airport. Can you tell us about it, Detective?

Downing: Yes, not a problem. Georgetown Municipal is an entire air transportation ecosystem of businesses all centered on private planes and small commercial business jets. It is one of the fastest growing small airports in the country and a majority of its clients hail from the wealthy residents south of here. In Texas, Oil & Gas are booming, High Tech is in full gear, and the Texas State Government in Austin keeps this airport humming eighteen hours a day.

Parker: You sound like an advertisement for Georgetown.

Downing: Well, Georgetown is a great part of the country to live in and since I do the bidding of the Mayor of the city, I do my best to promote our fine town. It's been a bad night, but the town is still a fine town.

Parker: Thank you for that introduction, Detective Downing. Can you tell us more about what happened here yesterday? We're standing in a field where a lot of action happened, right? Can you fill us in?

Downing: Yes, I can. Let's start with the aftermath. If you pan the camera around towards the freeway, you can see at least fourteen vehicles that were all destroyed during what might best be called an all-out battle between the Greater Austin Security forces and marauders from rural red Texas. Given the importance of Georgetown Municipal, this once empty field has been a semi hardened defense team home base for the past year. That is, until last night.

You can also see the remnants of a tented area for sleeping and eating and those container offices closest to the airport itself are the Operations and Command buildings. Twelve of the fourteen destroyed trucks in the field were defenders and thirty-five souls perished last night with those vehicles. You can see the blue pennants sticking out of the ground where the bodies were found. Another seventy defenders were injured and they are resting comfortably at hospitals in Austin.

Only two of the red marauder vehicles were stopped and both of their three man crews were killed. We've taken the bodies to the morgue for the medical examiner to determine cause of death. It will be a simple exercise for her this time as they were all blown to bits by two well aimed RPG rounds. Lucky hits actually because RPG's are a bitch to hit anything precisely, but these targets had stopped moving and a defense team was only about ten yards away when they fired two rounds. It was so close in fact that one of the shooters was immediately killed by his own hit and the other shooter ended up in the hospital with concussion head trauma from the blast wave.

The twelve defending trucks were all nailed almost simultaneously according to survivor reports. Around 9:00 PM local time, right at dusk, we are told that a huge buzzing sound erupted from the other side of the freeway and at least thirty camera-style drones came rushing in at about fifty feet altitude. They flew in rough formation and by that I mean they weren't organized into a line or a chevron, but they were a big mass of flyers all going in the same direction at the same speed.

As soon as they arrived at the edge of the compound, they acted independently instead of as one big noisy cloud and each one bee-lined for a truck. And when I say bee-line, I'm referring to a big mean, nasty and angry hornet with its eye on a prize and not taking no for an answer. The cloud of 'em crossed the freeway in a swarm and then "poof", each one picks a target, changes direction, and then, I'll use the words again, it bee-lines it to its target.

They weren't just camera drones either. When they hit their truck target, a stick of dynamite strapped on top detonated and that's what killed the twelve trucks. They hit hoods and windshields and sometimes the roof of the passenger area and as you can see, the explosions were fatal. At least four of the trucks were hit by two drones at the same time.

When the explosions started, it was a wave of destruction that flowed from the trucks closest to the freeway first, to the ones behind them to the ones that were farthest away. The entire drone attack took somewhere between thirty and forty seconds from first buzz at launch to the last of the twenty six separate explosions; buzz-buzz-buzz, then boom, boom, boom, BOOOOOOOOOM, boom, boom, boom... A witness from the airport proper said it reminded him of the carpet bombing during the Vietnam War; smaller bombs, but the same effect on the ground.

We recovered three of the un-exploded drones earlier this morning and it's a clever design in its simplicity; standard issue camera drone that can carry about a pound of payload. Half of that weight was the dynamite, a nine volt battery and a trigger circuit. The other half was an interesting circuit board and a six inch diameter coil of wire, powered by a bigger lithium ion battery that hung on the undercarriage of the drone. We think that this coil do-hickey is a really low tech metal detector that was used to do final targeting for the drone.

The trigger circuit was also something of a wonder. It was built with nine little reed switches that were mounted in a 3D pyramid with a magnet on springs suspended in the middle. If the drone hits something from any orientation, the magnet will bounce close to one of the switches and that sets off the dynamite. A tenth magnet/reed switch was also used, but this seems to be a self-destruct feature. It looks like once the drone gets up to attack speed, this circuit is activated and if the drone doesn't hit anything hard enough to set off the main trigger, eventually it slows down and "boom!" Once these birds are airborne and armed, they are not going quietly into the night. They'll self-destruct if they don't find a target. A couple of them didn't work this way, but 90% of the drones sent in last night exploded, so that's a really high success rate for a civilian design.

Back to last night's violence. Half of the defending trucks were on an "instant ready" status and their crews were inside with engines running. They were ready to pursue marauders at a moment's notice. These teams didn't stand a chance. When the drones struck, the men in the truck cabs were peppered with windshield glass, crushed by the explosion and burned in place. The ones in the truck beds were mostly knocked around. If they were lucky enough to be knocked out of the truck, then they flew maybe twenty feet and landed in a daze with mostly minor injuries. If they didn't get knocked clear, well, those poor bastards suffered like the cab crews.

The other half of the defense teams were in stand-down mode, and their crews were sitting at nearby tables having coffee or maybe something to eat. A few farthest away from the attackers were able to react quickly enough to run away from the burning trucks and then regather with their other surviving peers. A lot of the stand-down crews that were not fast enough are now in Austin hospitals.

The defending commander tried to reorganize the group into some sort of military posture, but that was short lived as within two minutes of the drone attack, a truck squadron of maybe ten trucks came flying off of the freeway access road right past Berry Creek and directly into the camp. Eight of the ten had a single .50 caliber machine gun mounted on a stand in the back and the other two were command units that only had passengers. It was these two trucks that stopped first and got nailed by the RPGs.

But the other eight trucks did mop up work and before another five minutes had passed it had become obvious to the defending commander that they were way shell shocked from the initial attack and way outgunned by the heavily armed trucks. He ordered his men to stand down and surrendered to the red marauders. He was fully expecting to be killed soon thereafter, but he was praying for a miracle anyway.

He was lucky. He got his miracle. After disarming the defenders and close questioning a few of them, the leader of the marauders approached the defenders and said, "You are free to go. We don't want any more death and we don't want prisoners; we just want the airport. Leave all of your weapons and equipment here. Go back to your families and friends and quit this amateur soldiering. We are bringing in a bus to take you down to Austin. If you come back with intent to do us harm or re-take the airport, it is then when you will die, but not now. Just go home and stay home."

Parker: That's an excellent report Detective Downing. Thank you so much. We have also heard that there were several other firefights last night and similar results occurred in those neighborhoods as well. Do you have information to share with us on those events?

Downing: Yes, but I've only been at this location since we arrived after the battle subsided and I have only gotten snippets over the radio. This is what I've heard, however. There were at least six of these attacks by red marauders last night, all of them with similar objectives and methods. These raids were spread across a thirty mile front that extends from Lexington and Rockdale to the east, all the way to Marble Falls and Burnett to the west. All of the attacks were timed for dusk and all were aimed at suppressing defense camps that had been set up north of Austin. All of them used drone bombs to destroy staged truck fleets and then were followed up by machine gun toting clean-up teams.

First estimates are that there have been over two hundred deaths across the red marauders and the blue defense teams, with by far the majority of the casualties taken by blue defenders. There may have been as many as forty-six trucks destroyed by the raiders and as far as we know, the only two red truck losses were the two marauding trucks taken out here at the Georgetown Airport raid. In each and every case, the bloodshed stopped as soon as the defenders raised a proverbial white flag and in all cases, the surviving defenders were returned to Austin city limits with no further harm.

The net effect of this battle - I don't know what else to call it - is that the line of demarcation between the Austin blue urban zone and the red countryside has moved approximately ten miles closer to Austin across the entire front of attacks. Georgetown is now red, not blue. The area north of Lake Travis is now red and not blue. On the east side, the red-blue front has moved almost twenty miles from Highway 77 to Highway 95. Three hundred square miles of land changed hands last night and Austin seems to be standing on a blue island that is shrinking in size almost every day.

Parker: So how does that work with you and your team, detective? Georgetown has changed from blue to red overnight. What is your relationship to the new red owners of this territory?

Downing: I told you earlier that I work at the bidding of the mayor. This morning, yesterday's blue mayor of Georgetown resigned peacefully and was put on a bus to Austin. A new mayor was sworn in immediately thereafter and now I have a new mayor to do the bidding of. He's a bright red mayor, but he's a friend of mine from high school, so we're going to get along just fine I think.

CHAPTER 34

The Bombing - Recording of a meeting aboard Air Force One

POTUS: OK, Bob, you've had the ninety minutes of prep time you asked for. We've been in the air for over two hours now and I need to know everything you know about what just happened. I know a bomb went off; we all saw the flash and that terrible noise. But why was I rushed out to Air Force One and why the hell did we take off from Dulles instead of Joint Base Andrews where we usually take off from? Talk to me and talk to me now!

SEC DEF: Yes sir, Mr. President. We do not know everything just yet; it's only been a few hours. But I can share with you what we do know and a few suspicions of ours, but many of your questions may not have answers yet.

POTUS: That's fine. I don't expect miracles, but I do expect to be a lot smarter about this when we're done talking. Fair enough?

SEC DEF: Yes, sir. Thank you, sir. I've got the Chairman of the Joint Chiefs of Staff on the video phone and he's going to give us the initial briefing. Harold, are you receiving our transmission? Can you see us and hear us?

Chairman: Yes I can, Mr. Secretary and Mr. President. I'd normally start out by saying "good evening", but it is definitely not a good evening, so I will dispense with that pleasantry.

POTUS: I understand your sentiments, Harold, but please jump right in. I am not a patient man to start with and keeping me in the dark for the last two hours has pushed my limits.

SEC DEF: Before you start, Harold, let me interrupt for one more moment. Mr. President, I risked frustrating you for longer than you wanted because this event is a huge problem; a make or break a Presidency kind of problem. Yes, we had a bomb go off in Washington DC and yes, it was a big bomb. But we've been getting conflicting information from all of our normal sources and we had to stabilize our understanding before coming to you.

We literally did not know what happened for sure until forty five minutes ago and since then, the teams have been answering my questions so that we can put a clear story in front of you. Until I get the same answer to my questions three times in a row, I don't believe I can trust the information. This is big enough that we have to get it right before reacting. We have to be sure of our situation and you'll understand why in a moment.

POTUS: Thank you, Bob, for doing your job and thank you for trying to keep me out of trouble. I seem to find enough of it on my own. But let's get on with it. Harold, please proceed.

Chairman: Yes sir, Mr. President. Here is what we know. At approximately 7:32 PM eastern time, a large explosion occurred in Washington DC, northeast of the Capitol Hill neighborhood. Ground zero of the explosion was Lincoln Park, which is just over one mile directly east of the Capitol Building proper. At the same time, coincident with the blast, a large number of our radiation detectors were set off and instrument readings from our satellite eyes in the sky have confirmed that this was a nuclear weapon detonation.

POTUS: A nuke? How come we're not all dead? Nukes takes down whole cities!

Chairman: Yes, sir. An ICBM warhead would have destroyed most, if not all of Washington DC. But this was a very small nuclear weapon and it didn't come from the sky. We believe it was brought there in a van. There is not much physical evidence left in the area, but we have a few cloud based security camera feeds from nearby residences that show a white van that proceeded west on East Capitol Street, jumped the curb, drove straight into the park and continued west on the sidewalk.

These cameras also showed that the van did not have a driver and we think that it was either remotely piloted, or it had an autonomous, pre-programmed driving route. Either of these schemes could have delivered the bomb to the middle of the park where it was then detonated.

Based on the nuclear signature, the White House evacuation immediately after the blast was staged to take you west, away from ground zero and not towards Joint Base Andrews, which is basically ten miles on the downwind side of Lincoln Park. Fifteen minutes after the blast, it was determined that it would be safe to fly and we had Air Force One expedited to Dulles International where you came on board.

We drove you west, away from the blast and used Air Force One to continue to fly you west to get as far away as possible, and as fast as possible. By the way, you are currently flying a figure eight pattern over Iowa and we expect to keep you and your family in the air for at least twenty-four hours as a precaution against other explosions should they occur.

POTUS: Yes, yes, thank you for your concerns and your caution, but please, back to the event. Please.

Chairman: Of course, sir. I just wanted you to know that your safety is our number one concern. I shall continue. Please take a look at the video screen on your wall which shows an aerial view of Lincoln Park, or I will be more correct in saying an aerial view of where Lincoln Park once was.

Now there is simply an eight hundred foot diameter hole in the ground. It's about forty feet deep in the middle and all of the town homes and apartments within the immediate blast zone have been destroyed. The buildings closest to the park simply no longer exist. Out at the eight hundred foot edges, the buildings are still there, but damaged beyond repair and most of them are still burning as we meet.

POTUS: Do you have any idea on casualties?

SEC DEF: I've been focusing Harold on the event itself; what happened, and how did it happen. I had two other teams looking into the casualty situation and we are <u>not</u> very close to understanding the full picture. There are upwards of one hundred thousand people that live in the area that was affected. There are maybe, it's hard to be precise, but there may be six hundred residents that were incinerated. We don't know who was home and who was not, but that many people lived in the homes that were vaporized.

Chairman: But it's worse than that, sir. This was a nuclear weapon and we'll have to deal with radiation effects. It was a small nuke in the scheme of things, but it still generates fallout and the prevailing easterlies are blowing fallout towards RFK stadium and points beyond. We're lucky that the radiation readings are low, but people are still going to get sick from this.<pause> So maybe we have another few hundred folks that will succumb over time. We're evacuating a few of the hot spots, but some calamity is inevitable with an event of this nature.

POTUS: OK, so the blast and the radiation combined impact is what, under a thousand people? This is a tragedy in any terms, but compared to Hiroshima, it's a drop in the bucket. That's good news.

Chairman: Not exactly, sir. Well, I mean you're correct in saying that under a thousand dead from a nuclear blast and fallout is the good news. But there is additional information we need to share and this is the bad news. One thing we didn't understand at first was the radiation pattern from the bomb. I mentioned earlier that we have radiation detectors around Washington DC and some of them registered hits. That helped us know we had a nuke.

We actually have hundreds and hundreds of these radiation detectors and they are spread around in all of the government buildings, the memorials, key intersections, hotel lobbies, some of the local restaurants; all over the place. These are there to give us early warning of anyone, absolutely anyone that happens to be transporting fissionable material into our capital. The second team Bob set up has completed a preliminary assessment of the radiation from the bomb and it has led us to a catastrophic conclusion.

POTUS: I don't like the sound of that.

SEC DEF: Let me jump in here, Harold. This is why I asked for the extra time before this meeting, Mr. President. I did not believe what I was being told and I wanted it confirmed and reconfirmed and re-reconfirmed before we brought it to you.

It's probably best explained on a map, so look at the screen again and now you see another aerial view, this time covering more of Washington DC. We've also added the mapping of the radiation detectors; you can see the two lobes to the east and those are the fallout zones. These areas are not very dark as the measured radiation is not very high.

POTUS: What's that deep red area that points west?

SEC DEF: That's our catastrophic conclusion. Have you ever heard of a neutron bomb, Mr. President?

POTUS: Yes, but it's been a long time. Isn't that a weapon that doesn't do much damage, but can kill people with radiation?

SEC DEF: Yes, Mr. President. This isn't exactly a neutron bomb kill pattern we're seeing on the map. Neutron bombs normally have a spherical distribution of neutrons - they go out in all directions pretty evenly. But this long dark lobe to the west of Lincoln Park implies that this neutron weapon had the ability to emit radiation in one direction only. And very intense radiation as well. Everyone that was in this lobe area at the time of the blast received severe doses of radiation. Enough radiation to kill you if you were unprotected.

POTUS: So what are you telling me? We have a lot more victims out there?

SEC DEF: Yes, Sir, that's the message. But these are not "now" victims, these people are "soon to be" victims. People unfortunate to be closer to ground zero will start getting sick this evening and will be deathly ill by morning. Those further away or off center to the radiation spike will take longer to feel the effects, but they will get sick. Everyone that was in this neutron lobe when the bomb went off will become very, very ill and most will die. We estimate that there will only be a 5% survival rate and that is after a long bout in the hospital.

POTUS: So how many people are we talking about?

SEC DEF: We don't have an accurate estimate yet. Thousands for sure. Maybe five thousand. Maybe more than that. But it's not the body count that made me ask so many questions, sir. It's the types of people impacted. This bomb was aimed at Congress. And the Supreme Court. And the Library of Congress. And several of the Smithsonian Museums. The kill pattern stretches halfway down the National Mall, but peters out before it got to the Washington Monument or to your White House.

Earlier this evening, there was a gathering going on in the United States Capitol building. Both houses were present to celebrate yet another veto override they've become so good at.

POTUS: What are you telling me? Be clear and quick, Bob.

SEC DEF: What I'm telling you, sir, is that your Congress is going to die; almost all of them. And we can do nothing about it. Some of them will start getting sick in the morning and think that they had bad food at the party. By tomorrow afternoon, they all will be trying to get to hospitals, only to find them jammed full of other victims that were closer to the bomb and got sick faster. Radiation poisoning cannot be cured and it cannot be stopped. Your entire Congress is going to die and within one week the only members left will be the ones who were out of town and a handful that may not have gotten full doses for some reason.

POTUS: I can't believe what you are telling me.

SEC DEF: Neither can I, but that's why it took me so long to verify the facts. All four doctors I spoke to claim the same result; a 90-95% kill rate. And I asked all of your cabinet for their thoughts on the country's reaction to this incident. Not only are you going to lose your Congress, but you are going to be blamed for it. They all died and you didn't - that's pretty convenient.

POTUS: I don't care about that; people hate me anyway. What I do care about is that nuke. How the hell did someone get a neutron bomb? Where did it come from? You don't build a nuke in your basement. I want to find out who made this thing and how it got to Washington DC. And I want those answers yesterday!

SEC DEF: Already on it sir...

CHAPTER 35

Call Up of the Reserves - Broadcast from the Oval Office

POTUS: We are all truly saddened and alarmed at the catastrophic event that occurred two days ago on Capitol Hill. The immediate death count due to the bomb blast in Lincoln Park is believed to be above seven hundred people, but we are still excavating the damage, so that number will rise even more in the days to come. Additionally, the number of people sickened and dying from lethal radiation doses is already above twelve hundred and that number climbs every day as well as people succumb to their invisible injuries. Over five hundred members of the federal government, including Congress and the Supreme Court, have already passed or have been admitted to hospitals for compassionate care as they live out their last hours.

This is a disaster with few comparisons. We have to go back to September 11, 2001 to find a similar atrocity and prior to that we have to go all the way back to December 7, 1941. All three of these calamities were brought on by cowards and inflicted untold trauma on American citizens. In this case, the attack was directly aimed at the government of the United States and even though your federal offices are open for business and everything is running, the loss of leadership is too large to describe with words. We have fewer than forty Senators and Congress people remaining out of an original cast of over six hundred. Half of those alive are terminally ill. The Capitol Building is out of commission and will be for at least two months. We have no Supreme Court. And we have nothing but a black hole in the ground east of where I am sitting as I speak to you. Our hearts go out to all impacted by this sudden and unpredictable chain of events.

Let it be known that all available resources have been assigned to determine the people that caused this disaster, to find them, and to arrest them and to bring them to justice. We will leave no stone unturned in this effort. The perpetrators will be found and they will be arrested. They will be tried and they will be found guilty and they will be put away for the rest of their lives – which may be a very short time for them if my request for reinstatement of the death penalty for this crime is approved.

In order to help stabilize the country while we clean up this damn mess, I am calling up the Army National Guard in all fifty states and putting over three hundred thousand men and women into active duty, starting immediately. All notified personnel are to report directly to their guard posts within the week and should be preparing for an extended assignment of at least three months. By that time, we should have been able to identify new Congress people and bring our federal law making capability back on line.

It is unfortunate that we live in a time with so much death and destruction. This is not like us. This is not the United States that I want to live in. I'm sure I speak for all of us in this sentiment. I am committed to bringing justice to bear in the immediate sense, but I am also committed to bringing our broader hostilities to a halt as well.

God Bless the United States of America.

CHAPTER 36

The Bombing (Part Two) - A meeting in the President's limousine

POTUS: OK, Harold, it's been two weeks since the bombing and we need to be moving from investigation to action. The hawks are clamoring for retaliation and I find myself wanting to throw a punch as well. We've been meeting everyday on this topic and so far you've just been confirming that a nuke went off and killed thousands. I want to know who did this and where we can find them, or I want your resignation.

SEC DEF: Yes sir, Mr. President. You've been totally clear on what you want me to find and I can assure you that we've been pulling out all of the stops on this one. I am prepared to give you a summary today of everything that we've discovered and I have also prepared a resignation letter if you want that instead.

POTUS: No, Harold, I don't want your resignation. Not yet. Despite my ramblings, I think you're doing a good job. But I'm so frustrated with this and all of America is frustrated with this, so I lash out. Keep your letter in your pocket and tell me some good news for once.

SEC DEF: I will let you know before I get started that some of the information you will be hearing today is new; new to you, but not new to me. For reasons of plausible deniability and the absolute need to not retaliate on an innocent party, I have held back inconclusive information until we can piece enough facts together to build proof. The major cause for delay as we have discussed is the fact that all of the physical evidence of this crime disintegrated in a ball of plasma fire from the detonation. So we've been literally chasing clouds and loose ends and believe me, everyone working this case is as frustrated as you and the hawks.

That said, I held a half day summit yesterday with the investigation team and here is everything we now know; no more hidden details.

Number one: we've completed studies on the radio isotopes from the weapon used in Lincoln Park. It's easy to ascertain the sources for weapons grade uranium. There are few uranium enrichment facilities in the world and we know where they are and who runs them. We've catalogued families of enriched uranium that is produced and if you give us a sample, we can tell you where it was made. But we haven't got a sample; all we have is irradiated debris and clouds of fallout to study.

What was reported to me yesterday is that the uranium that was used to construct the neutron bomb is a mixture from multiple enrichment sources. That nuclear core was made up of weapons grade materials from Russia, France, the UK, China, and North Korea. There was even material from two of our enrichment facilities in the USA and a trace of Iranian product as well. Bottom line? There are too many isotope signatures from this bomb to clearly determine where it came from as it came from everywhere.

This bomb was manufactured to intentionally display ambiguous isotope analysis results. At the summit, we officially declared this avenue of study a dead end, although we will continue a low-level, longer term study to complement the rest of the investigation.

POTUS: Seriously, Harold, two weeks of study by the best in the world and all you can tell me is "we don't know..." That's bad, Harold, really bad.

SEC DEF: I know, sir, but let me move on to point number two. We expanded our security video analysis to everything we can find up to seventy-five miles from ground zero. That's a lot of cameras and most of the video is not useful, but we believe we have been able to determine the origination of the delivery van and its travel path.

Origination first. The van that delivered the weapon was an autonomous vehicle from a company called "Auto Deliveries." Auto Deliveries owns a fleet of self-driving vehicles that companies can lease fractionally. That means they can rent a half or a third of a vehicle for use with their business and it saves them lots of money by sharing delivery capacity.

The van in our story was reported stolen by the company two days before Lincoln Park. It was on a routine delivery route and never returned to base. Our video work found this same van traveling southeast on Maryland Highway 586 forty-five minutes before the blast, and although we don't have 100% coverage of the entire drive, we have at least a dozen sightings that lead us to believe that it started its drive outside of Rockville, got on the Beltway near Silver Spring and circled east, outside of Washington DC proper. It then used the Baltimore-Washington Parkway to come back towards the Capitol, exited onto East Capitol Street near the stadium and drove straight to the detonation point. The entire drive was just over thirty eight miles and took less than an hour.

This vehicle story was pieced together last week which leads us to point number three: where did this bomb came from? Believing the device was loaded into the autonomous van somewhere near Rockville and then sent to Lincoln Park, we put over a hundred agents on the ground there. No fancy TV-show style electronics forensics or power consumption studies; none of that. We sent teams upon teams of people to go door to door and get into every facility in the city. We obtained a blanket search order from the federal court and buildings that were vacant or unoccupied were forcibly entered and inspected.

We searched almost a thousand homes and schools and churches and factories and warehouses before we found what we were looking for. But we did find it, sir. <pause>

POTUS: Well, spit it out, Harold.

SEC DEF: Yes, sir. I'll jump to the end and then we can fill in details if you want them.

POTUS: I said "spit it out, Harold", not "drool it out!"

SEC DEF: OK; yes sir. Mr. President, the Lincoln Park bomb was made in America; right outside of downtown Rockville. It was manufactured in an ex-auto repair building that was leased to a shell company eight months ago. We're chasing down the trail of ownership, but all indications are that we're looking at false identities and cash transactions and nothing much else.

This particular auto-repair facility had a decent machine shop and our team found plenty of indication of precision fabrication of metal parts and an entire area to assemble electronics and cables and what not. There were no plans or documents or messages left to study. All paper had been put into a fifty-five gallon drum, burned to ashes and then flooded with water. All of the numerically controlled machines had their controller taken apart and everything associated with running part making programs was smashed and burned. There were two laptops there; they were also smashed and burned.

POTUS: If there's no evidence left, why do you think they made a nuke there?

SEC DEF: Two reasons, sir. The first is the pile of dead bodies. Six individuals; all were male. Two were nuclear engineers, three were mechanical engineers, and the last one was an electrical engineer. All were from well-known schools and big companies. Two had military backgrounds as well.

POTUS: Red or blue?

SEC DEF: That's a confusing part. They're from both persuasions, sir. Far fringe left and far fringe right; anarchists every one of them. They are so far left and right, they actually found common ground. It looks like the team was assembled to continue the "deliberately ambiguous" theme, just like the uranium.

We have no doubt there were other players involved; I mean, who killed them after all? Probably the same person or people who brought in bomb plans and the uranium for what may have been the most sophisticated nuke in the world. The design was not home grown, only the team that made it and the place they made it in. And then they were killed and all of the evidence burned. My team thinks we hit another dead end.

POTUS: Well, keep at it Harold, you might find something else, soon. You said there two reasons to think this is where the nuke came from. What's the second reason.

SEC DEF: Good memory, Mr. President. This is the second reason.

At that point the Secretary of Defense reached into his jacket breast pocket and pulled out a piece of paper that was zip locked into a quart sized plastic baggie. He handed it to the President.

SEC DEF: It's a picture of the bomb, sir; the bomb and the bomb makers. Look at the size of it, sir. It could fit into a duffle bag. The picture must've been taken between the time they completed the project and when they were killed. It was pinned to a corkboard above one of the work desks so that we could find it with the bodies in the shop.

The picture was printed on a printer right there, probably with a wireless phone connection. And the printer was smashed and burned; just like everything else. We're following up, but it may be another dead end. The people that planned this whole thing were pros.

CHAPTER 37

All Hands Lost - Washington Post online article

"The Washington Post has just been informed by a communication specialist for the Joints Chiefs of Staff that less than thirty minutes ago, Air Force One suffered a catastrophic engine failure during take off from Andrews Air Force Base and has crashed into a small neighborhood called Westphalia Estates. It is feared that all passengers of Air Force One may have perished as well as an undetermined number of residents on the ground.

The President, as many as five cabinet members, the Chairman of the Joint Chiefs, the executive branch press corps, and perhaps twenty five members of the president's staff and Air Force One crew members are believed to have been on board when this tragedy occurred.

Based on the rapidness of the event and also eye witness reports, we project that there will be no survivors from the crash of Air Force One. Our hearts are with the families of all who suffered from this loss – there is barely any consolation possible, especially at this time of year.

The loss of the President and so many others comes at an unfortunate time so soon after the neutron bomb attack on the Capitol three weeks ago. Since that incident, we have reported on funeral after funeral for a broad swath of America. In addition to the more than six hundred and fifty deaths during the immediate bomb blast, over seventeen hundred citizens exposed to lethal doses have succumbed to their radiation poisoning. We have also shared that over five hundred Congress people along with the entire Supreme Court are no longer with us.

Eye witnesses to the crash have described that Air Force one was on a normal takeoff pattern to the north when the plane noticeably veered to the right. At that same time, a puff of smoke came from the outboard right engine and then some flame as well. Within a second or two, Air Force One seemed to lose lift on the right wing, and take a steep dip in that direction. It seemed to wobble for a moment, and then dove straight into Westphalia Estates, destroying at least six homes totally and another dozen partially. The plane never exceeded fifteen hundred feet in altitude and was in the air for less than seventy seconds. There was no time for anyone on board to have been able to take emergency measures or start any evacuation and we believe that all on the plane have perished.

There is no further information on this topic at this time, and we will keep you informed as news is available. Stay tuned to this online channel for the latest updates."

CHAPTER 38

The Downing of Air Force One - Interview with a drone pilot

Interviewer: Jonathon, do you need anything before I start recording - a coffee, some water, anything?

Jonathon: No, I'm good; maybe later.

Interviewer: OK, anytime you want something, just ask. Let me set this conversation up and then I'll sit back and listen as we talked about earlier. <pause>

As the whole world knows, the President of the United States and seventy-six other people were killed when Air Force One crashed into a small residential area just north of Andrews Air Force Base in Maryland. This was a little over six months ago and the investigation is predicted to take another twelve months before a report will be issued. The official cause of the crash has been tentatively identified as "catastrophic engine failure during takeoff", although there are a handful of conspiracy theories going around claiming intentional mischief. Is this all familiar?

Jonathon: Yes, absolutely. I remember it like it was yesterday.

Interviewer: <softly> Yes, and I think that is why we are here talking today. You were an eye witness to the crash, were you not?

Jonathon: You could put it that way. I didn't see the plane hit the ground as I was maybe a mile away, but I saw the whole sequence of events unfold before my eyes.

Interviewer: Why don't you take it from here, Jonathon; share whatever you remember.

Jonathon: Sure, fine. <slowly> Wow, where to start. You've said you want details. And you said you want the truth, the whole truth, and nothing but the truth. And you said we have plenty of time, even if it takes a few days for us to finish. And to state it for the record, I am getting paid and paid handsomely for this story so that you can send your report off to wherever it goes, guilt free of literary theft or plagiarism. And also to state it for the record, on top of my compensation for the story, I am to receive escorted and secure travel back to New York as well as "security support", shall we say, for at least one year duration.

Interviewer: That is all correct; thank you for the summary.

Jonathon: No problem, I just wanted some things spelled out before we start; I'm happy now. Actually, I've been happy since six months ago when the plane went down; very happy. But things have been heating up here around DC, and I think I should be getting back to the Big Apple. Sooner or later, this story is going to come out big time, and I don't want to be anywhere near here when it does.

The only reason the true story hasn't leaked so far is that Air Force One took off right at dusk, so few people could see much of what was going on. The truck squadron attacks from the suburbs had pretty much driven most families out of nearby neighborhoods and those that chose to stay behind? They pretty much stayed inside; especially at night. The public seemed satisfied with the explanation of "catastrophic engine failure during takeoff", and over half of the country hated the President anyway, so who am I to argue?

Well, except that even though "engine failure" is the truth, it's not the whole truth; not by a long shot. And you want the whole truth, right?

Interviewer: Yes, yes, absolutely. Jonathon, it might be best to talk about your role and what you were doing in Maryland that evening...

Jonathon: Oh, yeah, yeah, good idea. I forgot to do that, sorry. OK, so I'm a drone pilot in the Eastern Blue Free Militia Air Corps and I was there that day to participate in a dry run for an outgoing airline interdiction exercise. We'd formed up a few groups of specialized fighting units while the war started to blow up and we were into our second round of live trials.

This was our first night practice. And boy did we catch a whale; totally by accident. The truth of the crash is that Air Force One did suffer from catastrophic engine failure. But the whole truth is that we caused that engine failure. We took down Air Force One.

It was such a fluke. We didn't even know that Air Force One was flying that night. We were going to test our stuff on the little planes that take the big wigs on and off the base, not a 747 for God's sake. And our stuff is way too small and way too slow for real pursuit, but we're proud of our inventions and we were out there in full dress, so to speak, and we were going to practice some.

We were there more to learn about what our systems could not do - more than what they could do. We're still pretty crude when you compare it to real military gear. None of us are ashamed of our inventions and what we've created. Eventually we'll find a way to employ our drone attack force that is killer, literally and figuratively. But regular citizen tech is way different than aerospace company tech, and, well, we do our best I guess.

First I'm going to tell you about our little drone force and what we want to be able to do in the long run. That in itself is pretty cool. Then I'll tell you about what happened that crazy night, but after the force description. Bueno?

An airline interdiction exercise is a class of maneuvers we've defined to interfere with air traffic in general. It's easiest to think about this at takeoff and landing. When planes are flying around in free space, they are really high in the air and going really fast and they don't have roads or lanes to stick to. We call it coloring outside the lines. But at takeoff and landing, planes are way more predictable in their flight path, they are much closer to the ground, and they are going way slower than during cruising flight. They tend to color inside the lines at those times and that's where we plan our interdictions.

In an interdiction we are trying to keep a plane from taking off or preventing it from landing. You know, as long as our drones are in the area, it's too dangerous to fly. It's more of a deterrent than an actual threat. Our drones are pretty small compared to airliners, but nobody wants to hit anything when you are in the air. That's just not a good idea.

We want to be able to interfere with enemy air operations of all natures, so we practice and practice. We've designed a few new drone systems and have pulled together a team of people to operate them and a logistics crew that makes the whole concept work. Let me tell you about our drones first and then I'll cover the other pieces.

The Eastern Blue Free Militia Air Corps drone force is not your run of the mill camera carriers most people think about when they think "drone", nor are they the sophisticated ones operated by the military when they think "unmanned aerial vehicles". The consumer drones we've all seen are maybe one to two feet in diameter, can carry a pound or two of cargo, and fly at maybe twenty miles an hour max. They're intended to hover and take pictures for goodness sake. That's what they do.

There are also racing drones, and they reach speeds of maybe sixty miles an hour, but they don't hold any payload really and they just go fast. These consumer camera and hobby racers cost between five hundred and five thousand dollars for something serious.

The military UAVs are off the charts performance-wise and cost-wise as well, so off financial limits for our militia, that's for sure. Maybe they'll make a difference someday, but for now they are all grounded in the States. So we decided to try to use some upgraded consumer drone approaches to augment our other military affairs.

We have four specific drone designs that are a technology step above the consumer drones we all see and probably two technology steps down from Raptors and other UAVs that the military uses. Our drones are between three feet and six feet in diameter. Some fly as fast as one hundred and twenty miles per hour, and some can carry as much as seventy pounds of payload.

Some are designed to operate as a solo unit, and some are designed to operate in tandem with one or more other drones while they are tasked on a mission. All of them are designed with state of the art communication systems and we have an army of software engineers that can literally make these birds dance.

And oh yeah, three of the four drone types are armed and dangerous.

The first drone in our tailored force is the un-armed one and we call her a "Chaser/Caller"; or C/C for short. These are our fastest models and they are actually fixed winged airplanes, not rotating wing beasts or helicopters. These are the ones with a top speed over a hundred miles per hour and they are not intended to carry anything except some great cameras and a signal generator that calls out to our other drones with position information and deployment instructions.

The C/C's are each piloted by a drone driver like me and are used to provide coordinating information during an interdiction. Experienced drivers can operate up to four C/Cs at a time. The driver's purpose is to fly a C/C drone at best speed to a formation point and then call in all of our other drones as planned to create the interdiction.

Because we never really know how high, how fast, or exactly where an interdiction will need to occur, we use our C/Cs to fly as quickly as possible to a point in space where we think our other birds will need to gather to create the interference required to make an interdiction work.

Wow, that's a lot of words...

So my job as a C/C pilot is to assess the operating environment, pick a formation point, drive one of my C/Cs there and send out a "come over here" broadcast. When the formation signal is activated, the other drones assigned to my Chaser/Caller will high-tail it to the formation point and each will do their own thing.

Each of our models has their own deployment formation requirements and mission parameters to accomplish their part of the interdiction. It's hard to describe unless we get into model-by-model and mission-by-mission specifics. Like I said earlier; lots of code required.

During an interdiction mission, we will actually launch all of our drones as quickly as possible. Because they are all different sizes and speeds, we sequence the birds into the air in order to get the most effective gathering at the formation point.

So think of trying to block an airplane from taking off. To cover one end of a runway we would send up maybe six Chaser/Callers along with thirty to fifty other drones. Probably only two or three of the C/Cs would reach a formation position that makes sense, and each one of these would eventually call a half dozen to a dozen other drones to set up a perimeter. Once the in-position C/Cs are activated, the others in less important locations return automatically to a recovery point and the original Callers will orbit in position in case the formations need to maneuver around.

Total time from launch to formation in place is typically three to five minutes and this is usually too long. By too long I mean that our target has usually left the vicinity while our forces are still getting into position. We're just too slow to rise and get to position/altitude to intercept planes in real time. The target usually just flies over us while we are swarming up and most of the time they don't even knowing we are there.

Yet we keep improving our designs and mission strategy and who knows what impact we might have in the long run?

A second member of our drone force is called the "Metal Seeker"; or MS for short. These are our smallest drones and third fastest at about sixty miles per hour. These fly solo and when they are summoned to a formation point, maybe ten will be sent in and begin to hover in a hundred foot by a hundred foot pattern in the air. They point their sensors in the direction from where we expect an enemy to come and if they see something that has the right parameters, they shift from hover to hunt and move as fast as they can to close with the target.

Think of these as a smart minefield in the sky. Our Metal Seekers form a moving wall of destruction. They're not like surface to air missiles as they are already positioned in the air near where the target is expected to be. Surface-to-air missles are point to point weapons that need huge accelerations to catch up to their prey. MSs lie in wait and provide a two dimensional attack front that allows our less sophisticated explosives to hopefully create enough damage to kill an enemy.

Each MS drone has a two pound plastic explosive charge surrounded by armor piercing shrapnel coverings that shatter into a hundred different finger sized pieces when the charge goes off. Each of these drones have a visual trigger to set off the bomb if they are literally about to hit something. They also have a proximity fuse that will trigger the bomb if a large metal object passes by. Effective damage distance is maybe ten feet, so these drones need to get really, really close to be effective. As of the date of our Andrews Air Force Base interdiction exercise, we had achieved zero, count them, zero detonations of these MS's during our practice runs. We use them for other missions as well, so they have their purpose, and they are just one piece of our air interference force.

Another drone system we have is a pair of drones operating in tandem. We call them our Cable Traps; or CTs for short. These are our slowest drones, coming in at around forty miles per hour. These drones are paired at launch with a quarter-inch steel cable stored on reels on each drone. When flying to a formation point, the drone pairs are coupled together by this cable and fly close to each other to reduce cable drag. Upon reaching a formation point, these pairs separate to about one hundred feet and then hover or fly patterns together to try to achieve a snag upon enemy aircraft.

If and when a snag occurs, two things occur. The first thing that happens after a snag is that the cable reels retract the cable as fast as possible. The reels are spring loaded and when snagged, they pull the drones together quite rapidly so that they get closer to the wing or the tail or whatever was snagged.

Imagine a wing being snagged by a Cable Trap drone exactly halfway between the top drone and the bottom drone. The chord of the wing might be twenty feet deep, but we have a cable separation between drones of one hundred feet. If we simply let the CT drones get dragged, they will detonate thirty feet behind the wing, which is too far away to cause real damage. So instead of a passive snag trigger, the snag event now causes the reels to retract cabling to get the bombs closer to the airplane.

After that, a timer detonates the bomb on each drone after half the cable is retracted. These are the same bombs that are on a Metal Seeker, that two pound plastic explosive with the shrapnel shell. Remember that these interdictions want to occur to a plane that is going a couple of hundred miles per hour, so when things happen, they happen fast. We don't want a snagged Cable Trap to blow up after the plane has flown past, so we detonate as quick as makes sense after the snag occurs.

As opposed to the Metal Chasers, where we have had zero detonations on interdiction missions, our Cable Traps have taken four planes down during testing and that's just with our prototype systems. I like Cable Traps.

In a typical interdiction, we'll send up maybe ten pairs of CTs and we try to position them to cover a five hundred foot by five hundred foot window. Most of the pairs are cabled vertically aimed at snagging a wing, but we throw in a few horizontal pairs just in case a tail comes by. We've tried building stationary walls, i.e. the CT formation forms in one place and then sits there. We've also tried roaming CT formations where the CTs fly around in some pattern, typically a zig-zag or a circle. We hadn't fully determined the best mission doctrine at the time, but the night we took down Air Force One, we had three CT formations of five pairs each - two formations were stationary and one was roaming.

The fourth member of our drone force is called a Net Dragger; or ND for short. Net Draggers are configured with three separate drones that form the corners of the formation and strung between these corners is a wire net that uses thinner, lighter and stronger cables than the Cable Traps. When fully spread out, an ND net is over three hundred feet along the edges.

The birds themselves are really specialized and they are faster than CTs, topping out at maybe eighty miles per hour. That speed is only the setup speed and once deployed in formation, they move much more slowly.

Net Draggers also have stationary and roaming interdiction modes. We did not utilize CT cable retractors with this system to pull the drone and their bomb into the target. Instead, we place a small four ounce explosive charge at each cable intersection across the net and when a snag occurs, we wait maybe two seconds for the net to be dragged into hugging the wing or the body of the aircraft. Then the whole net goes off at once - a hundred different explosions simultaneously like a big blanket bomb.

The idea is that at least one of these bomblets will break something important, or just as likely, a dozen or more holes across the body of an aircraft will blow out some windows or whatever to cause a catastrophe.

Net Draggers were also designed to be our most rapid deployment. At launch, the three drone bodies are lined up axially one right after the other, and this allows the combined thrust from all three machines to create the eighty mph setup speed. To help hit this speed, the cable net is initially loaded into a long thin plastic shell covering that is dragged behind the third drone. The whole formation of an ND system during setup is about six feet long and about three feet in diameter with a six foot by one foot net canister behind.

The three up drones and the net pod are actually pretty aerodynamic and this allows the whole system to get to the formation point as quickly as possible. Once at the formation point, the three drones separate in space. The rear most drone flies vertically upward, and second drone goes down and to the right and the lead drone goes down and to the left. Cables tied to each drone become taut during this maneuver and this literally cuts the plastic shell off of the net inside. As the drones move further and further apart, the net spreads out until full deployment is reached and the bomblets are armed.

It's actually a pretty sight to see up close, kind of like a flower blooming at high speed. But typical deployment altitudes are above a thousand feet and so it's pretty much invisible from the ground. The night Air Force One went down, we had four Net Draggers in operation. And just saying, one of them worked really, really well.

My design by the way... Did I tell you that? <pause>

OK, so that's the drone force - Chaser/Callers, Metal Seekers, Cable Traps and Net Draggers. But they can't accomplish their mission without lots of support, so I need to talk about the trucks next.

Due to the nature of the interdiction mission, we can't launch drones from very far away. The batteries last much longer while hovering or roaming than when rising and flying fast. If they would have to fly, say, from five miles away, their dwell time in formation would be really short at that point. That's a lot like military fighters and choppers that have to watch their fuel really carefully.

To get the drones closer to their mission/target, we use trucks; trucks of all kinds, but of three major varieties. The first we tried were standard pickup trucks and we can fit one drone in each truck; sometimes two like with a Cable Trap. We have to build special carriers for the truck beds to secure the drones while we're hauling ass down the highway. Due to wind turbulence, pickups have to stop for a successful launch.

We've got a motorized tarp cover for the pickup trucks. It unrolls after loading and reels up the tarp right before launch. It helps with road debris not damaging drones and probably more importantly, you can't just look at a loaded pickup driving down a freeway and see a four foot diameter Metal Seeker packing a two pound bomb. That's a good way to get caught, if you ask me.

We've also converted several sizes of box trucks into drone launchers and they have specialized carriers as well. We cut the top panel out of most of these and mount the tarp spools there. Most of our box trucks carry twice as many drones, so two, maybe three Metal Seekers or two pairs of Cable Trap drones. Again due to wind turbulence, the box truck launchers need to all but stop for a launch. That costs time and exposes them to being identified and caught.

What we're really proud of though, are the container truck launchers. These are really cool. We take standard size forty feet by eight feet by eight and a half feet shipping containers and convert them to produce three types of launchers.

The first is for the Chaser/Callers. We have a racking system where we can set up as many as twenty C/Cs in one of these. We end up with two abreast, two vertical, and five deep. What is really good about these launchers is that we don't have to slow down to launch. The birds are mounted facing forward, i.e. the same way as the truck is driving, and they are spit out the back. Since these are fixed wing, airplane looking things, they take the launch buffeting well.. At launch, they are actually going like sixty miles an hour already because of the truck speed.

We can cycle a launch about every two seconds, so one of these trucks can puke out all twenty birds in under one minute. At highway speed, one of these beasts can launch a C/C every two hundred and fifty feet and it will cover nearly a mile during a full twenty-up launch. We usually run partial loads, so a common configuration would be eight birds launched over a two thousand foot distance.

A second container truck configuration is designed for Net Draggers. We can only get three ND systems into a container because the launching racks are more complicated and these drones are launched from rails that are tilted about twenty degrees up and to the front. We have developed a little sling-shot that accelerates the ND drone groups to fifteen miles per hour faster than truck speed at launch, so they come off the rails at almost full flying speed.

These launchers are also our most camouflaged in that we have a cute overhead door system that is closed for transit. It opens like a garage door for launch and then re-closes immediately after launch. The only thing you can see from the air when they are closed is a really thin seam across the top of the container and that isn't really visible farther away than fifty feet or so.

Launch cycle times for the Net Draggers can be really fast at under three seconds between launches. This is so fast that you have to use special flight programming to get the lead birds out of the way of the next-to-launch birds. We've found that this fast of a launch actually puts the NDs too close together for best deployment, so we usually use a ten second launch interval. This puts a Net Dragger up every eight hundred feet or so and we program the birds to turn at a right angle towards the formation point in sync and this covers about a third of a mile of patrol zone from a single launch series.

We're also working on a new container launch design for Metal Seekers that has the same two up by two wide storage matrix as the C/C launchers. But with forty feet of container we can get at least twenty five rows in and have a one hundred bird load from one launcher.

It's also supposed to have a three-quarter second launch cycle that would put up all one hundred birds up in under one minute. That would look a lot like a parachute formation during a military drop, but kind of the opposite in that instead of dropping to the ground in a big long line of parachutes following the plane, our birds will be flying up in a big long line following the truck and they will be doing it at their forty miles per hour MS flight speed.

We'll see how this massive launcher works when it's done. It looks really complicated on paper.

So that's it for the launchers; now let's talk about the people. It takes lots and lots of people to run an interdiction. A driver and a shotgun for each truck and we'll have dozens of trucks for each mission. The night of Air Force One, we had over thirty pickup trucks, ten box trucks, and a half dozen container truck launchers. So that's maybe a hundred people there.

We also had six spotters, which is basically a sports car with a sunroof and some headsets where the driver and spotter can talk to each other and to other vehicles without wind chatter; so another dozen people for spotting.

We always have one vehicle for the pilots, and this is a Sprinter van with a bunch of high tech consoles and video screens that can seat three pilots at a time so five people here. And the final crew is Mission Control, which is another Sprinter van with less complicated video, but more comprehensive spoken communication capability to direct the overall interdiction effort; another five people here. Sometimes we have a few camera vans in the area to collect mission results, but with Air Force One, it was getting dark, so we left the cameras at home.

Oh, yeah, I forgot about the Drone Recovery Auxiliaries. These are folks that protect the backs and flanks of the launchers and pilots and all. That's during the interdiction. When the mission is complete and we want to recover, we've found that there may be strays. If we lose a bird, we try to go look for it. These things are really expensive and we don't want the designs to get into the wrong hands. A hardware failure, a code bug, who knows, but we have maybe a dozen of these Auxiliary trucks that drive around at the edges of the interdiction to find birds afterwards. Because the recovery team hasn't been involved in the interdiction, it is not as suspicious if they dwell in the area longer. If we lose a bird or one gets out of range then drone recovery starts.

So adding the Recovery teams to the total, all in all, there were sixty seven vehicles, somewhere around eighty drones, and right at a hundred and fifty people making trouble on Air Force One night. That was a huge exercise for us... And I guess it turned out alright.

I mean I hated the bastard and I had several, no, I'll be honest; I had many shots of whiskey to celebrate the downing of Air Force One. Our country is in shambles due to the policies of the Gump administration. My opinion? If he dies? We all get better.

Except that, well, he died. But we didn't get better. In fact we've gotten very much worse.

CHAPTER 39

The Downing of AF1 (Part Two) - Interview with a drone pilot - continued

Jonathon: Thanks for letting me take a break and thanks for the sandwich, too. I'm borderline diabetic and when I get stressed and hungry, well, I've had some anxiety attacks. It's been happening a lot since that night, so I try to stay chill and eat right. Thanks again.

Interviewer: Not a problem. Like I said earlier, we have all the time we want to take and everything is on us, comfort-wise. We'll put you up for the night if we can't get this done in one session.

Jonathon: I think that we'll be finished today, unless there are a ton of questions.

Interviewer: I'll just say "maybe" to that, so let's get the recorders started. I think you were just about to tell us about the details of the interdiction that night. Why don't you just pick up there when you've had a chance to gather your thoughts.

Jonathan: Yeah. Good idea. Sometimes I don't know where to start. Some people want to talk about all the planning and coordination of the drone fleet and the launchers and the crews, but that's a really, really long conversation. Why don't I start when we let the birds fly and if you want the planning info, too, we can cover it later.

Interviewer: That sounds good. Let's play it by ear.

Jonathon: Good, that works for me. <pause> Remember that this was a trial run, and our first one at night. So we were pretty inexperienced compared to now. And it was clearly the largest team we'd ever put together and we were spread all over the maze of freeways that surround Andrews Air Force Base. We didn't inform the authorities that we were having an exercise and we wanted to see what kind of response we'd get when launching seven dozen UAVs into their flight path.

What usually happens is that we get a reaction, but definitely a delayed reaction. We can't put the drones up and leave them in the sky, because even though they are small and don't have much of a radar profile, they do have a big overall footprint. Radio waves, motor noise, and heat are the big culprits. If we go up too early, then the air traffic controllers get spooked and all the planes get held on the tarmac. To counter for this, we end up waiting until a target plane has started their takeoff roll to launch our birds and this is what we did that night.

Also what usually happens is that while the plane is going down the runway at a hundred and fifty or two hundred miles an hour and accelerating with two jet engines, we're out in front of them launching a bunch of propeller birds that have to climb, climb, climb to intercept. Most early tests resulted in the target plane flying past the drones like eight hundred feet in altitude above them. The best we've done was a five hundred foot gap between where we were and where they were when they flew by. But we were out that night trying it again with some different attack plans and felt good about our living laboratory, so to speak. I told you it was a fluke that we took down Air Force One, and it truly was. There were like four different things that went wrong for the President and his team that day and we just happened to have been in the right place at the right time.

One of the things that went wrong was the weather. We were getting the front end of nor'wester and we had this thirty miles per hour blow from west-northwest and that made the take-off direction and flight path pretty predictable.

Another thing that went wrong for them was that there were two planes taking off. Air Force One was the second plane. It plummeted down the runway only two minutes after a smaller, private jet took off. This private jet was a regularly scheduled shuttle between Andrews and I think, Colorado, but I'm not positive on that. It doesn't matter. Anyway, we had picked this shuttle as our target for the exercise, so our launch was synchronized to match their 5:45 PM departure time.

Third thing wrong: we found out right after the crash that this particular Air Force One flight was a test run for a new emergency departure protocol. It wasn't a real flight, it was a fire drill. The neutron bomb thing had freaked everyone out, and the secret service teams revised their evacuation procedures to shrink the "decision-to-departure" time for the President by 50%. That's like down below ten minutes from the White House to wheels up on Air Force One.

That night they were doing a dry run on the new emergency evacuation protocols and everybody was focused on the time, not what was going on around them. When they got into the air and turned their attention to normal security affairs, it was too late to do anything.

Plus they left the AF1 fighter escort on the ground that night to save some money. It was just an exercise right? Start the timer; helicopter to Joint Base Andrews; take off in Air Force One; stop the timer; then circle and land. No big deal, right? <pause> Wrong!

We'll never find out if they hit the goal. Everyone who knew that was on the plane when it went down.

Fourth thing wrong: I lost track of two of my Chaser/Callers during the interdiction exercise while focusing on the other two I had successfully directed to the middle of our interdiction sweet spot. It happens when you get thick in the middle of things and since they orbit, who cares, right? Well, Air Force One should've cared, that's for sure.

OK, so back to the story. Our truck launchers had been split up into six groups. Two of them with mostly pickup trucks were going north and south on Forestville Road, which is north of the base and east of I-495. Two groups were going north and south on I-495 and the last two were going east and west on Hwy 4. All the groups were synchronized to be approaching north of Andrews Air Force Base right at the shuttle departure time, i.e. 5:45 PM. The Colorado shuttle is pretty timely and usually takes off within a minute or two of schedule, so our arrival was pretty well fixed in time.

The pilot and mission control vans were staged northeast of the base near Westphalia and the recovery teams were out about ten miles in all directions, but they knew the recovery area would be to the east of I-495 due to the strong winds and all had routes planned to that location.

Our spotter was able to see the shuttle plane turn and line up with the runway and issued a "launch imminent" command which in our code words is "baby bird is standing." Within thirty seconds, right at 5:45 PM on the button, the launch command was sent - "the chick has left the nest." This started all of us going.

Without getting into all of the nitty gritty sequencing, I'll just talk about a generic launch and then pick up when all the birds were hustling to the formation points. Remember that the pickups and box trucks have to all but stop to launch, and when they got their launch order they were spread out all over Forestville and District Heights.

Each truck has already retracted their cover tarp - that was done on "baby bird is standing", so they each found a convenient parking lot, side street, strip mall alley, whatever seems to be the best at the time. But when the launch call comes, they have to be stopped and shooting up drones within ten seconds.

When they hit the launch button, the drone rotors spin up to full thrust and then about two seconds later, three hold-down pins are automatically removed. Most of these trucks were carrying Metal Seekers and these birds just bounce into the air - straight up for at least two hundred feet, and then they turn on their C/C links and wait to be called. They'll continue vertical to five hundred feet if they don't get a call, and then hover and wait.

The Chaser Callers were all launched from the I-495 groups and eight of those spit out one right after the other and continued at full speed to an invisible east-west line at one thousand feet altitude and about two miles north of the runway. Once in place, they will automatically go into tight circles, unless a pilot directs it to some other location.

The Cable Traps and the Net Draggers were launched from the groups on Hwy 4 as well as I-495. Since the wind was strong, we pre-programmed their dwell stations to be above the Penn Mar Shopping Center and Forestville itself. We knew they would drift some from the wind, so we pushed them east to start.

The launches went just fine for the most part. Two Metal Seeker launchers jammed and one box truck developed some nasty engine noise, so those vehicles left the scene quickly. But everything was pretty much clockwork, and at 5:45 PM and thirty seconds, we had our seventy-five drones up in the air and rushing to the shuttle to "cut it off at the pass" so to speak.

I vectored two of my C/Cs to fifteen hundred feet altitude and north of the Penn Mar Shopping Center and hit the Call button. We have this very cool tracking display in our vans that uses a point of light for each drone - different colors for each type - and we can see the action in real time. As soon as the call went out, every drone system responded and immediately shifted direction to go to their formation points. All the drones and their lights on the display are pretty spread out by this time in a launch and so there is just this reverse waterfall of rainbow colored motion on the screen s the drones try to get to altitude quickly enough.

And then what usually happens, happened again. That dang little jet used a steep flight path and veered quickly into the wind and at 5:46 PM and twenty two seconds, it flew right over our flotilla's head by at least three hundred feet. We had expected that, but it was good news in that we had cut the miss distance almost in half, so that was something to celebrate later.

It was really a deployment to see with all of the different systems getting into formation, albeit a bit late. Metal Seekers formed invisible walls of death, Cable Traps split their pairs and went into their 3D snag lattice and our Net Draggers formed their triangles and either hovered or roamed. We can see all the action on our displays and at 5:47 PM and forty-five seconds, our interdiction force was in full bloom. We let it stay that way for a minute or two and then sent a recovery call, which told all of our birds to start their landing sequences.

Remembering the wind again, the interdiction area was just west of I-495 and our recovery area was planned to be on the east side of I-495 where it is a bit more rural and less crowded. When we recover, it's not as big of a rush as it is at takeoff. We basically put the drones on a predictable flight path and they just kind of float down with the wind and we can pretty much pinpoint where they will touch down.

So, fast forward about two minutes and everyone is heading to their recovery zones. All the birds are dropping down on path and then, all of the sudden, a spotter calls out "Oh, holy crap; there's a huge bird standing in the nest!" And immediately following "Correction, correction: Air Force One is standing in the nest. I repeat Air Force One is in the nest!"

That got our blood going! Are you kidding me? That rat bastard is taking off right in front of a deployed takeoff interdiction formation? That's amazingly bold of them, but then again, not very many people know about us. And all of our coverage has been very blue, blue, blue, so pro-government, right? Why on earth would anybody be flying a fleet of drones right on top of Andrews Air Force base?

And still I couldn't believe it - the rat bastard is flying right into a full-fledged deployment.

Wait a second; we're not in deployment, we are in recovery. The whole fleet is disarmed and totally <u>not</u> dangerous! All the birds are really just floating to the ground at leisure. Not good, not good. I want this plane and our whole drone force is brain dead with no fingers on triggers.

Mission Command chimed in: "AF1 is doing a rolling takeoff and is already accelerating; estimated twenty seconds to lift-off. <pause> "five, four, three, two one... AF1 is in the air; due north departure off of the west runway. Reaching three hundred feet. Six hundred and fifty feet, now veering into the wind. One thousand feet. She's climbing fast. Where are our forces?

Voice from my partner pilot: "Everything is in recovery mode and drifting east southeast with the wind. Drones are spread out between five hundred feet and eighteen hundred feet, mostly east of I-495 by now. AF1 is flying away from the pack."

"What's at eighteen hundred feet and where?" "A squadron of Metal Seekers, but they are already past the freeway. And a Net Dragger, which is the closest bird we have as well, but it's folding up and they're going to miss it by at least a half mile."

"Try to get that Net Dragger online and spread. And where are the Chaser/Callers?" "Oh, wow, hadn't checked. There they are. OK, OK; the two mission drivers are hovering at twelve hundred feet but way to the north. The backup C/Cs are in their orbits all over the place, but two of them are riding tandem and they are very close to the AF1 projected flight path."

"Get those two back on line and start them screaming. See if we can restart any other birds to follow..." "Uh oh, one of those C/Cs just went off line. No fade or degradation or distress beacon. It just went dead. I wonder what that was. The other one is resetting - now! It has a ten second re-boot time." "That's going to be too long. AF1 will be past them by then."

"Wait a second... AF1 is taking a huge turn to the east. It was veering into the wind since leaving the ground, but it has changed heading by about ninety degrees. I feel sorry for the passengers; the plane must've been on its ear. OK, AF1 has also just leveled out at fifteen hundred feet. She looks to be taking evasive maneuvers and sacrificing increased altitude to gain additional speed."

"Evasive maneuvers from what? Us?"

"Where is she heading now? I mean relative to our drones." "She's flying east-northeast in a straight line and will be crossing I-495 in about seventeen seconds.

Fifteen hundred feet constant altitude, but flying back towards our force cloud. Gaining speed fast, that's for sure."

"Metal Seekers status? That squadron at 1800 feet." "A quarter mile to the south of her track." "Net Dragger? Any luck?" "Let's see. Back into operational mode, but still drifting down at sixteen hundred feet." "Can we get a Caller there?" "No way; too far." "What about manual flying?" "That's a far stretch." "Damn."

Right at that instant, the remaining Chaser/Caller that had been in orbit came online, punched its forward speed, and slammed on its calling signal. It was over a mile away, but the signal was strong and the only other mission-operational bird heard its call.

The Net Dragger that had been too high and floating away from the target now began organizing itself for high speed flight. The drone segments drew together to form a coupled set of three with the net dangling not too far below. As it did this reassembling maneuver it fell in an organized fashion, losing altitude along the way.

After the ND drones reassemble, they climb together as a unit and ramp up in speed to make sure the net is trailing behind. Once a critical speed is achieved, it then performs a barrel roll and a compass turn maneuver to wherever the call is coming from.

In this case, the Caller was five hundred feet down and to the southwest, so the Net Dragger would climb maybe fifty feet to gain speed and clear the net, and then do a magnificent over the shoulder spin dive to hightail it to the new formation point. Great aerobatics. Did I tell you this was my design?

"What just happened? What just happened? My ND telemetry shows red and the beacon is going nuts. Talk to me." "I don't know; it never completed assembly! It didn't speed up on its own, but it's now going two hundred and sixty miles per hour to the northeast! What in hell?"

"It's been snagged, it's been snagged" "Yeah, could be. But why hasn't it detonated? We've got good triggers; no duds at all so far on this model."

Then we all got it. And we all shouted into at least three separate mics at the same time: "It's disarmed! It's disarmed!" "Rearm sequence takes fifteen seconds. OK, started." "It'll be ripped to shreds by then. Damn it!"

But then there was this bright flash in the distance; followed by an ominous darkness. About two seconds later, more light and then a streak of flames arching down with a smoke trail behind. At five seconds after the first flash, there was a loud boom and a stream of screeching and metal tearing and then a roar that drowned out everything, including our people in the control trucks that were no longer talking to each other.

Seven seconds after that, the flaming, roaring arch met the ground and there was yet another blinding, silent flash. In yet another five seconds the sound reached us and the shock wave knocked my coffee off of the counter in the truck.

Holy Shit.

CHAPTER 40

The Downing of AF1 (Part Three) - Interview with a drone pilot - continued

Interviewer: I know I've asked this before, but each time we get off track and I'm still trying to put the pieces of the story together. Talk to me again about what happened between realizing the Net Dragger was disarmed and the crash. You said earlier that the bird was disarmed, but then it detonated? What happened?

Jonathon: Yeah, OK, we kind of skipped over that. A lot was happening right then and we cycled through emotions pretty quickly that whole evening. We didn't really know what had happened for a few hours. When AF1 went down, we scrambled like hell to recover and get the hell out of dodge. A recovery is bad enough at any time, but when the space floods with emergency vehicles, it's a bit of a nightmare.

And these emergency vehicles were from off base, not your normal dirty and dented city machines we see all the time. Brand new, cleanly washed, polished and waxed military fire trucks and ambulances and hummers by the dozens. We thought we were going to get caught for sure, but they drove right through us to the crash site and then they just wanted everyone to leave the area. We actually got escorted out to the freeway. The trucks were zipped up by then, and we were coming from all over the place in ones and twos, but still. Our whole team just drove away without being confronted.

Back to the detonation. The next morning we were all still pretty psyched that we took down Air Force One. We had no idea who was on the flight until later when the news got going. All the coverage then was about the event and the immediate search and rescue. The flames were still burning in the morning, mostly in the neighborhood that got nailed. We were having a normal post-operation debrief and the detonation topic came up.

“I don't get it... Every bird was disarmed. That's supposed to be fail-safe. Why did it blow?” “Maybe the ND went into an engine and the engine blew up.” “Maybe our birds got smashed and it was just lucky.” “Maybe...”

“Sammi did it.” <pause> <silence>

“What do you mean Sammi did it?” “Sammi, who? The intern?”

“I know, I know, but she was shadowing us that night. Remember, we were testing and evaluating, not attacking. I brought her along.”

“So what happened?” “As soon as we all screamed “disarmed!” most of us froze. There was no way to turn on the detonators fast enough. But Sammi's smart and she's been with us on a few trips.” “What did she do?” “She reached in between us at the console, lifted the safety cover and slammed her fist down onto the “fleet self-destruct” button. That's when the ND blew...”

“My God, why didn't the whole fleet go up? That's what's supposed to happen.” “I know, but they were all disarmed and the self-destruct was ignored.” “It's not supposed to happen that way. They are supposed to go, no matter what!” “I know, I know. It was a code bug. We verified it this morning. A damn code bug saved the fleet.” “And saved the intern.” “Yeah, there's that, too.”

Anyway, that code bug saved the fleet, or most of it anyway. We lost three total birds that night; the ND that nailed Air Force One and the lit Chaser/Caller that blew into about twenty self-destruct pieces when Sammi hit the button. Plus the other C/C that went off line earlier before all the excitement. The rest of the fleet recovered well and we were pretty much intact.

We didn't really know exactly what happened for a few days and this still may be wrong explanation. Until the official report comes out, we won't get any new data to go on. But we had our drone telemetry information, a few really good eye witnesses on the team, and some immediate news footage over the next day or two until they clamped things down and other war stories grew.

Our version of the crash goes like this: we think that Air Force One snagging the ND was totally a fluke. Our fleet was drifting in the sky and AF1 was going to miss us high and to the west by a half mile at least. And then AF1 turned and leveled out and drove straight into a Net Dragger that was all but dead in flight. The

ND was falling down with the wind and trying to re-couple her three drones into an axial configuration, and AF1 ran right into her. Fluke, fluke.

So the best we can tell from where we sit now is that the ND got snagged by the right wing out next to the fourth engine. We think the net was collapsed; stretched across the back half of the wing and probably off the trailing edge as well. When the detonation occurred, all the little bomblets had gathered in one long, thin pile and the detonation caused enough damage to the wing for it to start to come apart. Fluke, fluke, fluke.

With Air Force One engines in full take off throttle, the rightmost engine itself did the rest of the work, ripping away from the wing root and taking the wing tip with it. Once separated, the engine and wing tip tore apart from each other as well and were found about a quarter mile apart on the ground. There was no fire damage on either part, but there was clearly some hitting the ground really hard damage.

The original flash was the Net Dragger detonating and the flames were from the fuel bleeding from the right wing after the engine had flown the coop. With half thrust on the right side of the plane and 30% loss of lift from the right wing, the left wing rose up and over the body of AF1 and overpowered the right side - right into the ground. The big explosion was obviously AF1 itself and all the fuel went up at once as the entire vertical wing crushed itself open for a hundred yard swath right through Westphalia Estates. The impact was on the edge of the neighborhood with a direct hit on the park and playground, but the swath was wide enough to take out one edge of the development and kill, what did they finalize on? I think it was twenty seven people on the ground.

From the Net Dragger flash to the boom on the ground - it was maybe ten seconds. Nobody on the ground or in the air had a chance. Can you imagine being in the plane? Normal takeoff except for a steep climb, then there is this loud bang and the plane executes a huge right turn, putting the plane on its ear. It probably flattened out within five seconds, but if they were really going for speed over altitude, the engines would have been spun up to full military throttle and they would have been screaming. Everyone inside would be gripping their arm rests from the turn and now pressed back into their seats from the acceleration and pretty much freaking out.

And then the coup d'etat with a blinding flash and a deafening boom on the right side of the plane. Then the metal rending and bellowing as the engine removes the wing tip from the plane and flies off on its own. Then the rolling to the right and the flames and the smoke and the alarms and then dipping all the way onto everyone's right ear again, but this time facing almost vertically downward and then? Then nothing; from flash to nothing in under ten seconds. <pause>

Definitely crap in your pants time for them, but hey, the head bastard has been criminally ruining our country for years, so good riddance I say. Plus we got the pile of cronies getting the hell out of Dodge with the head crime boss, so they'll be doing a lot less damage from here on out as well. I feel sorry for the innocents on the ground and we had a few true blues in the press corps on the flight, but we rooted out the number one source of US pain, so I sleep well in spite of the collaterals.

Interviewer: You said something about a bang before the plane turned east. That's the first I've heard of that. Can you tell me more?

Jonathon: Yeah, but we made that part up kind of to put some twos and twos together. It comes down to the question: "Why did Air Force One go into evasive maneuvers in the first place?" This was a normal, nothing-going-on takeoff and then all of the sudden AF1 freaks out and kills itself by running into a bomb.

We don't have a recording that has a "loud bang" in it for proof, but remember the Chaser/Caller that went off line? We think that it hit AF1 right in the left temple, you know, right behind the cockpit. Really, we think that AF1 and our C/C hit each other and a seventy-two pound drone hitting something at two hundred and fifty mph would leave a mark and make some noise.

Two pieces of evidence point to support this idea. The first clue is from a wreckage photo that displayed a piece of the unburned left side cockpit. Right behind, like maybe two feet from the window is a shallow dent and a bright blue scratch. That's why we think there was a collision.

Interviewer: Blue scratch? I don't get it.

Jonathon: We didn't get it either for a while. All of our birds are painted grey. And then someone remembered that one of the C/Cs that night had an experiment going on with it. We were trying out some new radar scattering materials and this one drone was covered with it. And the paint is bright blue, not grey.

The second clue is from other crash footage. There were a few news shots that showed what would be a random piece of debris to most people, but when <u>we</u> look at it, we see a C/C drone that is all smashed up on the front right. It was pretty much pushed flat on one side and a lot of parts dangling and wires and cables from all but breaking totally up because of the collision. And it was painted blue. Fluke, fluke, fluke, I tell you.

We've got no hard proof, but we know that's what happened. Air Force One head-bumped one of our birds, freaked out, changed direction, and then flew right into the other more deadly bird. It was a fatal mistake for them.

Fluke, fluke, fluke, fluke, fluke.

CHAPTER 41

The Sacking - Interview with the Chief of Police

Police Chief: The morning after Air Force One went down, everything was pretty quiet. It was a nice day with a good dose of the spring to come in the air and promises of sixty-five degrees by mid-afternoon. Cherry blossoms were starting to bud, plenty of happy birds bounced between branches, and there was very little traffic. It was going to be a beautiful day. Well, except for two big black holes here in the DC area and the smoke from fires still drifting to the east. What a mess.

Everyone in the US and all over the world had heard about Air Force One. The morning news covered the now-dead passenger list, which had just been corroborated by whoever was left at the White House. Missing and presumed dead: the President and Vice President of the United States, the Attorney General, five cabinet Secretaries, the Chairman of the Joint Chiefs and three of his staff, two Senators and three Congress people that happened to be in a meeting with the President when the evacuation call was sent, the crew of Air Force One and the entire White House press corps. All incinerated in an instant. Plus the twenty seven people on the ground. And nine of those were from two families that were playing in the Westphalia Estates park at the wrong time. What a mess.

The whole nation was shaking from the magnitude of the onslaught over the past three weeks; a thousand government officials and not-quite twice that many civilians dead and dying from political upheaval. Nowhere in the world was it more intense than in Washington DC itself. We witnessed the carnage first hand and most everyone had family or friends that were killed or injured.

I mean, the whole government was all but gone - Executive Branch, Judicial Branch and the Legislative Branch. Somebody did a headcount, and we realized there were maybe two dozen elected politicians still alive at the federal level - many of them really, really old - the ones that couldn't make it to the Congressional celebration.

The morning after the crash the city came out in small groups, stunned and not sure what to do. We wandered aimlessly, sharing quiet whispers and conversations over Starbucks drinks. Everything was driven in this town by political agendas. You go here because the Senators are meeting. You go there because someone is giving a press conference. You go to breakfast, lunch and dinner hoping to catch a glimpse of someone who is destined to fix our country and you want to be able to say "I was there when..."

But not that day; there would be no meetings. There would be no press conferences; not by anyone that matters anyway. So we wandered. All of us; the families, the teachers, the students, the parents, the police, the corporations, the small businesses, everyone was outside looking for some sort of solace, some sort of guidance.

By mid-afternoon, a lot of the families had retreated home so there were fewer youngsters around. But there were still lots of people and more foot traffic than cars and there were plenty of Ubers to bring folks to wherever they were going. Some groups were coagulating out of the currents of people and started having lively discussions. One set of college students started handing out some placards. And then another group a few blocks away bought some posters and markers and started making signs of their own. A couple of portable PA systems came from somewhere and the soap-boxing started. This was at dinner time now and it was getting pretty loud. I think people were just hungry and tired and should've taken a break.

But that didn't happen. Remember that Washington DC is deep inside the eastern blue zone and after two years of moving the red families out and moving more blue families in, well, let's just say that there hasn't been much pro-Gump sentiment recently. Certainly not in the three weeks after the neutron bomb. When the crowds got louder, they didn't get louder with "Long live the President!" On the contrary; even though the President and anyone else connected to him were all dead. I mean, really; have we no shame?

We did a study and compared Gump's first and second level connections to the victim lists. Of his first level connections in the government, 86% had perished over the past weeks. With his second level connections, 44% had perished. On the family side, it was not as bad, just 25% of the family was or would be gone soon. Bryan had been attending a school event in the Smithsonian Air & Space Museum and was in a hospital fighting for his life.

But Gump, even though everyone knows the crash could be an exact copy of what might happen in their family or one of their friend's families; even with that, the dead Gump became a focus point for a lot of unhealthy energy that night.

Our patrols started pulling evening crowd control shifts around 4:00 PM and we had over five hundred men and women all across the city in groups of twenties and thirties. On foot for the most part, full riot gear and hand guns only. There was back-up nearby with more firepower, but the crowds that were approached only saw camouflage and helmets and the conversation was respectful across the board.

They say it takes some sort or trigger to go from crowd-loud to crowd-ugly and I agree with that. And I also think that everyone, well, all the groups that were getting loud, they were all set on hair-triggers and worked into a frenzy by enterprising loud mouths with points to make. And all of those points were really similar: "Better off without him..." "Just desserts..." "Who cares..."

Yeah, nice huh? But it got worse.

"I wish they had taken the rest of his family too." "Fuck Gump." "The rat bastard is dead!" There were a lot of other more derogatory and more lewd and more cruel things that I won't detail. It was bad and getting worse and a lot of people were getting tired of the noise and confusion and anger.

And then right around 6:45 PM, some passing adult couples drifted by one of the loud groups that had gathered on a big pile of debris a few blocks away from where Lincoln Park had been. There was lots of debris in this neighborhood and still some smoke drifting. The group had just finished a really crude chant regarding some of Gump's body parts.

I guess she had had enough, because a thirty something lady from the passing couples stopped and rotated to face the noisemakers on the pile. As her friends moved past her they could see her saying something softly, but then she let it rip:

"The man's dead for God's sake. Why can't you leave him alone!" <pause> <long, silent pause>

We've found the person who threw the first stone; plenty of video available on that. It was terrible. One rock comes from the left side of the debris hill about halfway up and lands about four feet from the woman. Then three separate chunks of debris - you know, bricks, concrete, whatever - they land even closer. The brick actually took a bounce and hit her in the leg.

Everybody in the crowd was standing in silence and watching as the woman looked down at her foot and then back at the pile and at last raised a big right middle finger. She started to shout a big "fu..." when an angry fifth rock came in on target. About the size of a baseball, the concrete was rough and when it glanced off her forehead, it left a bloody gash and snapped her head back in a nasty way you never want to see again.

She didn't fall, just stumbled back and started bleeding like a stuck pig. She was turning to flea when all hell broke loose for her. Almost instantaneously, a dozen rocks at a time from the pile were targeting her. Some were hitting, but most were not. Her friends ran in to shield her and drag her away and a few of them picked up some bricks and threw them back.

That was a big mistake. After the second wave of defensive throws from the couples, the debris pile disgorged its entire populace, and, well, there were a lot more chanters than there were couples. Hand to hand combat with sticks and stones, literally. A second group of trouble-makers joined the first and the assault intensified frenetically.

My guys in the area were a block away to the east. When they got the call about crowd violence, they double timed it to the west and flew around a corner to find a pile of humanity swinging and yelling and kicking and just one big mass of pummeling. Knowing that someone in the middle of that mass was probably the subject of all that attention, the patrol leader pulled out her pistol and shot three times into the air. It had the desired effect of stopping the attack as the crowd jerked three times involuntarily and then fled away at full run. Left behind were eight bodies and only one was moving, trying to straighten an obviously broken arm.

The unintended side effect of the gunfire was that it touched off the hair triggers I mentioned earlier. The police weren't the only ones with guns that night and we started hearing gunfire. First from a block away, then a half mile away and before long, guns were going off everywhere. People were mad all over the city and as word spread of the "upstart Gump supporters getting their comeuppance..." it just let go. Most of it was celebration and shoot in the air stuff. People are stupid. We counted two dead and twelve hurt that night due to bullets dropping from the sky.

But some of the gunfire eventually shifted towards more intentionality; store fronts and automobiles were decorated with holes. You can predict what was coming. A few fires; then a few more. Some people with masks to cover their faces to filter the smoke just happen to go into some of the businesses and do some free shopping. And light some more fires. And do some more free shopping. And shoot each other if they wanted to. All of this was more random than planned. Many of them had been drinking pretty heavily by that time.

So Washington DC gets a neutron bomb attack that maims thousands and kills Congress and the Supreme Court. Three weeks later it gets a plane crash that eliminates the Executive branch. The next day there are fourteen square miles of riot destruction, seventy-two dead and four hundred twenty-six injured in the "Gump is Dead!" celebration.

What have we come to?

Epilogue - Interviewer commentary

About four months ago, I woke up in a cold, cold sweat. The result of a bad dream probably. All I remember from it was the wailing at the funerals. If you listened with your ears, it was a thousand mother's painful voices in sad harmony. If you listen with your heart however, it is beautiful tribute to those that they mourn.

My sweat smelled of frustration and futility; two of my most familiar friends for the past years. My country, the United States of America, has plunged into a dark period. Civil War Two has danced through its first and second phases and is showing no promise of subsiding. Not anytime soon; not before thousands more die.

After the sack, the country just seemed to give up. It was like there was no wind anywhere to fill our sails. The burials from the Washington DC events lasted for months. With so many politicians dead and gone, the ones that were still alive headed back to their states to connect with their constituents or get medical care or just as likely, both.

And then the not so funny thing happened; the politicians never came back. There was no one left in Washington to come back to! Whatever mechanisms that were put in place to start up the election cycle and find replacements for Congress sputtered and failed. There was no heart in it. No one was left to hold anyone accountable.

I continue to generate my periodic reports and have terabytes upon terabytes of source information. My sponsors continue to pay my bills and send me plane tickets for those infrequent cold trips to the north lands. I have never seen impact from my reports, let alone the mention of the research in any broadcast or online news sources I frequent.

The chorus of my dream-moms rattles me to my bones and leaves me not satisfied. Not satisfied with where things have been. And not satisfied with where things are. And certainly not satisfied with where things are going. So four months ago in my cold, sweaty pajamas, I started to cauterize my research into a publishable and meaningful slice of history.

The material you have just absorbed is all about the beginning of Civil War Two; America's Second Attempt At Suicide. It covers many of the ungainly events that led America to its present insanity. This part of the story concludes at the end of Phase One, when America's federal government goes missing and most of our binding principals fly out the door.

Not everything I discovered is included in this Phase One story. But enough of it is here to help draw a straight line between America's original red, white, and blue thinking about "we" and "our" to our current and sickly red-only and blue-only thinking about "me" and "my".

Enough of recent history is here to track the implications of rude behavior, bad manners, and lack of respect for others which has become the backbone of our modern media messaging and the centerpiece for our modern political soap-boxing. Our leaders sit smugly in tiny circles with their other smug friends. They cast dispersions of hate and lies about their opponents while ignoring their own issues, defects and the garbage they call fresh thinking.

And enough of recent history is here to give life to so many, so many deaths that were unnecessary should we have collectively chosen a different path.

Shame on us.

Shame on us for allowing the one percent on either end of the political spectrum to drive the agenda for <u>us</u>, the 98%.

Shame on us for not speaking up and following those that stand for sanity and centrality.

Shame on us for putting people into power that manipulate the polls and the voting and break laws so that they can assemble their graft-taking engines that only service "them and theirs" and then move on to repeat the process with their most recent pretty platform that never gets implemented.

Shame on us.

I don't know where our future will take us. The violence subsided for a bit after Washington DC fell silent; maybe for six weeks. That's when the cash ran out and the federal checks weren't sent for the first time since Social Security began.

Right after that the food supply chain broke and the grocery stores emptied. And right after that all hell broke loose.

This story is not a complete story and America is still embattled in broad fashion. But this story is enough for now until the next round of ugly truths from Phase Two can be assembled. Between the abyss we've descended into and the lack of reconciling efforts between any source of blue/red leadership, we have years of penance to pay. There will be plenty of new stories to come along; plenty of violence and blood and gore to share in the future.

God help us.

America's first Civil War pitted brother against brother. Politicians split the countryside on a map with an east-west horizontal line. Those on the opposite sides of the line, well, they were on opposite sides of the war.

Since then, we have fewer brothers. Families are smaller across the board and many, many Americans are choosing not to bring life into a world such as this. Can you blame them?

We have a social fabric that continues to morph as more and more people come to the United States. They come for opportunity. They come for safety. And they come for pillage; it has always been this way.

We may have fewer brothers, but we have many more neighbors than in times past. Not just in density, but in diversity as well. Diversity in background and family history and religion and skin color and gender and sexual orientation and education and financials and goals and aspirations and intents.

Civil War One pitted brother against brother.

Civil War Two is about neighbor against neighbor.

God help us all.

Quotations

When everything that we've known and loved disappears and becomes a sad bit of history, perhaps then it is time to truly study the wise words of those that have come before us.

They have lived through the changes and have thought deeply about what they learned and what they would do differently.

James Stewart

It's sad when someone you know becomes someone you knew.
Henry Rollins

War is a symptom of man's failure as a thinking animal.
Unknown

Death is not the greatest loss in life. The greatest loss in life is what dies inside us while we live.
Norman Cousins

If you want a happy ending, it depends, of course, on where you stop your story.
Orson Welles

Whoever wants to win a war has to stop it right away.
Unknown

We must fight for peace as bravely as we fought in war.
Lai Bahadur Shastri

When will mankind be convinced and agree to settle their difficulties by arbitration?
Benjamin Franklin

A single death is a tragedy; a million deaths is a statistic.
Joseph Stalin

The tragedy about history - personally and globally is that while we may learn it, we rarely learn from it.
Rasheed Ogunlaru

Darkness cannot drive out darkness; only light can do that. Hate cannot drive out hate; only love can do that.
Martin Luther King, Jr.

War does determine who is right; only who is left.
Bertrand Russell

Life's tragedy is that we get old too soon and wise too late.
Benjamin Franklin

A million words would not bring you back, I know because I tried.
Neither would a million tears, I know because I cried.
Unknown

Tragedy, for me, is not a conflict between right and wrong,
but between two different kinds of right.
Peter Shaffer

Truth will always be the path to peace.
Tsang Lindsay

War means violence that begets new violence.
Unknown

There is nothing that war has ever achieved
that we could not better achieve without it.
Havelock Ellis

It's not the military that starts wars, it's the politicians who do it.
Unknown

Refusing to fight for what someone thinks is right isn't an act
of cowardice. It's the realization that wars are pointless.
Unknown

When the power of love overcomes the love of power,
the world will know peace.
Jimi Hendrix

Excerpt from Civil War Two; The Rise of the States

When Albert woke up he was groggy; groggy, uncomfortable and aggravated.

He was aggravated because he had lost his plane. Good pilots don't lose their planes. Good pilots bring their planes back to their base to fly another mission. They bring their planes back because they're amazing machines and wonderful partners and they're expensive and useful and someday they may help this sad country get back on its feet. Someday America may return to normal, but not with the help of his plane. His plane is dead; just as dead as a half million people across the nation.

He was uncomfortable because he was on the ground in some antique barn someplace with his arms wrapped around a wooden pillar behind him that was just large enough to put his shoulders in an awkward backwards twist. His feet jutted in front of him and his ankles were wrapped with three loops of a rope that looked even older than the barn itself. They were tied with a surgeon's knot that was snug enough to cut off circulation to his feet. He was sure his wrists were tied with some of that same rope and the wrist knot was even tighter than the ankle knot.

He was groggy because he had ejected from his plane at 16,000 feet altitude and had plummeted to the ground in his ejection seat much too quickly under a parachute that was tangled and had only opened up most of the way.

He was lucky groggy in that he dropped through a wind gust just as he approached the ground and it put him into spin like a tether ball at the end of a rope. That spin had saved his life as he had hit the ground seat-first with enough horizontal velocity to tumble and bounce him the length of a city block through a cornfield, as opposed to crushing him like a tin can under an angry boot.

He remembered the flames from the plane and the ejection sequence and the three mile fall and his parachute panic and the roller coaster tumble and now he's tied up in a barn. So when Albert woke up he was aggravated and uncomfortable and groggy and confused.

He closed his eyes and inventoried his body. Headache? Yes. Cut lip? Yes. Broken teeth? None he concludes, but a sore jaw throbs and his right cheek is probably bruised. Gut check? No sharp pains anywhere but he's hungry and that's normal. Broken bones? His legs had looked fine and if anything was wrong with his upper torso, the arms around the post would have been excruciating.

So OK enough, I guess. I can probably walk at least. But how in hell did I get into this barn? And where is this barn? And why am I tied up? I remember the corn stalk whipping and then waking up in the barn; but nothing in between.

He opened his eyes and looked around to assay his environment. There were blood stains down the front of his flight suit confirming the cut lip. One boot was untied. Six feet away at eleven o'clock was his flight helmet. It was scraped all across the right side and a spider web crack scarred the visor. Corn crop remnants were jammed into two or three of the helmet joints.

Oh, man; that confirms the jaw and the cheek. I liked that helmet; it was the first one that really fit me well. It probably saved my life. <pause> I'm gonna miss that helmet. And my plane, damn it. Best ride I've ever had, that's for sure.

Albert continued looking around the barn in the brightening morning light. Further off to his left his parachute was gathered up on a shallow stack of hay. It would never be used again, that's for sure, with its tangled and snapped lines and a number of ragged holes from the ground tumble. A few blood stains were visible, but nothing that hinted at larger issues than a cut lip. There were corn leaves and stalk pieces and even a few ears of corn strewn across the parachute and the hay stack, and also across the scraped dirt between the closed barn doors and where he lay.

Was I dragged here? And then tied up? Not taken to a hospital for a med check? OK, not good.

He pushed his eyes around the rest of the barn that was now showing itself with the light beams coming through the cracks in the barn siding. In the dimness, it looked like a Norman Rockwell painting of the inside of a working barn. There were yard tools; two rakes, two pitch forks, and an assortment of shovels. There were six or seven pegs hammered into beams with various rope coils hanging from them and just as many pegs with chains of various lengths and sizes.

There was shelving with unorganized piles of tractor parts, fencing materials, boxes of nails, wooden stakes and a few other odds and ends. On the other wall, there was a peg board that held a collection of hand tools; hammers, screwdrivers, box knives, tin snips, mallets, wood saws, hack saws, loppers, hedge shears and pruners.

OK, OK. Not good; not good. If this turns into an inquisition, there's everything here to make me buckle; no need to go to Home Depot first.

He was still looking around and testing the tightness of his knots when he heard someone walking up to the barn door. Actually, the approach was silent, but he could see the shadow scream as it moved from right to left in front of him. As it crossed, it interrupted the light beams and strobed the hay dust floating in the air.

Shit.

The shadow figure stopped between the barn doors in the middle of the largest light crack and raised its arms. Albert's heart stopped and his breath held as the giant wooden panels began to creak softly open. The sun had just risen moments before and Albert was blinded by the direct sunshine behind the doors and the figure now glowed with a bright halo. He blinked the sunspots from his eyes and began to focus on the single person that was standing in the doorway.

OK. One torso only; definitely not a goon squad; definitely not. That's good. Six feet tall? But it's still too bright for me to be sure.

As the uninvited guest swung into the barn while pushing the left door fully open, the foggy torso sharpened into a less foggy silhouette and Albert squinted to force his vision into clarity. Dull lines sharpened and blurs diminished as Albert noticed something.

What is that? He has a helmet on; a flight helmet! What the heck? If this is a flyer and he has me tied up, then this blue bastard is definitely not good news.

The sunspots receded and Albert's focus improved as the silhouette spun to open the right barn door. In that move Albert noticed something else.

He has a flight suit on as well; definitely with blue trim. Not good, not good, not good.

Albert began to sense panic setting in as bile jumped up from belly to throat. He realized how dehydrated he was as his tongue swelled to fill his mouth. Having opened both doors fully enough and now standing in the bright sunlit doorway, the confirmed blue bastard rotated slowly to face Albert head on and placed his gloved hands on his hips; his face still shrouded in the eclipse-like sunglow.

I don't like the stance; there's something up this bastard's sleeve. This is really not good.

What was up this bastard's sleeve was actually on his hip and as he raised his right hand, Albert could see a new silhouette. This time a semi-automatic pistol was casting the shadow.

Not good. Not good. Not good.

For Alfred, that silent moment lasted an eternity as he continued to squint through the sunshine that was full face on with the barn doors now widely open. He strained his vision to pierce the blinding brightness, still trying to understand why he was tied up and who this person was when it spoke to him.

"Wake up lover boy. It's time to get moving."

What the hell? My hearing is all fucked up too. That voice is all wrong.

The blue bastard stood there silently with one hand on a hip and the hand with the gun in the air while Albert's heart raced and sweat beaded across his brow. Albert could almost see the grin on the blue bastard's face when the figure started tapping his right toe. And then he noticed the posture was as wrong as the voice.

What the hell? It's like one leg is shorter or something. I've seen that before. And wait a second; that's long hair coming out of the helmet. This is not a blue bastard, it's a blue bit…

"I said wake up lover boy. It's time to get moving."

Albert's mind raced as he re-compiled all of his observations from masculine to feminine; size, stance, swagger, hair, figure, voice.

<pause>

"Joyce, is that you?"

"Oh, good. Your brain is still working. We've got a long way to go. It's time to get moving."

Albert smiled on the inside, but the adrenaline intensity kept him frozen in place. Same old Joyce…

"Joyce, what's happening? Why am I tied up? Why do you have a gun? What are you doing here?"

Joyce took advantage of a pause in Albert's interrogation to step across the barn and squat down on one leg about eight feet from him. She was off center from the door and the light was now showing her face from behind her left shoulder. She had face scratches of her own and Albert noticed a few strands of corn silk caught up in one of her flight boots. She slowly raised the pistol to a dead aim position and began answering Albert's questions.

"I'm here because I saw you fall from the sky and in some sort of useless sense of loyalty, I came back to make sure you were OK.

I have <u>your</u> gun because I took it from you right after you shot it at me which was right after I untwisted you out of your broken ejection seat, you ungrateful bastard.

You're tied up because you were insane after your crash and you tried to kill me. I had to back heel kick you down to get you to shut up. You were out cold so I dragged you into this barn and tied you up so that I could check out the area without having to worry about you trying to kill me again.

What's happening, lover boy is that I'm arresting your red butt and taking you back to my base. You're my prisoner, asshole."

Albert thought things through for a bit and a few puzzle pieces jumped into his brain. His memory started adding chapters after the corn whipping scene where he lay immobilized in his ejection seat. He had been beaten up by the tumble, wrapped up in the parachute and cords, and the face of his helmet had been smashed into the ground by the weight of his broken throne.

Someone had come up from behind and had silently cut lines to free him from his predicament. After the chute came off, the rescuer toppled the ejection seat up and over and Albert had been thrown a few feet into a row of corn.

When he rose to his feet he realized he was facing the blue trimmed flight suit of an enemy pilot and reacted instinctively from years of military training, drawing his pistol and squeezing off a shot or two.

But there's nothing in my memory after I fired the shots until I woke up just now. Was that Joyce standing there in the field? Really?

"Joyce, OK, wow. I think I'm catching back up. That was you I shot at?"

"Yes it was, you dork. I'm lucky you always had terrible aim."

"I don't have a terrible aim..."

"Then why am I standing here with your gun and not out there face down in the corn?"

"I was pretty shaken up; lots of adrenaline, like now."

"Yeah, sure. It doesn't matter; we are where we are. I have your gun, you are my prisoner, and as soon as I think you are safe enough to travel with, we will be going to my base and I will introduce you to my friends there. I have all sorts of friends who would like to talk to you."

"Look Joyce, you and I both know how this is really going to end. We're a lot closer to my base and we'll go there first. Then I can get you a ride back to O'Hare or wherever you need to go."

"Yeah, right. Except you forgot about the parts where you're tied up, not me; and I have your gun, not you. You're going to do what I tell you to do and you're going to like it. "

"Joyce, this is not going to end pretty if you don't untie me right now and give me my gun back."

"Really? It won't end pretty? What are you going to do? I'm thinking about walking away and leaving you here tied up. I just checked; there is no one around for miles. I'd close the barn doors, of course, to keep the dogs away. But I really don't know what you are going to do about food and water."

"You wouldn't do that; I'm a superior officer!"

"Not right now you're not. Right now you are a prisoner of war. And I'm calling the shots, not you."

"Look, Joyce, this has been fun, but I need you to get over here and untie me and let me get you back to safety. It's dangerous for a girl to be so far deep into enemy territory by herself. You need my help."

"You're incorrigible. I need your help? You need to look in a mirror right about now and start thinking about what facial expressions you'll use when you explain to your buddies about getting your ass kicked by a girl and getting hauled off from inside your own territory by that same girl to be a POW. You've always been this way with me. You suck."

"I'm getting to you, aren't I, Joyce. I'm telling you, it's the stress of the situation. You need to let me go so that we can pool our ideas and energy and figure this out together."

"I have a better idea. You need to think more deeply right now about whether you really want to get out of those ropes or not. I've determined that you are definitely not fit to travel with at this time so why don't you sleep it off for a while."

That said, Joyce stood up and immediately executed her second back heel kick of the day with her right boot catching the left side of Albert's face this time.

He went out like a light and she checked him for a pulse, breathing, and made sure his neck was not broken.

As she walked away she thought to herself "I'm glad I pulled back at the last second. He didn't have his helmet on this time..."

www.ingramcontent.com/pod-product-compliance
Lightning Source LLC
Chambersburg PA
CBHW070636310726
48982CB00001B/290

9781499906790